CRITICAL PRAISE FOR *SLIGHTLY SETTLED*

"Readers who followed Tracey's struggles in
Slightly Single, and those meeting her for the first
time, will sympathize with this singleton's post-breakup
attempts to move on in this fun, lighthearted
romp with a lovable heroine."
—*Booklist*

"Tracey is insecure and has many neuroses, but this
makes her realistic.... And like many women, Tracey
needs to figure out when to listen to her friends
and when to listen to herself."
—*Romantic Times*

CRITICAL PRAISE FOR *SLIGHTLY SINGLE*

"...an undeniably fun journey for the reader."
—*Booklist*

"Bridget Jonesy...Tracey Spadolini smokes, drinks
and eats too much, and frets about her romantic life."
—*Publishers Weekly*

D0061656

WENDY MARKHAM

is a pseudonym for *New York Times* bestselling, award-winning novelist Wendy Corsi Staub, who has written more than fifty fiction and nonfiction books for adults and teenagers in various genres—among them contemporary and historical romance, suspense, mystery, television and movie tie-in and biography. She has coauthored a hardcover mystery series with former New York City mayor Ed Koch and has ghostwritten books for various well-known personalities. A small-town girl at heart, she was born and raised in western New York on the shores of Lake Erie and in the heart of the notorious snow belt. By third grade, her heart was set on becoming a published author; a few years later, a school trip to Manhattan convinced her that she had to live there someday. At twenty-one, she moved alone to New York City and worked as an office temp, freelance copywriter, advertising account coordinator and book editor before selling her first novel, which went on to win a Romance Writers of America RITA® Award. She has since received numerous positive reviews and achieved bestseller status, most notably for the psychological suspense novels she writes under her own name. Her previous Red Dress Ink title, *Slightly Single,* was one of Waldenbooks' Best Books of 2002. Very happily married with two children, Wendy writes full-time and lives in a cozy old house in suburban New York, proving that childhood dreams really can come true.

Mike, Mike & Me

Wendy Markham

**RED
DRESS
INK**™

First edition January 2005

MIKE, MIKE & ME

A Red Dress Ink novel

ISBN 0-373-89507-0

www.RedDressInk.com

Printed in U.S.A.

Dedicated with love and friendship to the Siegel family,
Joan, Richard, Rory and Nicholas, and to
the three guys I adore: Mark, Morgan and Brody.

With special gratitude to the brilliant David Staub
of Network Expert Software Systems.

one

The present

So in case you've been wondering, I married Mike after all.

Which Mike, you might ask?

And rightly so.

For a while there, it was a toss-up. But when I finally made my choice, I honestly believed it was the right one—that I'd chosen the right Mike.

Only recently have I begun to question that…and everything else in my life. Only recently have I been thinking back to that summer when I found myself torn between the guy I'd always loved and the guy I'd just met.

That they shared both a name and my heart is one of life's great ironies, don't you think?

Then again, maybe not. According to the United States Social Security Administration, Michael was the most popular boys' name in America between 1964 and 1998. Odds are, if you're a heterosexual female who was born between those years—as I am—you're going to date a couple of Mikes in your life. As I did.

Meanwhile, if you're a heterosexual male who was born in those years, you're going to date a couple of Lisas. That was the most popular girls' name the year I was born.

I'm not Lisa.

Remember that song? All about how she wasn't Lisa, her name was Julie. It was a big hit when I was a kid. I remember singing it at slumber parties with my best friends—two of whom were named Lisa.

But I'm not Lisa. I'm not Julie, either.

My real name is Barbra. Spelled without the extra "a," like Barbra Streisand's. That's not why mine is spelled that way; I was born back in the mid-sixties, before my mother ever heard of Barbra Streisand.

My father—who if his own name weren't Bob probably wouldn't be able to spell *that*—filled out the birth certificate while my mother was sleeping off the drugs they used to give women to spare them the horrific childbirth experience.

That, of course, was back in the Bad Old Days when they didn't realize that the fetus was being drugged as well—otherwise known as the Good Old Days, when nobody was the wiser and nobody was feeling any pain.

I always figured that when it was time for me to give birth, I'd want those same drugs.

Am I a wimp? you might ask.

Um, yeah. I've never been good with pain—I'm the first to admit it. I stub my toe; I scream. I get a sliver; I cry. I see blood; I faint.

By the time I got pregnant, I had heard enough gory details from my friends to know that it would be in everyone's best interest if I were knocked out before I reached the stage where it was a toss-up whether to call in the obstetrician or an exorcist.

I envisioned drifting off to a medically induced la-la land, waking up feeling refreshed, and having somebody hand me a pretty, pink newborn, even if my husband spelled its name wrong while I was out.

Alas, that wasn't to be.

For one thing, we knew that our firstborn son would be named after my husband, who is conveniently familiar with the spelling of Mike.

For another, when—about five minutes into my first pregnancy—I asked my doctor about drugs, he recommended a childbirth class where I would learn to use breathing and imagery to control the pain. Call me jaded, but I didn't see then and I don't see now how huffing and counting and focusing on a flickering candle or, God help me, a favorite stuffed animal, can possibly make you forget the nine pounds of wriggling human forcing its way out of you the same way it got into you nine months—and nine pounds—ago.

As the scientific theory goes, what goes in must come out. Eventually. Somehow. And the coming-out part is never as much fun as the going-in part.

Whose scientific theory is that? you might ask.

It's mine. And you should trust me, because I'm an expert.

If you've ever eaten all your Halloween candy before the calendar page turned to November—or if you've ever done too many shots of tequila on your birthday—then you're an expert, too.

But if you can't relate to childbirth or vomiting up a pound of chocolate or a pint of hard liquor, think about this: back when Mike and I were first married, he and my father carried our new couch up two flights of stairs to our one-bedroom apartment in Queens. When we moved a few years later, the movers we hired couldn't get the couch out. No matter which way they turned it, they couldn't make it fit through the doorway. They finally told me that the only way to get it out was to remove one of the legs.

Now, normally, I don't balk at being the decision maker in our marriage. But, normally, strange men don't request a saw to disfigure our furniture.

I tried to reach Mike at work to see what he wanted me to do—in other words, to ask his permission for the couch amputation—but he wasn't there.

So the movers sawed off a leg; the couch fit through the door; they moved it to our new house up in Westchester.

When Mike arrived that night, fresh—not!—from his first train commute and ready to collapse, he immediately noticed that the surface he was about to collapse onto was tilting dangerously.

I explained what happened.

He was incredulous.

Okay, not just incredulous. He was other things, too. Including royally pissed off. Now that I've had almost a decade of enlightenment regarding Mike's daily commute to the city, I can attribute his fury that night, at least in part, to an hour spent on an un-air-conditioned railroad car sandwiched in a middle seat between two large businessmen who carried on a conversation across his lap. But at the time, in my seminewlywed overanalytical self-absorption, I concluded that everything was all my fault.

Him: "How the hell could you let them cut the fucking leg off the goddamn fucking couch?"

Me: "I had no choice."

Him: "We got the fucking couch in. They're goddamn professionals and they couldn't get it out? And what kind of movers carry a goddamn fucking saw around to cut the legs off people's furniture?"

Me: "They don't. I ran out and bought one."

Him: "You bought the saw?"

Me: "The goddamn fucking saw. They told me to."

Him: storms off, spends sleepless night trying to keep balance on the aforementioned—and seriously listing—goddamn fucking couch.

Me: spends sleepless night sobbing into pillow over first significant married fight.

When I say significant, I refer to the fights that stand out in a couple's mutual memory. Not the arguments that happen along the way: arguments about the thermostat or what color to paint the bedroom or who should buy the Mother's Day cards for his side of the family. I'm talking Fight, fights. Lying-awake-at-dawn-crying fights. Who-are-you-and-what-have-you-done-with-the-man-I-married fights.

Actually, I can count on one hand the number of fights and sleepless nights we've had in our marriage.

After the moving ordeal, our next sleepless night—and, incidentally, our next significant married fight—was a year or so later, when I was ten centimeters dilated and pushing. Does that fight count? I mean, I truly wasn't myself at the time.

Who was I? you might ask.

I was Lizzie Grubman meets Shannon Dougherty meets Valdemort—a temporary state brought on by the sheer physical agony of childbirth.

And Mike—who was supposed to be coaching me—was just plain stupid at the time, a temporary state I'll chalk up to low blood sugar. I'll admit that it was due in part to the fact that I wouldn't let him visit the hospital cafeteria—or even the vending machines—for the twenty-four-hours-plus that I was in excruciating labor, lest he miss the big event.

That's how stupid I was. I kept thinking that any minute now, there would be a baby. I kept thinking that for, oh, sixteen thousand minutes or so before it actually happened.

Anyway, here's how stupid Mike was: He brought up the couch story in the midst of my agony.

"You can do it, hon," he crooned. "You can get this baby out. Unless you want me to run out and buy a saw so that we can cut off one of its legs?"

Har de har har, right? Funny guy, that Mike.

Of course, he then found it necessary to make like Jay Leno and regale the nurses, the doctor and a passing orderly with the Couch Monologue. They all had a good laugh at my expense while I writhed and moaned and cursed the epidural that didn't work and swore that if the baby ever came out I would be a single mother because I was getting a divorce.

As it turned out, I didn't.

As it turned out, neither did my parents, although they're such opposites that most people say it's a miracle they've stayed together all these years.

Anyway, as I was saying before I went into my longer than anticipated digression, my father—who is good at many things, including, fortuitously for us, fixing freshly sawn-off couch legs—has never been good at spelling. He likes to tell people that's because he's an accountant—as though an accountant requires prowess only with numbers and not with that pesky alphabet.

So when he filled out the paperwork after I was born, he left out the second "a," and by the time anybody figured it out, it was too late. My mother woke up and I was Barbra and that was that.

My three older brothers used to tease her—and me—that it was a good thing he had left off the second "a" instead of the third one along with the first "r," in which case, I'd have been named after the large gray elephant in the French children's story.

My mother wasn't amused. It isn't that she has anything against children's literature; she is, after all, a middle-school English teacher. She is also a fanatic about all things spelling- and grammar-related. From what I hear, she didn't speak to my father for a few days after she discovered the spelling mistake in my name. But, like I said, they managed to stay married.

Around the same time I came along, Barbra Streisand became a household name and validated the unorthodox spelling of mine. I can barely remember anybody ever calling me Barbra anyway. I was dubbed Beau early on, and I have never since been anything but.

My parents gave me the nickname because it's short for Beaulieu, as in Priscilla Beaulieu Presley, Elvis's wife. They thought I looked a lot like her. Which I do. In fact, complete strangers have come up to me and said that over the years.

I never mind when people do that. I mean, it's not like they're telling me I look just like Cyndi Lauper or something.

Priscilla was, and still is, beautiful.

Three pregnancies and a lifetime ago, I was also beautiful. Now I've got a seven-year-old, a preschooler and a baby. I've also got flab, stretch marks, varicose veins, dark circles under my eyes, sagging breasts that have nursed three children, with nipples that hit my belly button, and a childbirth-traumatized crotch that leaks pee if I laugh.

Which I don't, lately.

That, I suppose, is a blessing. But it doesn't feel like one.

Damn, it used to feel good to laugh until tears streamed from my eyes instead of my bladder.

Things that used to make me laugh that hard: being tickled by my dad. The scene in *Planes, Trains and Automobiles* where Steve Martin and John Candy are in the car that catches fire. *Seinfeld*—even the reruns I've seen a dozen times.

Oh, and my husband, Mike.

He really cracked me up back when we were dating. When we were first married, too, even after we moved up here to the suburbs.

He used to do this dead-on imitation of our crotchety old neighbor, Mrs. Rosenkrantz, that was hilarious—and, I suppose, cruel, if anybody but me had ever seen it. But nobody ever did. It was our special thing.

We'd be doing some mundane task—folding laundry or grocery shopping—and I'd say, "Do Mrs. Rosenkrantz for me, please," and he would. He'd be Mrs. Rosenkrantz folding laundry or Mrs. Rosenkrantz grocery shopping, and I swear I'd be on the floor gasping for air.

Mrs. Rosenkrantz died right before I gave birth to our second son. I was in labor for the wake and in the hospital for the funeral, so we didn't go. We came home with our tiny blue bundle to find a rented wooden stork on our lawn and a For Sale sign on hers.

Once or twice after that, I asked Mike to "Do Mrs. Rosenkrantz," and he obliged, but it wasn't the same.

A lot of things haven't been the same since then. Some are better, some are worse—but nothing is the same. Lately, I find myself missing the way things used to be.

I don't miss Mrs. Rosenkrantz, though—I just miss laughing at her. Or, rather, laughing at my husband's impression of her.

A young family from the city bought her house. Where we live, in the leafy northern suburbs of New York, young families from the city always buy dead old people's houses. This was a nice family, the Carsons. They have a daughter my older son's age and a son my second son's age and twins on the way any second now. The mom, Laura, is a lot of fun when she isn't eight months pregnant with multiples in the blazing dead of July, and the dad, Kirk, coaches Little League with Mike.

On hot summer days we grill and drink beers on their deck or ours while the kids play in the sprinkler, and on cold winter days we shovel while the kids build snowmen. The Carsons pick up our mail and *Journal News* when we're on vacation and we pick up their mail and *Journal News* when they're on vacation, and we keep saying that one of these years we should vacation together.

It sounds good, doesn't it?

Yeah. Suburban bliss.

Three kids, a raised ranch, an SUV and a 401K. We have everything but a dog, but the boys have been begging for one, and sooner or later I know I'm going to give in and we'll have the dog, too.

They, like I, will have everything they always wanted.

I was born under a lucky star. That's what my mother always said, shaking her head and laughing. Things came easily to me from day one. Friends…contest prizes…school elections…boyfriends.

If I wanted something, I got it.

This life is what I've always wanted. Isn't it?

Well, *isn't* it?

Back when I was young and single and dating my husband—along with the other Mike, the one I didn't marry—I dreamed of the life I have now. I figured it would be mine for the taking, because most things were.

Be careful what you wish for—or so they say.

They being the same *they* my grandmother is always quoting; the *they* who say beauty is only skin deep, and when the cat's away, the mice will play, and love and marriage go to-gether like a horse and carriage.

Or was that Frank Sinatra?

Not that it matters. Grandma Alice quotes him, too.

The thing is, there's truth in all clichés—that's why they're clichés.

So here I am, a living cliché, on the cusp of my fortieth birthday, reminding myself that I have everything I ever wanted—and trying desperately to remember why the hell I wanted it in the first place.

two

The past

"If I were you," Valerie told me, lounging on her unmade bed and polishing her toenails that stifling July night, "I'd wear the red. Mike likes you in red, right?"

"He does, but…" I surveyed my image in the full-length mirror we had bought at Woolworth's and tacked to the back of our closet door only a few days ago. God only knew how we had managed to live in that apartment for almost a year without a full-length mirror.

But Valerie claimed that when she couldn't see the thirty pounds she had to lose, she didn't worry about them.

The day after we bought the mirror—my idea—she went back on her diet. It was the same diet she had been on—and off—for the past year or two.

You would think something as drastic as eliminating all fat grams from one's diet would work. At least, Valerie would think that. It seemed a little extreme to me. But then, I was blessed with a normal weight and a high metabolism. I couldn't imagine giving up ice cream, chicken chimichangas with cheese, or Popeye's fried chicken with mashed potatoes and Cajun gravy.

Whenever Valerie was on her low-fat diet, I had to sneak my indulgences so that she wouldn't be tempted to stray from her oat-bran-strewn path. Of course, sooner or later, she always did, but at least I knew it wasn't my fault.

"This is new. Don't you like it?" I asked Valerie, gesturing at the black spandex minidress I was wearing.

I wiped a trickle of sweat from my forehead as she contemplated my appearance. Damn, it was hot, despite the open window and the rotating floor fan in front of it. This was my second summer in Manhattan. Last year, I was so thrilled to actually be living here that I guess I didn't notice the heat in our fourth floor, un-air-conditioned one-bedroom walk-up.

I do remember noticing the street noise—the round-the-clock horn-honking, sirens, construction-site jackhammers, the throbbing bass from passing car radios and neighborhood bars. It took me a while to get used to the incessant din that accompanied daily life on the Upper West Side. After I did get used to it, whenever I went upstate to visit my family, the nights seemed preternaturally quiet.

Valerie shrugged, set aside the bottle of pale frosted pink polish and said, re: my outfit, "I don't know, Beau. Don't you think it's kind of…"

"Short?"

"Yeah, that. And…"

"Dark?"

"That, too. But also kind of…"

I opened my mouth again, but this time Valerie finished her own sentence.

She finished it with "slutty," and I grinned.

"I haven't seen Mike since April, Val. After three months apart, maybe I want to look slutty."

"No, you want to look sexy. The red one is sexy. This one is slutty. There's a big difference. Hey, I love this song!" She reached toward the stacked plastic milk crates serving as a nightstand between our two beds and turned up the volume on the boom box.

"I hate this song," I grumbled, recognizing the all-too-familiar opening strains of Paula Abdul's "Forever Your Girl."

"I thought you loved it."

"I didn't 'love' it, I liked it. And that was last month, before they played it every five minutes on every radio station in New York."

As Valerie sang the opening, "Hey, baby," in an off-key falsetto, I couldn't resist adding, "Anyway, I like new-wave stuff much better than pop. Pop is so over."

"That's what you said about Madonna last year, and now look. She's everywhere again."

"I give her five minutes," I said darkly. "And Paula Abdul gets ten. Nobody will ever have heard of either of them in a few years. But INXS and The Cure will be around forever, like the Beatles. Mark my words."

She was too busy singing along with flash-in-the-pan Paula to mark my words, so I picked up the hanger draped with the red dress. It was a month old and I had worn it at least three times already, but of course Mike had never seen me in it. Holding the hanger against my shoulders, I surveyed my reflection.

The short skirt had a ruffled flare, reflecting the lambada craze that had overtaken everyone's wardrobe that summer. My light brown hair was pretty much bigger than the skirt:

long, kinky-permed and teased on top, with the bangs sprayed fashionably stiff and curving out from my forehead like a tusk.

"I don't know," I told Valerie. "I think I like the way the black clings better."

Lying on her back and waving her legs around in the air to dry her toenail polish, Valerie interrupted her singing to say, "I'd kill to like the way something clings on me."

I never knew how to respond when she made comments like that. It wasn't easy being five foot seven and a hundred and twenty pounds when your best friend was six inches shorter and a good thirty pounds heavier.

I know, I know…it was probably much harder to be the shorter, heavier one. But I couldn't help feeling awkward whenever Valerie looked at me with blatant envy…like she was right now.

I tried to think of something nice to say about the neon-blue spandex bicycle shorts she was wearing with an oversize neon-orange T-shirt, but I was at a loss. Spandex wasn't the most flattering trend if you weren't built like a pencil. Which, fortunately, I was. And which, unfortunately, Valerie wasn't.

"My toes are never going to dry with this humidity. Wouldn't you kill for a window air conditioner?" Valerie asked, still waving her legs around in the air.

"Maybe we can scrape up enough money to buy one."

"Yeah, right." She snorted.

So did I. Naturally, we were both broke. She made eight bucks an hour as an office temp and had yet to land a full-time job with benefits. I had the full-time job and the benefits, but I made a mere seventeen thousand dollars a year. Back in my small hometown, that would have been a fortune. Here, it barely covered the absolutely vital three Cs in every girl's life: cocktails, cigarettes and chimichangas. At least, those were the things that were vital in mine.

"I suppose you want me to clear out of here tonight," Valerie said, getting off her bed to join me in the mirror, wielding a tall pink and black can of Aqua Net. She sprayed her towering blond hair liberally, then offered me the can.

I misted my head and handed it back. "Is that all that's left? Didn't you just buy that yesterday?"

She shrugged. "I'll pick up more during lunch hour tomorrow."

Ugh. Between the hair spray and the sweat, everything north of my neck felt sticky. I stripped off the black dress and stepped back into my own bike shorts—neon pink, with fluorescent green stripes up the thighs—and oversize neon-green T-shirt, which I knotted over my left hip.

"So, like, do you want me to see if I can sleep at Gordy's tomorrow night?" Valerie asked, taking a cigarette from the open pale green box of Salem Slim Lights on her dresser and offering the pack to me.

Gordy had been our friend since the three of us met at college upstate freshman year. He moved to New York after graduation, same as we did. He was the ultimate cliché: an aspiring actor/waiter who came out of the closet only after his staunchly Roman Catholic parents finished putting him through college. They promptly disowned him, leaving me and Valerie as his only "family." He had a studio apartment in Hell's Kitchen, a scary neighborhood we ventured into only in pairs, and only in broad daylight.

"You don't have to stay there," I said around the cigarette in my mouth as I held a lighter to it. I took a deep drag, then told Valerie, "I mean, it's a work night and everything."

Naturally, I was hoping she would protest.

She did. Sort of. "Well, don't you want to be alone with Mike on his first night here?"

"Yeah, I do, but…"

I waited for her to say that it was no problem; that she was absolutely going to Gordy's. She didn't say it. She just blew a smoke ring and shrugged.

Dammit.

Don't get me wrong. Valerie was a great roommate. She didn't snore, she washed her own dishes, she ogled Officer Tom Hanson aka Johnny Depp on *21 Jump Street* with me religiously every Sunday night.

But she didn't have much of a social life, which meant that unless she was at work—currently a temp job at a textbook publishing house—she was pretty much always home.

That wasn't a problem when my boyfriend wasn't coming to visit me for the first time since he'd finished grad school in Los Angeles in May.

Mike, who now had a master's degree in computer science, had set up a bunch of interviews in Manhattan. I was praying he'd land a job and move back East, because I was starting to realize that the alternative was me giving up my dream job as a production assistant on a television talk show and moving out West. I had been born and bred in New York State, and I had no desire to move to southern California.

I sensed that Mike was going to try to convince me that I should, though. He was from Long Island, but he had fallen in love with California. When I visited him there in April, he kept talking about how I could get a great job in the television industry. When I pointed out that I already had a great job in the television industry, he pointed out that the quality of life on the West Coast was so much better than in New York.

"See, Beau? You don't have to step over homeless people every time you walk out the door," he said as we crawled along in his convertible on the 405 one sunny afternoon. He gestured at the blue skies and palm trees overhead. "Everything's clean, there's no snow and you don't have to be jammed on the subway with a million strangers."

"No, you just have to be jammed on the freeway with a million strangers in a million cars."

That he so obviously preferred the L.A. traffic to the N.Y.C. crowds scared me then, and it scared me now.

He was really excited about some independent computer research project he and a couple of other grad students had been working on. The project was supposed to end when school did, but it had apparently morphed into something bigger, which was why he was still in California.

He hadn't actually come out and said that he was considering staying on the West Coast for good, but I got the hint.

But thanks to my pushing, he had arranged these interviews in Manhattan. I had my heart set on living happily ever after with Mike, à la Michael and Hope on my favorite show, *thirtysomething,* and I was determined to do it right here in New York.

I figured that while he was in town this week, when he wasn't busy interviewing or spending time with his parents, he and I could do some preliminary apartment hunting. He'd have a job lined up before he flew back West; I'd go with him; we'd load up his car with all his belongings and drive back here together. He could stay with his parents—or, better yet, with me—until our new place was ready. I was sure Valerie wouldn't protest.

Never mind that our place was almost too small for us two women, and I hadn't actually checked with her. Never mind that I had already used up my first year's allotment of one week's vacation. And never mind that Mike and I hadn't yet discussed the prospect of living together.

I figured everything would fall into place the second I fell into Mike's arms. Which, I saw, glancing at my new Keith Haring Swatch—was less than twenty-four hours from now. If the plane was on time.

I felt a ripple of anticipation. After all, Mike was the love of my life. We had met at summer camp in the Catskills during high school and fallen madly in love over roasted marshmallows and color war. We reconnected every summer, first as campers, then as CITs, and finally as counselors. We went to separate state universities but managed to keep up a long-distance relationship all through college.

This last year had been the hardest, though, by far. Instead of sixty-some miles of New York State Thruway between us, there was an entire continent.

Absence makes the heart grow fonder.

That was what my cliché-spouting Grandma Alice always said. She was—and still is—a big believer in true love triumphing over the odds. After all, she and Grandpa Herman started dating before he was shipped overseas to the Battle of the Bulge. Their relationship survived a world war.

My parents' relationship survived the Vietnam War—not that my dad was sent to Southeast Asia or anything. But he did serve in the military back then, stationed in Alabama for more than a year when my sister and I were really young.

I couldn't imagine that Mike and I would ever live through a war in this day and age, but I honestly believed, in my young and foolish heart, that we could make it through anything the future was going to throw at us.

three

The present

Splat.

"Shit!"

No, not *literally* shit. That would have been even more disgusting, but this is pretty vile. I have just been sprayed with Earth's Best Organic First Sweet Potatoes.

"Beau! Watch your mouth!"

Startled by the voice, I turn to glower at my husband, who is standing in the kitchen doorway, fresh from his shower and wearing a crisp white button-down and maroon tie unmarred by pureed orange root vegetables.

"Well, I wish he'd watch *his* mouth," I snap, gesturing at my squirming five-month-old, whose chubby cheeks are ominously puffed again. "He does this spitting thing because you taught him."

"I didn't teach him to spit food. I taught him to do this.

Didn't I, Tyler?" Mike leans over the high chair and blows a vibrating raspberry into our son's face.

Tyler squeals with glee.

"Stop it, Mike. You think it's cute, but lately he does that whenever he has a mouthful, and I'm the one who ends up wearing his breakfast, not you." I reach for a cloth diaper from the basket of clean, unfolded laundry on the table and mop the mess from my face.

"Yeah, well, I'd trade feeding him his breakfast for getting on the train," Mike says darkly.

Tyler does another loud raspberry.

"No, Tyler, that's bad, bad."

"No, don't say bad like that—he'll think you're saying *he's* bad," I reprimand Mike for the millionth time since I read that parenting magazine article that claimed telling your children they're bad will create self-esteem issues they'll carry for a lifetime.

"Oh, right. What am I supposed to say again?" Mike doesn't roll his eyes at me, but I can tell that he wants to.

"Tell him 'that's naughty.'"

"That's naughty, Tyler," Mike says, even as he strides over to the polished granite counter and peers at the coffeemaker.

A moment goes by. I pretend to be oblivious, focusing on circling the rubber-tipped spoon just below the rim of the jar until it's coated with orange goo.

"Oh…no coffee?" Mike lifts the empty glass carafe, as if to be absolutely certain that steaming black brew isn't somehow concealed inside.

I swallow a snarl as Tyler swallows the spoonful of sweet potatoes I've cautiously slipped past his drooly pink gums.

"No coffee," I inform my husband curtly. "I haven't had a chance to make it yet. I've been busy with the laundry and the baby."

"Mmm," he says, or maybe it's "hmm." Either way, the message is clear. He, the commuting husband, is feeling neglected by me, the stay-at-home wife.

"You can stop at Starbucks on the way to the station," I inform him.

"You know I don't like their coffee."

I do know that. He thinks it tastes burnt, making him the only grown human in the tristate area who doesn't patronize the place.

"Go to Dunkin' Donuts, then," I tell him. "You like their coffee."

"It's too out of the way. I'll miss my train."

I shrug. What the hell does he want me to say?

I clear my throat. "Sorry."

That, I know, is what he wants me to say.

But now that I've obliged, he merely shrugs and strides to the sink, where he reaches for the orange prescription bottle on the windowsill.

You'd think he'd tell me that it's okay. That, for once, he can live without his caffeine fix for the hour it will take him to get to his office in midtown. You'd even think he'd offer to get up five minutes earlier from now on and make his own goddamn coffee.

Nope, nope and nope.

He swallows the small white pill he's been taking for his high cholesterol ever since the doctor prescribed the medication last winter.

You'd think he'd be grateful to me, his loving wife, for caring enough about him to insist that he get a physical after years of neglecting to do so.

Nope again.

If I'm in the vicinity when he takes his daily dose, as I am most mornings, he makes a big show of making a face as he swallows. Sometimes—like today—he throws in a heavy sigh for good measure, as if to illustrate how tragic it is that his very life depends on modern medicine.

Not that it does. His cholesterol wasn't *that* high. But early heart attacks run in his family, and I don't want to be a young widow.

Really, I don't.

Shoving aside a twinge of guilt, I spoon more baby food into Tyler's gaping mouth.

The fact that I have found myself fantasizing lately about being single again has nothing to do with wishing my husband dead.

I love Mike. I've loved Mike for almost half of my life.

It's just that I've loved him more passionately in the past than I happen to love him right now.

Right now—as in, these days—he gets on my nerves.

Right now—as in, right this second—he's *really* getting on my nerves.

"I thought Melina came yesterday," he says.

Melina is our cleaning woman, and I know where this is headed. Teeth clenched, I scoop more baby food onto the spoon and say tersely, "She did come yesterday."

"The sink doesn't look clean."

"It was clean after she left."

He bends over to inspect the caulked groove where the white porcelain meets the black granite. "There's a speck of red gunk that was here yesterday morning. It's left over from the lasagne pan you washed," he informs me. "It's still here."

"Then why don't you scrub it off?" I snap.

"Because that's Melina's job. That's why we pay her a hundred bucks a week. Why are we paying her if she's not doing her job?"

Why, I wonder, are we having this conversation yet again?

"If you don't want to tell her that she has to shape up, Beau, I will."

"I'll tell her," I say quickly, driven by the inexplicable yet innate need to protect Melina from the Wrath of Mike. "It's just hard. She doesn't speak English."

"Then show her. Bring her over to the sink and point to the gunk. Then bring her to the corner of the upstairs hall and show her the cobwebs that have been there for two weeks. Then bring her to the boys' bathroom and show her the grunge growing on the tile behind the faucet. Then—"

"Okay! I get it, Mike."

"Right. So will she, if you show her."

I sigh. "Yeah, well, I can't follow her around the house every time she's here."

"Then maybe you should fire her and hire somebody who doesn't need to be shown how to do their job."

"We can't fire her. She has two kids to support here and three more in Guatemala. She needs the money."

Mike shakes his head and mutters something, his back to me.

"What?"

He doesn't turn around. "I just said, I don't understand how a mother can leave her kids behind like that."

I bite back another defense of Melina. I don't understand it, either. The thought of leaving my babies behind—even when they're adolescents—to go live and work in another country is as foreign to me as...well, as Guatemala is. Intellectually, I understand her reasons. Maternally, I'm at a loss.

I'd never heard of such a thing until I moved to Westchester and had my first brush with domestic help. In the past seven years, I've met countless nannies and housekeepers with children and spouses back in South America or the Ca-

ribbean or wherever it is they're from. I used to find it shock-
ing; now it's merely unsettling.

I, after all, didn't think twice about leaving behind a promising career in television production to become a stay-at-
home mom after Mikey was born.

All right, maybe I thought *twice*. Maybe it wasn't exactly
a no-brainer. Maybe I believed I could have it all: marriage,
children, glamorous career.

Maybe some women can.

But when my six-week maternity leave was over, I found
myself crying daily on the commuter train that carried me
away from my precious child. I lasted two weeks, until
Mikey—poor sacrificial lamb—caught his first cold from a
sick toddler whose working mother sent him to day care with
a green runny nose.

That was when I knew the jig was up.

Hadn't I been weaned on seventies TV? Didn't I know
that if you were going to make it after all, you had to be
spunky and single and living in a bachelorette pad with a big
gold initial on the wall?

I was never going to be Mary Richards. It was too late for
that. No, I was destined to become Ma Ingalls meets Olivia
Walton meets Marian Cunningham.

Tyler gurgles adorably and swallows more food.

I smile at him, spoon in another orange glob, and watch
Mike try to catch his reflection in the window above the
kitchen sink. He fusses with the dark hair that fringes his forehead, a forehead that seems to be getting taller with every
passing day.

I never imagined that my handsome husband would have
a receding hairline by his fortieth birthday. Most men do, I
know. It's just that Mike has always been as effortlessly good-
looking as…

Well, as *I* was.

On that grim note, I watch him turn abruptly, cross back to the table and take his suit coat and briefcase from a chair. He asks, "Do you think you'll be able to pick up my dry cleaning today, Beau?"

Oops.

"Yes," I say. "I'm sorry I forgot yesterday. I took the boys to the mall to get them out of Melina's way, and I forgot to stop at the cleaner's on the way home."

"I need my gray suit for tomorrow."

"Your gray suit?" I frown. "I don't remember dropping that one off."

"I wore it last Friday and then I put it into the dry-cleaning hamper."

"Well, I dropped off the dry cleaning on Friday morning, so it must still be in the hamper."

"Beau, I needed that suit by tomorrow."

"I'm not your wardrobe mistress, Mike," I snap.

"Fine. Whatever. Bye." He plants a kiss on Tyler's head and heads for the door.

"Bye," I say as it slams behind him, remembering that there was a time when he wouldn't leave—or come home—without kissing me, too.

Tyler coos. I flash an absent smile in his direction, my thoughts drifting back over the years, remembering the path that led to this place—and wondering what would have happened if, when I arrived at the inevitable fork, I had chosen instead to head in a different direction.

four

The past

So life was good. I was young, pretty, living in New York and madly in love—not to mention happily employed.

I adored my job as a production assistant on *J-Squared*, aka *J2* or the *Janelle Jacques Show.*

Back when I was fresh out of college and interviewing for the position, I thought I'd be the luckiest entry-level drone in the city if I actually got it—which I doubted I would. Ironically, most of the other candidates competing for the job were huge fans, but I'd never even heard of Janelle Jacques before I moved to New York. She was a fairly well-known soap opera actress, but I rarely watched the soaps, aside from a few months leading up to Luke and Laura's wedding on *General Hospital* my senior year in high school.

Turned out, I was wrong about my not getting the job. I was also right about being a lucky drone when I did. My job was one of those too-good-to-be-true things fate throws at you, so good that you just know the bottom is going to fall out somewhere along the way...and then it never does.

A year later, the freshly hired glow had yet to wear off. It was hard work, but I was still fascinated by the whole behind-the-scenes television studio process. Disillusioned, yes, but fascinated just the same. Perhaps even more so as the months went on and I realized that in the entertainment industry, nothing is ever what it appears to be.

As an actress, Janelle Jacques had won a decent fan following and was even nominated for a daytime Emmy. As a talk show hostess, she left something to be desired.

It wasn't that she didn't have stage presence, because she did. She was svelte and statuesque, with a flaming-red mane, porcelain skin and delicate bone structure. All she had to do was walk onto the set and the rest of us instinctively stopped whatever we were doing or saying to focus on her.

But when it came to interviewing her guests, she just wasn't very...good.

Yeah, okay, she sucked at it. I mean, even I knew, courtesy of my high-school journalism class, that you don't ask simple yes-no questions when you're conducting an interview; nor do you ask questions that can be answered in one word.

Apparently, Janelle Jacques never took a high-school journalism class. Her Q&A sessions were almost painful to watch.

Janelle Jacques: Did you have fun making your new movie?

Up-and-coming starlet: Yes, I really did.

Janelle Jacques: That's great. Great!

Up-and-coming starlet: Yes.

Janelle Jacques: Where was the movie filmed?

Up-and-coming starlet: In Paris.

Janelle Jacques: And do you speak French?

Up-and-coming starlet: No. (Beat.) No, I don't.

Janelle Jacques: So was it hard to live in Paris and not speak French?

Up-and-coming starlet: Yes, it was.

I mean, come on, Janelle! I kept expecting one of her guests to respond to one of her vacuous queries with an eye roll and an exasperated "Duh," but nobody ever did.

Sometimes, as I watched the show taping from behind the scenes, I could see Janelle's eyes glazing over and realized that she wasn't even listening. And sometimes, when I had a clear view of the guest's eyes—or more specifically, the guest's magnified pupils—I realized that they'd ingested—and/or smoked—something stronger than Jolt Cola and cigarettes as a pre-greenroom pick-me-up.

But like I said, I was still enchanted by my job. Despite the inept host and the competitive late-night time slot—opposite Arsenio Hall's new hit show—*J-Squared* was doing fairly well, so far, in its ratings. It didn't hurt that the week before the pilot aired, Janelle eloped with Caleb DeLawrence, her former costar.

Naturally, the tabloids were all over the marriage, proclaiming the madly-in-love and stunningly beautiful newlyweds king and queen of daytime television. Almost immediately, the *Star* had Janelle trying to get pregnant, the *National Enquirer* had her well into her first trimester, and the *Globe* had her on bedrest expecting triplets, with Caleb hovering at her side, massaging her swollen feet.

Meanwhile, backstage at the show, an infinitely juicier rumor had it that the marriage was a publicity stunt. Supposedly, rugged heartthrob Caleb had a male lover and so did Janelle—only hers was married to a conservative congresswoman up for reelection in November.

At first, I didn't believe any of it. After all, whenever Caleb was on the set, he and Janelle were nauseatingly lovey-dovey. Then I caught a reluctant glimpse of Caleb with his purported lover when he thought they were alone in the wardrobe room one night. I may have been a small-town girl who had never knowingly met a gay man before Gordy, but even I knew that straight men didn't ruffle each other's hair. And they sure as hell didn't kiss, which my best work friend and fellow production assistant, Gaile, swore she'd seen them do.

Whatever. I mean, Janelle's sham marriage was the least of my concerns that summer. I was preoccupied with dreams of—okay, plans for—my own matrimonial future with Mike.

The day of his arrival from California plodded along. The taping seemed to take forever, and when it was over, Gaile caught me looking impatiently at my Swatch.

"You've still got an hour to go before we're off work," she pointed out as we carried tubs of dirty dishes and utensils from a cooking segment to the kitchenette backstage.

"I know, but I thought I could cut out early and get a head start on a cab to the airport."

"What are you going to do when you get there and have a couple of hours to kill?"

"I don't know…read?" I was in the middle of a Danielle Steel novel the hopelessly sappy Valerie had forced on me.

"You could read," Gaile agrees. "Or get drunk in the bar. That's what I always do in airports."

I laugh.

"I'm serious. Then I don't have to worry about plane crashes."

"Why did you have to bring that up?"

"Sorry. Don't worry, he'll be fine."

I scowled at her. "That's easy for you to say. Why did I have to go and rent *La Bamba* last weekend?"

"La Bamba?"

"You know, that movie with Lou Diamond Phillips as Richie Valens. You know…the day the music died." I sing a few bars of "American Pie" for her.

Apparently, Gaile has no idea what I'm talking about.

"Never mind," I say, giving up. "So, will you cover for me?"

"You're going to stick me with all these greasy pans?"

"I promise I'll clean the whole stage on my own the next time Janelle has that animal guy on the show."

Gaile tilted her cornrow-and-turban covered head, considering it. "I'll take grease over piles of monkey shit any day," she concluded. "Deal."

"Thank you!" I squealed, giving her a hug.

She laughed. "You knew I'd do it, Beau."

"No, I didn't."

"Sure, you did. You always get people to do what you want."

I bristled at that until I saw the twinkle in her brown eyes. Still, I asked, "What's that supposed to mean?"

"Nothing bad. Just that you're a little bit spoiled, girl-friend."

"Spoiled? Me?" I feigned shock, but I'll admit it: This wasn't the first time I'd ever heard that. People were always saying it when I was growing up.

I guess, when you're the youngest child of four—and the only girl—you grow accustomed to people doting on you. Back home, I was the princess.

Here in New York, I sometimes had to remind myself that not everyone was going to drop everything to cater to my needs.

Then again, people often did. Especially men.

"I'm going to go change my clothes," I told Gaile.

"What did you decide on? The red or the black?"

"The red," I told her. "What do you think?"

"I think that it's the least blah out of two blah choices."

I rolled my eyes and grinned. When it came to fashion, Gaile was anything but blah. She'd jumped wholeheartedly on the currently hot Afrocentric-garb bandwagon, decking herself out daily in exotic headdresses and flowing robes. The contrast of bright-colored native fabrics against her ebony skin was dazzling, but if you asked me—which she never did—her jewelry, invariably made of bones, tusks and teeth, made her resemble a one-woman archaeological dig.

And if I asked her—which I frequently did—my jewelry and my wardrobe were in desperate need of pizzazz. But whenever I tried to follow Gaile's fashion advice, I wound up feeling as if I belonged on MTV with an all-male, eye-liner-wearing backup band.

"Let's face it," I told her now. "I'm a blah girl, Gaile."

"You're gorgeous and you know it."

"Well, I have blah clothes. What can I say?"

"You don't have to be blah."

"Yes, I do. I have to be blah. Blah is my style."

We deposited the tubs of dishes on an already cluttered countertop, next to a basket of bagels that had been sitting out since this morning, and half a dozen red-lipstick-stained, half-filled coffee mugs. Janelle was a caffeine hound, and she refused to drink out of the foam coffee-service cups. Only real porcelain—and just-brewed, steaming hot coffee—would do. As soon as the contents of her mug grew lukewarm, she pushed it aside and had an assistant—often, me—bring her a fresh cup.

But for today, I was finished with catering to Janelle's

every whim and cleaning up after her. Thanks to Gaile, I was free.

"Good luck, Beau," she said as I headed for the door.

"Luck?" I stopped short. That struck me as an odd thing to say. "Good luck with what?"

"You know…"

"Not really." I waited.

She looked me in the eye, as Gaile likes to do. "Your plans," she said simply. "For you and Mike. I hope they work out."

"They will."

She ran water into the sink.

"They will," I said again.

"I didn't say anything."

"You said good luck."

She shrugged.

"You don't think Mike's going to want to move here after all?"

"I don't know what Mike's going to want to do, Beau." She squirted Palmolive into a pan.

"He'll want to be with me," I assured her with confidence.

But what if he didn't?

What if, for the first time in my charmed life, things didn't go my way?

In the ladies' room, I slipped out of my blah black leggings and tunic and into my red dress. Being blessed with a good complexion and nice features, I rarely wore much makeup. But this was a special occasion.

I stood in front of the mirror and outlined my green eyes in dark liner, coated my lashes with black mascara and painted my lips the same color as my dress. When I was finished, I sprayed Obsession in the hollows behind each ear and each knee, and Aqua Net all over my head. I teased my bangs a little higher, sprayed again, and surveyed my reflection.

Perfect.

Okay, not perfect, perfect. I mean, I still looked like Elvis's Priscilla, but by then Elvis was long gone and his ex-wife had faded from the spotlight. And I wasn't really a dead ringer for bombshell model Cindy Crawford, despite frequent assurances that I was, from Ramon, one of the show's security guards.

For one thing, I was almost a head shorter than Cindy. I knew that because Gordy and I spotted her in the Scrap Bar one night when she wasn't famous enough to be recognized by anyone other than my celeb-crazed friend.

Nor did I have Cindy's mole, nor Cindy's voluptuous build.

My figure back then was straight and flat as the Long Island Expressway out East: no boobs, but no pesky hip, gut or thigh padding, either. Sometimes, I fantasized about cleavage, blissfully unaware that it would one day be in store for me—or that it would be bestowed only with cracked, sore, milk-spurting nipples and a baby attached to them 24/7.

Satisfied with my reflection, I snuck out of the studio and into the subway station. Too broke to pay cab fare all the way from Manhattan, I took the jam-packed, un-air-conditioned number seven train out to Queensborough Plaza, descended the elevated platform down to Queens Boulevard, and spent almost fifteen minutes trying to hail a taxi.

By the time I sank into a disconcertingly sticky back seat, my hair had wilted. Luckily, I'd tucked the can of Aqua Net into my oversize black bag, and I'd have plenty of time at the airport to repouf.

Fifteen minutes—and almost fifteen dollars—later, I did just that in a ladies' room down by the gate.

Unfortunately, the lyrics to "American Pie" were still running through my head. I hoped it wasn't an omen.

According to the monitors, Mike's plane was on schedule, but I still had a couple of hours to kill.

Sometimes, even now, I look back and wonder what might have happened that night if I hadn't forgotten my Danielle Steel novel back at the office.

Would I have plopped down in a chair and plodded my way through a few more chapters of *Daddy* until Mike's plane landed?

Probably.

Would I have avoided the chance meeting that turned my life upside down and made me question every choice I'd made since?

I don't know.

I mean, did I believe in fate?

Did I believe that my life was preordained?

Did I believe that what happened would have happened even if I hadn't settled on the only vacant stool in an airport bar?

I ordered a gin and tonic, and drank it too fast, still uneasy about Mike's flight.

Yes. I would look back on that day in years to come and see it as a turning point. Nothing would ever be the same again.

I would wonder time and again what would have happened if the television hadn't been on above the bar.

Or if it had been a different night, any other night of the year.

Or if *he* hadn't been sitting next to me.

five

The present

E-mail is an amazing new invention, don't you think?

Okay, maybe *you* don't think of it as a new invention. Maybe you've been online for years, along with the rest of the world beyond my cozy little domestic one.

Me, I've been online for three months, ever since my in-laws bought a computer for our family room. Technically, it was a birthday present for Josh, our middle son, and they gave him a shitload of *Blue's Clues* and Disney software to go with it.

But Mike and I suspect the real reason they gave us the home PC is so that we can stay in constant touch with them now that they've moved to Florida year-round. Until recently, they've only spent winters at their retirement condo in St. Petersburg, and even then, they dropped hints that we need to call/write/visit more often.

Okay, not hints. They've been known to come right out and say, "You need to call—or write, or visit—more often."

But Mike only gets two weeks of vacation from his job, and we always spend one in Vermont over Christmas with my family at a rented ski chalet. He doesn't want to spend the other with his parents in Clearwater Beach. Naturally, my in-laws must assume that I, the daughter-in-law and only non-blood relative in the family, am the holdout.

In truth, I'd be thrilled to spend Mike's second week off in Florida—or anywhere other than here, working on the house. But Mike doesn't believe in hiring somebody to do something he can do himself—or misguidedly *believes* he can do himself.

Two Augusts ago, we dry-walled the basement; last August, we painted all the trim. I say *we* because although my job was technically to keep the kids out from underfoot and provide takeout pizza and ice water, I eventually wound up on my knees and on ladders right alongside my hapless home-improving husband.

This August, Mike wants to stick a half bath under the stairs. That's how he says it—"stick a half bath under the stairs"—as though it's as simple as sticking a magnet over Mikey's latest crayoned depiction of a dinosaur on the fridge. Yeah. Right. Plumbing is not his forte. Is it anyone's forte, other than a real live plumber's?

But Mike doesn't want to hire one of those. No, he wants to stick a half bath under the stairs all by himself.

Me, I want to stick my feet in saltwater.

Not necessarily the Gulf of Mexico, because according to my in-laws, it's warmer than a bathtub in August. That, to them, is a positive thing.

That, to me, is not the least bit positive. I'm not sure why. Maybe because if August is so freaking hot in the New York suburbs, I sure as hell don't want to go someplace where it's even hotter. Or maybe because warm water makes me think of pee. For that matter, so does the word *bathtub.* That's probably because I have a four-year-old who thinks of our tub as a walk-in urinal.

Anyway, re: the saltwater thing…I was thinking more along the lines of the refreshingly chilly North Atlantic.

You know, the beauty of being online is access to vacation information. I've been researching Cape Cod "family vacation packages." For the unenlightened, "family vacation packages" come with accommodations that include bed rails and cribs, kiddie pools, well-supervised day camps and evening baby-sitters so that Mommy and Daddy can eat overpriced shellfish and drink watered-down frozen margaritas.

Yeah, yeah, I know. But trust me, it beats Kraft mac-and-cheese and Capri Sun fruit punch in a pouch.

Which is what I—and my two older boys—had for lunch this afternoon. Now, with the July midday sun too hot to venture outdoors, I've opted to keep the kids in the comfort of central air, at least for now. Mikey is building a Lego city in his room with Laura Carson's daughter, Chelsea, and Josh is captivated by *Dora the Explorer* on television in the master bedroom and Tyler is dozing in his swing in the living room.

Here I am down in the family room at the computer, checking e-mail for the third time today. Why didn't anybody warn me that it was so addictive? Every day, I wake up wondering who I'm going to hear from next.

Since I became Beauandco@websync.net, I've been in touch with my old friend Gaile, my favorite middle-school teacher and my campus alumni association. I've also heard from my in-laws on a daily basis, have deleted countless offers to enlarge my penis, and have been temporarily convinced that if I forward an e-mail to everyone on my list, Bill Gates will send me a dollar.

Since then, I've become more savvy about Internet hoaxes and spam, not to mention my mother-in-law. For example, I've learned not to respond to her e-mails during hours when she might actually be sitting at the computer, because then she'll know I'm home and she might decide to call me and I'll have to answer the phone and I'll have to talk to her for an hour. More, if she puts my father-in-law on.

Now I know that the best time to respond to her e-mails is at four o'clock, when she and my father-in-law are likely to be at an early-bird special, or after nine o'clock, when they're sound asleep.

Today, I sign on for the third time, and once again, I've got mail. Woohoo!

Okay, maybe not woohoo. I skim past two e-mails from MIL, several spams and a couple of lame jokes from my cousin in Ohio, who forwards everything that crosses her electronic path.

Then it happens.

A legitimate woohoo moment.

There, amid the junk mail, is a screen name that suddenly has my heart beating faster.

Okay, it's probably spam, I tell myself as I grip the mouse and maneuver the arrow toward HappyNappy64@web-sync.net.

I mean, it has to be a coincidence. More than likely, a pornographic one. I'll probably click on the screen name and be treated to a nude twelve-year-old girl reclining on leopard-skin sheets.

I stare at the screen.

HappyNappy64.

It can't be *him*. It can't be, yet I hear his voice echoing in my head from fifteen years and a lifetime ago.

You know what I feel like, Beau?

No, what do you feel like, Mike?

A happy nappy.

Then he'd pull me to the bedroom and we'd make love in broad daylight, then fall asleep in each other's arms.

Happy Nappy.

That was what he called it, and it always made me laugh.

Somehow, despite all the details that have drifted back to me—especially lately—about the time we had together, I forgot all about *Happy Nappy*.

Now it comes back to me in a rush, all of it—not just the sound of his voice in my head, but the smell of his skin when I cradled my head on his naked chest, and the sunlight filtering through the crack in the blinds, and the way his mouth tasted when he kissed me after eating chocolate ice cream; his lips and his tongue sweet and cold and luscious.

Happy Nappy.

I forgot all about that, but not all about him.

I could never forget him if I tried.

And I had. Tried, that is. For a long time, I tried to forget him. I thought it would be better. Easier.

Then I realized nothing would ever be easy, and I stopped trying.

Lately, what I've been trying to do—maybe subconsciously, I realize now—is *remember* him. Remember Mike. Remember what we had.

Remember why the hell I was so willing to leave it behind, to leave him.

But for all the things I remember, I can't remember that and I didn't remember Happy Nappy.

Now, my heart beating in my throat as I stare at the screen name, I highlight *HappyNappy64* and click on it.

Please, I beg silently as the battery–operated swing clicks back and forth behind my desk and animated televised Dora chatters in Spanish from the next room and Mikey and Chelsea argue upstairs over how many Legos are necessary for a properly tall Empire State Building...

Please don't be porn.

Please don't be porn.

Please be him.

Be Mike.

The Other Mike.

The Mike I didn't marry.

The Mike I can't forget.

Please, HappyNappy64, please turn out to be him.

And it does.

SiX

The past

"Can I get you another one?" the bartender asked, gesturing at my glass that now contained only melting ice cubes and a sliver of lime.

I contemplated the question. The first drink had gone down pretty easily, and I still had more than an hour to kill in the airport bar before Mike's plane was due to land. But I didn't want to be wasted when he got here, and the drinks weren't exactly a bargain.

"Go for it," a voice urged, and I glanced up to see that it had come from the guy on the next bar stool.

I immediately noticed that he was good-looking. I mean, how could I not? I was a red-blooded female, even if I was just biding my time until the love of my life stepped through the jetway.

Yes, this guy was good-looking. He had a brooding,

Johnny Depp thing going on around the eyes. Plus he had style, no doubt about that. His dark hair was cut fashionably long on top, short on the sides, and brushed his collar in back. In other words, he had a mullet.

Don't laugh.

Back in the summer of 1989, mullets were not reserved for rednecks and butch lesbians alone. No, mullets were the happening hairstyle of the moment, and this guy had one.

He also had on a pair of baggy jeans, a white T-shirt and a short black-and-white patterned jacket with shoulder pads.

Hair and clothes: A plus for effort.

But he was a babe even beyond those variables that were within his control. His dark eyes were fringed by thick, sooty lashes. There was a deep cleft in his chin and deeper dimples on either side of his mouth when he grinned.

He was grinning at me, and God help me, I found myself grinning right back at him.

He told me to go for it.

Yeah, and he was talking about the drink, I reminded myself.

Aloud, I said, "Go for it? That's easy for you to say."

"Well, why not? Oh, I get it. You're a plainclothes pilot, right? You're about to take off for Paris or something, and it would be irresponsible to take the controls after a couple of drinks."

It wasn't that hilarious, but I laughed as though it were the funniest thing I'd ever heard. "No, I'm not a plainclothes pilot. I'm just…"

"Broke?" he guessed, a little too close to truth for comfort.

"Not exactly."

"Well, this one's on me anyway. Another round," he told

the bartender, who nodded and headed for the top shelf and two fresh glasses before I could protest.

"Mine wasn't Tangueray the first time," I pointed out to the good-looking and fashionable guy, who shrugged.

"Mine was. And I'm treating."

"Thanks. But…"

"But?"

I wanted to tell him that I had a boyfriend. But I didn't know how to do it without making it sound as though I thought he was interested in me, which I didn't. Or, even worse, as though I was interested in him. Which I wasn't.

I mean, he was just a polite guy politely buying me a drink. To be polite.

Did I mention that in addition to being polite, he was very good-looking? Fashionable, too.

"Never mind," I told him, and attempted to shift my attention elsewhere. Because he might be buying me a drink, but that didn't mean we were now a couple.

I mean, he was a total stranger, and I was on the verge of being reunited with Mike.

"Mike," the total stranger said just then out of the blue, and I looked at him, startled.

"Excuse me?"

What was he, some kind of mind reader?

Or maybe I'd just imagined it. Maybe he hadn't said Mike at all. Maybe he'd said something similar. Like…

Might.

Or *bike.*

Oh, yeah. *Bike.* That made a lot of sense.

"Mike," he repeated, sticking his hand out in front of me.

"Mike?" I echoed.

"That's my name."

No way.

He was *Mike?*

I decided the coincidence was some great cosmic sign. A sign that meant...

Well, to be honest, I had no idea what it meant. But it couldn't be good.

"I'm Beau," I said, because he was waiting.

"Nice to meet you, Beau."

As I watched the bartender twisting lime into our fresh drinks, I told myself that I had to get out of here. Now. I would pretend I had to go to the bathroom and just not come back.

"Where are you headed?"

Again with the mind reading? I stared at him in disbelief, wondering how he could possibly know.

"To the ladies' room," I admitted, starting to slide off my stool.

I stopped when he burst out laughing.

"Hey, I hear it's great at this time of year," he said.

"Huh?"

"The ladies' room. Never mind. Bad joke."

The bartender set down our drinks. I reached for mine, needing it desperately.

He went on, "I meant, where are you headed from here? Flying someplace on vacation? Or business?"

"Oh! No, I'm just...I'm meeting somebody's plane." *And I'm head over heels in love with him.* So stop flirting.

Are you flirting?

Or is it my imagination?

"How about you?" I asked him, after taking a sip of my second drink. The second drink I shouldn't have been having in the first place.

"I landed a while ago. My luggage missed the connection at O'Hare so I have to wait for it to get here on the next flight."

"You're in New York on vacation?"

"I just moved here a few months ago."

"Oh."

He just moved here. Which meant that he lived here. Unlike Mike. My *Mike*.

"So you live here, too," he pointed out conveniently.

"Yes."

"Where?"

"Upper West Side." I didn't want to ask him where he lived because it really didn't matter because I was never going to see him again.

Then again, it seemed rude not to ask, so I did.

"Lower East Side."

"East Village?"

"Lower."

"SoHo?"

"Lower," he repeated with a shrug. "Chinatown, really."

"You live in Chinatown?"

"Yeah. But I'm not Chinese," he said, deadpan.

"You're kidding. You're not?" I asked, also deadpan.

"No. People make that mistake all the time, though."

"They do?"

"Yeah, you know, they'll ask me for my recipe for kung pao chicken or they'll want to know how to play piaji, and I—"

"Piaji?" I cut in.

"Yeah, it's a traditional Chinese game." He grinned.

"Really?"

"Really. And actually, I really do know how to play. You soak up a lot when you live in the neighborhood, you know?"

"Yeah."

"Like, I bet you know how to eat Sunday brunch like nobody's business."

"What?"

"Living on the Upper West Side. Forget it. I was trying to be funny again."

"Oh." I cracked a smile.

"I should probably give up my dream of starring in my own sitcom, right?"

I laughed.

So did he. Then he said, "Actually, I'm serious."

"You are?"

"Yeah. I really do want my own sitcom someday. Dream big, I always say."

I honestly couldn't tell if he was kidding or not, so I just shrugged and said, "Yeah."

"But for now, I'm working entry level at an ad agency. What do you do, Beau?"

"For a living? I'm a production assistant."

"What kind of production assistant?"

"You know that show *J-Squared?*"

"Janelle Jacques? Yeah, I know it. You work for her?"

"Yeah. I'm a production assistant on the show."

"You're in the industry?"

"The Janelle Jacques industry? You bet," I quipped.

He was already reaching into his pocket. "Here," he said, and pulled out a small pale blue rectangle.

"What is it?" I asked, though it was obviously a card. His card.

"My card," he said unnecessarily. "So you can get in touch with me if…"

"If Janelle becomes a sitcom producer and is looking for somebody to star in a new show?"

He smiled. "Yeah, or if you just feel like, you know…"

I did know, and I again wanted to blurt out that I was in love. With somebody else. Some other Mike.

But we weren't talking about love.

"…getting in touch with me," this Mike finished with a shrug.

I felt guilty taking his card, but I did. I shoved it into my bag without looking at it.

"Thanks," I told him. "For the card and for the drink."

"You're welcome. What time does your friend's flight get in?"

"Any second now," I lied, and looked around as though I almost expected to see Mike—my Mike—lurking behind a potted palm, spying on us.

Not that there were any potted palms in the airport lounge. Even if there were, Mike wasn't the spying, lurking type. He totally trusted me.

Poor sap.

No, just kidding. I was entirely trustworthy. I had no intention of cheating on him.

Yet.

"Oh, my God…look at that," said the guy with whom I would not be cheating on Mike.

Yet.

I followed his gaze up to the television over the bar, where a special news bulletin was unfolding. The room had fallen silent as everybody seemed to notice the television at once. In mute horror, we watched a passenger jet crash-land and burst into a fireball.

"Where is it?" I heard somebody ask.

"Somewhere in the Midwest," came the official-sounding reply.

My stomach turned over. Mike was flying over the Midwest.

Calm down, Beau. Thousands of people are flying over the Midwest right now. What are the odds that it's his plane?

"What airline is it?" somebody else was asking.

"Looks like United."

I gripped the arms of my bar stool to keep from toppling over. Mike was flying on United.

"Beau…are you okay?"

I looked up to see my companion watching me worriedly.

"My…friend is on United, flying from California. What if—?"

"Shh, listen…" He reached out and squeezed my hand re-assuringly as the news bulletin proceeded.

I was too frantic to focus; I couldn't see, couldn't hear. I wanted to bolt, but I was afraid to move. I was afraid to breathe. It was as though the slightest movement could carry the tragedy home.

Still fixated on the television screen, Mike told me, "That plane was headed to O'Hare from Denver. Your friend was flying from California? Was it a direct flight?"

"Yes. But what if—"

"Do you have the flight number?"

"Yes." Somehow, I managed to produce the scribbled information from the bottom of my bag, and handed it over with a trembling hand. My heart was racing and it felt as though a giant rubber band were compressing my chest.

Mike compared the scribbled flight number to the television screen, double-checking a few times before telling me, "The plane that crashed was flight 232. Your friend was on flight 194."

"Are you sure?"

"Positive."

I could feel tears springing to my eyes. I'd never been so relieved in my entire life.

Then I remembered that I had just held hands with a stranger.

Shit.

Reaching for my glass, I drained what remained of my drink in one long gulp, thinking it might steady my nerves. I plunked the glass back on the bar, heaved a shuddering sigh and imagined hurtling myself into Mike's arms in the near future.

"The friend you're meeting here…is she a she, or is she a he?"

I looked up to see the other Mike watching me. It dawned on me that even in my panic a few moments ago—my hand-holding panic—I couldn't bring myself to say the B word in front of him.

"Boyfriend." I said it now, then spelled out for good measure, "She's a he, well, he's a he, and he's my boyfriend. Not my friend. I don't know why I called him my friend."

"Maybe because you didn't want me to know you were involved with somebody else?"

I feigned shock. Now my heart was racing all over again, dammit.

"I know what you're thinking," he said before I could respond. "You're thinking I'm a cocky son of a bitch. Right?"

Fortified by gin, I said, "Well…kind of, yes."

"The thing is, I would have asked you out, and not just because you work in TV. I would have asked you out before I knew that, because you're gorgeous and I like your laugh and like I said, I'm new in town."

"How new?"

"New enough not to have a girlfriend."

Yet.

I was sure that wouldn't last long. The city wasn't exactly teeming with cute, stylish, witty, straight guys.

But I already had one of those, so I had no choice but to release this one back into the wild.

"Listen," he said, "if it doesn't work out with your boyfriend, give me a call."

"It'll work out with him," I assured him with more confidence than I felt.

"Well, if you find yourself casting a sitcom, give me a call."

I laughed. "Will do."

But I was sure I wouldn't.

So sure that the next morning, as Mike lay snoring in my bed, I crept across the room and removed the blue business card from my bag. I tossed it right into the garbage can without a second glance.

After all, Mike was back. *My* Mike. And I wasn't interested in anybody but him.

Yet…

seven

The present

Hey Beau, Bet you're surprised to hear from me. I Googled your name and found your e-mail address and figured I'd drop you a line. Where are you living now? I've moved around quite a bit, but now I'm pretty settled in Florida. Anyway, I'd love to know what you're up to, so please write back. Take care. Mike

And that's it.

I reread the e-mail at least a dozen times, just to make sure there isn't something more. Some hidden meaning between the lines. Some clue as to why he suddenly decided to get in touch after all these years.

Unless…

No. It has to be him.

Of course it's him.

He didn't sign his last name. He didn't have to. He knew

I'd know who he was the second I saw Happy Nappy. Happy Nappy 64—the year he was born.

So...

Why?

Why is he barging into my life now, after all these years? Because he Googled me?

Why did he Google me?

Okay, confession time: I Googled him, too.

It's not as though he's been on my mind every second for the past decade and a half, but like I said before, he does tend to pop up now and then. I can't help getting lost in memories sometimes, and I can't help occasionally wondering where he is, what he's doing, whether he's married with children.

Back when we first got the computer, I entered his name in the Google search engine and held my breath until it came up with thousands of hits. His name was too common. I gave up after the first few hundred. But I knew that if I really wanted to get in touch with him, I could have done it. I could have tracked down his parents, or old mutual friends, or hell, I could have hired a private detective.

Not that I would have gone to that extreme.

Still, now that he's found me...

Now that I know where he is...

I have this sudden, pressing need to know more.

Like, what is he doing in Florida? He never said anything about wanting to move to Florida.

And...

Is he married with children?

But I can't come right out and ask him that. I can't write *Dear Mike, Thanks for writing. Oh, by the way, are you married with children?*

After all, his marital and paternal status doesn't matter. It *can't* matter, because, oh yeah, *I'm* married with children.

Not that he's proposing anything in his e-mail other than an innocent e-mail in return. I could write and tell him what I've been up to.

But what could that possibly accomplish?

I read the e-mail again, then tear my eyes away, forcing myself to focus elsewhere for a minute. I have to clear my head.

The sun is streaming through the windows. It's a beautiful summer afternoon. I should take the kids over to the pool. Or the park. Or for ice cream.

But it's so hot. And the baby is sleeping. And...

And I would rather stay online and write back to Mike.

But that would be wrong.

Wouldn't it?

I don't know. I mean, I struck up an e-mail correspondence with Gaile after all these years.

But Gaile and I never took a Happy Nappy together. Gaile never tried to steal me away from the man I loved.

And still love, I remind myself. *You still love Mike. Nobody is going to try to steal you away from him now. He's your husband. You built a life together.*

Yeah, and keeping that life running smoothly is my full-time job.

I look around the family room, noticing all the things that need doing. There are a few stray orange Goldfish cracker crumbs on the rug, which the incompetent Melina missed, which I was about to vacuum yesterday before somebody interrupted me. Beside the television is a scattering of kiddie videos and DVDs I was in the midst of matching with their boxes earlier in the week before somebody interrupted me. On the desk is a stack of bills I started paying last night before somebody interrupted me. And after that I decided to settle in and watch a movie before somebody interrupted me, forcing me to TiVo the rest.

TiVo might just be the most revolutionary invention known to man or harried suburban mother. We've had it for a year now. It's nice to be able to hit Pause when the home-room mother calls you just as *CSI: Miami* is starting, to remind you that you signed up last fall to bring two dozen homemade cupcakes for snack in the morning. Or you can hit Fast Forward when one of the kids shows up in the room just as some unfortunate soul is getting violently whacked on *The Sopranos*. Or you can hit Instant Replay when your husband erupts in a deafening sneezing fit just as Alex Trebeck is giving the right answer on *Jeopardy*.

You know, it's too bad the trusty TiVo remote doesn't work on anything other than the television set, because I could use a version of it to Pause, Fast Forward and Rewind real-life moments all day, every day. No matter what I'm doing, somebody is always interrupting me.

So why isn't that happening now?

Why isn't one of the kids bugging me to give them Gummi Worms or to wipe their poopy keister or to tell so-and-so to stop *kicking/biting/looking-at-me* so that I can forget about answering Happy Nappy?

I don't *have* to answer him. I can delete him from my life with the press of a button.

Too bad it wasn't that easy the first time around.

Back then, I didn't know how to let go.

Maybe I still don't.

My fingers are flying over the keys before I can stop them.

Dear Mike, Thanks for writing…

Good. Now what?

I was so surprised to hear from you!

Good. Now what?

I've been thinking of you a lot lately.

Not good.

I replace it with I'm sorry things ended the way they did, and I've always hoped for the chance to tell you how sorry I am that things didn't work out for us.

Definitely not good.

I backspace over that and sit with my fingers poised on the keyboard, trying to think of something to say. Something that will lead us not into temptation. Something that isn't trite yet won't dredge up the painful past.

I mean, I broke the guy's heart. I let him believe we could have a future together, even though I was in love with some-body else.

The somebody else I married.

The somebody else with whom I have three children, a mortgage and a retirement plan. I should probably point that out first and foremost.

I immediately type I'm still married to Mike.

Then I realize it sounds as though I thought we might not last.

I backspace quickly. Of course I'm still married to Mike. Why wouldn't I be?

I try again.

Mike and I have three beautiful sons and a house in Westches-ter. He's working at an ad agency in Manhattan and I...

I pause, frowning.

Hmm. How can I make my hausfrau existence sound glamorous and exciting?

Perhaps the more pressing question is why do I feel the need to make my hausfrau existence sound glamorous and exciting?

I delete the last line, all the way back to Westchester. That was probably TMI, anyway. He doesn't need to know the intimate details of my life.

I just can't help wishing there were some.

Time to wrap things up quickly.

I'd love to hear from you again when you have time. Take care! Beau

There. Short and sweet.

I hit Send before I can read it over and change my mind.

Time for a reality check.

I log off, march over to the phone and dial Mike's extension.

His secretary answers.

"Hi, Jan, it's Beau."

"Beau! We were just talking about you."

"You were?" I say, wondering who *we* is.

I hate when somebody says they were just talking about me. Not that it happens regularly, but still…

What could anybody possibly have to say about me? I don't do anything. I don't go anywhere. I don't see anyone.

"Yes, I was just telling Mike how lucky he is to have a wife who's willing to stay home and be with the kids. If I had to be at home with my kids, I'd kill myself."

"Oh. Well…" What does one say to that? "It's not so bad."

"Well, I told Mike he needs to bring you some flowers once in a while too, to let you know how much he appreciates you."

Too?

"He's such a sweetheart, Beau," she goes on. "I can't believe he always remembers that purple is my favorite color."

"Oh…he's got quite a memory."

So do I. I remember when my husband used to stop at the florist in Grand Central on his way home every once in a while. He'd come in the door with a paper-wrapped bouquet of my favorite flowers, heavenly scented stargazer lilies.

He hasn't done that in months.

I hadn't even noticed until now.

"Hang on and I'll go get him for you," Jan says, and puts me on hold.

It's not that I'm jealous. If Mike's secretary were the least bit buxom or beautiful, I might be jealous. But Jan, a married mother of toddler twins, has crow's-feet, prematurely gray hair, saddlebags and an upper lip that desperately needs electrolysis. She and I are about the same age, but she looks a good decade older. She's so not a threat to my marriage.

In fact, until recently, I didn't think anything could be a threat to my marriage.

"Hey, what's up, Babs?" my husband's voice asks.

I hate when he calls me Babs. But at least he sounds cheerful, so I say, just as cheerfully, "Hi! I just…I wanted to see how your day was going."

"Crazy. How about yours?"

Upstairs, I hear the clattering of a million tiny plastic pieces against hardwood. Apparently, the Lego city has met its demise.

"Crazy," I tell Mike.

Because if an out-of-the-blue e-mail from an old lover isn't crazy, I don't know what is.

"Crazy how? Are the boys okay?"

"They're fine. One is playing, one is watching Dora, one is sleeping. When are you coming home?"

"Late" is his prompt reply. "I have to take some people out for drinks. Don't wait for me for dinner."

"I won't. Will you be home before I put the kids to bed?"

"I'm not sure. I'll try. Kiss them for me if I'm not, okay?"

"Okay. I wish you were coming home soon."

"Believe me, so do I. I'd rather be home with you and the boys than drinking Grey Goose and tonic at the Royalton on an empty stomach."

And I'd rather be drinking Grey Goose and tonic at the Royalton on an empty stomach. Ironic, isn't it, that we long for what we can't have?

Like...

No. Stop that.

"Let's go away," I tell Mike spontaneously.

"Away? What do you mean?"

"Let's go on vacation. Instead of staying here and working on the house. Let's just go somewhere. Please?"

"Beau, I spend every weekday of my life somewhere other than at home," Mike points out, sounding weary. "I'm tired of going somewhere. I want to go nowhere for a change."

"But if we went out to the Cape for the week, you could go nowhere once we got there. You could sit in a chair on the beach for six straight days."

"Do you know what the traffic on 95 is like between here and the Cape in August? It would be a nightmare."

"But—"

"I want to sit in a chair in my own backyard for six straight days, Beau. And when I'm not sitting in a chair, I'm going to be working on that bathroom under the stairs. Believe me, you'll thank me when you're flushing that toilet at the end of the week."

I don't think so. Not if it means also flushing any hope of a real vacation this summer.

I sigh. "It's just hard to be at home with the kids day in and day out, Mike."

"Maybe you should get a hobby."

Is it my imagination, or is he being condescending?

"What do you suggest?" I ask in a brittle tone. "Macramé? Model airplanes?"

"You know what I mean. You need something to do, other than taking care of the kids. I don't blame you for being bored."

His unexpected sympathy catches me off guard.

Before I can respond, I can hear a phone ringing on the other end of the line.

"We'll talk about it over the weekend, okay?" he asks, slipping from sympathetic to distracted in a matter of seconds.

"Yeah, okay."

We hang up.

I don't want a hobby. I want…

I don't know what I want, other than for this sudden restlessness to go away.

I stand there in the family room, listening to the overhead hum of childish conversation, Dora's theme song, the rhythmic, battery-charged rocking of the swing.

I almost wish Tyler would start whimpering, just to give me something specific to do.

When did I get to be this aimless housewife?

Mike and I have three beautiful sons and a house in Westchester.

It sounds so fulfilling when you put it in writing. So much better than the reality.

Reality is—

I hear a thud overhead, followed by the inevitable "Mommy!"

"Coming," I say, heading for the stairs and reality.

eight

The past

Two days into Mike's visit to New York, he had landed a second interview at a software firm and a lead on a possible commercial-banking position with a decent starting salary.

Things were looking up.

Rather, I assumed they were.

But then, I also assumed that Michael Jackson would always be a superstar.

And black.

Anyway, Mike didn't seem particularly enthusiastic about anything other than being with me. He was his usual romantic self, buying me roses, taking me to a fancy dinner at Windows on the World, giving me a full-body massage with patchouli-scented oil he'd brought with him from L.A.

But nothing about New York itself—not the superior bagels, not the breathtaking view from Windows on the World, not even the two orchestra tickets Janelle Jacques herself had given me for an evening performance of *Jerome Robbins Broadway*—seemed to thrill him.

Janelle was always giving away freebies to the under-lings, but she'd never offered me anything more valuable than an ugly red nylon fanny pack before now. She definitely had great timing. Now Mike would see that my job was not only fulfilling, but had great perks. Maybe he'd realize that moving to Los Angeles—which he hadn't officially sug-gested, but which definitely hovered unspoken between us—was out of the question for me.

"The great thing about New York," I told him as we stepped out of the Imperial Theater after the show, "is that you can see a Broadway show whenever you feel like it."

"Yeah," Mike agreed with questionable enthusiasm, lead-ing me through the after-show throng and across Forty-fifth street, weaving between the cabs and limos lined up outside the theater.

I brushed a clump of Aqua Net-sticky hair from my fore-head. After the air-conditioned Imperial, the July heat felt especially oppressive. Kind of like going from a raging bliz-zard to my grandmother's overheated nursing home in the dead of winter. Your instinct was to start shedding clothing immediately.

But I was already sleeveless, with bare legs and open-toed shoes. The only possible thing I could possibly shed was my rumpled blue linen shift dress, and believe me, after a few minutes trudging through that heat, it wasn't out of the ques-tion. The night air wasn't just hot, it was oppressively soupy. If it were any more humid, we could swim uptown.

"You want to go get something to eat?" I asked hopefully, thinking an air-conditioned restaurant and a big rare ham-burger would be perfect right about now.

"Now? You mean like an ice-cream cone?"

"I mean like dinner."

He checked his watch. "It's too late for dinner, Beau."

"Aren't you hungry? You said you were starving before the show."

"That's because it was way past dinnertime then."

"It was only six-thirty."

"Exactly."

"Who eats dinner before six-thirty?" I asked, and decided not to point out that we didn't have time then, anyway.

The reason we didn't have time was because I got hung up in an emergency meeting late this afternoon. Increasingly jealous of Arsenio's success, Janelle wanted us to implement some kind of audience-participation stunt, on a par with Arsenio's barking-dog pound. After three hours of brainstorming, one of the assistant producers finally came up with the idea of outfitting the studio audience in matching straw sombreros emblazened with Janelle Jacques's trademark initials.

Personally, I think she was kidding when she said it, but narcissistic Janelle loved it. Next thing I knew, Gaile and I were being given detailed instructions for purchasing the sombreros wholesale.

So I was late meeting Mike, and he wasn't thrilled to have stood on a street corner for forty-five minutes thinking, as he so eloquently put it, that I had been crushed by a crosstown bus.

"Who eats dinner at ten-thirty?" he was asking now, acting as if I had a hankering for fresh croissants and was insisting we board a plane for Paris *tout de suite.*

Stomach growling ferociously, I gestured around us at the street lined with crowded restaurants. "A lot of people."

"Not in the rest of the world, Beau. That's a New York thing."

"Yeah, well, when in Rome…"

He sighed. "If you're still hungry when we get uptown, we'll eat there. I can't stand the crowds here. Let's get a cab."

I looked around at the traffic-clogged side street that led to the traffic-clogged avenue. There had to be a few dozen cabs in the vicinity, but none of them were moving, and all of them were occupied.

"No cabs. Are you sure you don't want to grab a bite here?"

"Positive."

Mike and I headed uptown toward my apartment on foot. He seemed to be brooding, so I kept up a running commentary on the show.

"I really love that one short bald guy," I said.

"Which one?" Mike looked around.

"The one in the show. Him," I said, leafing through my *Playbill* and pointing out the actor's picture. "His name is Jason Alexander. Wasn't he great?"

"Yeah. Great."

His mind was obviously elsewhere.

I tried again. "My favorite part of the show was the scene with the three sailors from *On the Town*." I proceeded to sing a few bars about New York being a hell of a town.

Hint, hint.

But before my one-woman tourism campaign could launch the lyrics about the Bronx being up and the Battery down, Mike cut in with a brisk, "Beau, we have to talk."

"Can't we just sing?"

He didn't laugh.

I did, but only for a second. Then I saw the look on his face and reluctantly asked, "Okay, what's up?"

"It's just…this." He gestured vaguely with his hand.

I looked around, pretending I had no idea what he was talking about.

There were people everywhere: strolling, gaping tourists with cameras and maps in hand, striding grim-faced locals mowing them down, drag queens, cops that were outnumbered by gangs of wandering thugs and pickpocket types, lone vagrants, food-delivery people, flamboyantly gay couples, honeymooners, dog-walking matrons, weary corporate drones just leaving the office.

Towering skyscrapers. Neon signs. Open manholes. Con Ed repair crews. Round-the-clock construction sites. Bright white spotlights and blue police barricades that betrayed a movie shoot down the cross street. Honking, bumper-to-bumper traffic. Open cellars in front of all-night Korean groceries; dripping window air-conditioner units overhead.

Noise. Traffic. Litter. Stench.

"What?" I asked, all innocence.

"That."

I debated the wisdom of pushing it with another *what?* I knew damn well what he was talking about.

But in case I didn't, he added helpfully, "New York."

"Oh. That."

"You really want to live here forever, Beau?"

Uh-oh. I so knew this was coming.

"Yeah," I said promptly, with the hometown pride of a Trump. "I really do. I love this city. It feels like the center of the universe."

"So does L.A."

"No, it doesn't. It's only the center of the entertainment industry. Which, if you think about it, Mike, really has nothing to do with you, so I don't know why you—"

"It has something to do with *you,* Beau. I mean, think about it. You're building a career in television. You should be in Hollywood."

Damn, it was hot. I stuck out my lower lip in an attempt

to blow the hair that was plastered to my sweaty forehead, but it didn't budge.

"I don't want to be in Hollywood, Mike," I told him resolutely, sidestepping what looked like a heap of rags on the sidewalk.

I realized it was a human being only when it snarled at me.

"Whoa, Dude, chill out," Mike said, hustling me past.

Dude? Chill out? Who was he, Keanu Reeves in *Bill and Ted's Excellent Adventure?* I opened my mouth to inform him that things might be different on the West Coast, but here in New York, we didn't call the street people Dude, nor did we advise them to chill out.

But Mike was still speaking, and what he was saying was, "That's disgusting."

"What's disgusting?" I looked around.

Truth be told, there were plenty of disgusting things to be seen in this neighborhood at this hour. Hookers, overflowing trash cans, discarded syringes.

"The dude," Mike said with a shudder.

Oh. Right. The dude.

"He was filthy. And he stunk."

"Yeah."

I was accustomed to the homeless now, just as I was accustomed to the noise level, the crowds, the lines, the waits, the astronomical cost of living.

I was also accustomed to getting what I wanted.

I didn't want to leave New York. And I wanted Mike to be there with me.

"See, it isn't like that on the West Coast."

"What, there are no homeless? Come on, Mike. I know they're there. They're everywhere."

"They're there, yes, but you don't have to step over them every time you go someplace."

"That's because you have to be in a car every time you go someplace."

"What's so bad about that?"

"Nothing. I guess. If you like that sort of thing."

"What sort of thing? Driving?"

"I don't know, Mike...I guess I just think it's really overrated."

"Driving?"

"L.A."

Since I was still in a musical mood, I sang a few bars of Billy Joel's "Say Goodbye to Hollywood."

Hint, hint.

"Very funny," Mike said. "I'm being serious."

"So am I. I don't want to move across the country."

"I'm not sure I do, either."

"But the East Coast is home for you."

"Not at the moment."

"You know what I mean. You're from here. You'd be coming home."

"I'm not from Manhattan. I'm *from* Long Island. There's a big difference."

"Why don't you just see how you do with your job interviews, Mike?" I asked him in what I hoped wasn't too pleading a tone. "You have great opportunities here. And if you hate living in the city, you—*we*—can always commute from the suburbs."

"What, you mean like Jersey?"

"God, no. I was thinking Westchester."

"There are beaches in Jersey."

"Oh. Well then, maybe Jersey," I conceded, having forgotten his newfound affinity to sand and saltwater.

"Yeah. I need to have the ocean nearby," said Mike, who had grown up a stone's throw from Jones Beach, yet never dreamed of catching a wave until he moved to la-la land. "I can't live without beach access."

The riff from "Surfin' USA" replaced the Jerome Robbins score running through my head.

"Well, you already know that Long Island has great beaches," I assured him.

"I don't want to go back to the Island. I spent the first eighteen years of my life trying to get *off* the Island."

You can take the boy off the Island... I thought, trying not to grin at the pronounced accent he had tried so hard to lose. Mike's "off" was still "oh-awf," just as "coffee" was "coh-awfee." When I first met him, I had a hard time understanding what he was saying half the time. Now I was used to it, but still found it charming.

Not charming enough to want to move with him to Long Island and develop an accent of my own, though.

"The Jersey shore has great beaches, too," I pointed out, much to my own surprise. I mean, what was I doing? I didn't want to live in Jersey. I wanted to live in New York.

"Yeah. I guess Jersey wouldn't be so bad. Because I know I couldn't deal with the city in the summer."

I attempted to shove aside images of sidewalk cafés in the West Village and Shakespeare in Central Park and the Farmer's Market in Union Square. Eating hot dogs and watching the Bronx Bombers play at historic Yankee Stadium. Italian ices from street vendors, fireworks over the Statue of Liberty, sunning on a blanket in Central Park's Sheep Meadow on a Sunday afternoon.

I'd miss all of that if I had to live in Jersey.

Then again, anything was better than *Californ-eye-yay,* per the *inside-outside-USA* sound track in my head.

I mean, deep down I knew that I wasn't always going to have things exactly my way. If a compromise was what it would take to make our relationship work, then a compromise it would have to be. Because if Mike left, I'd miss *him* a hell of a lot more than anything New York had to offer.

The suburbs were better than nothing. I had to make him see that we could be happy here. Or at least in a thirty-mile radius of here.

"Great," I said with a *there, it's settled* gusto.

"Mmm," he said with a maddeningly noncommittal *nothing's settled* ambivalence.

But I, in my newfound The Donald mode, needed to seal the deal.

"You know, maybe we should go apartment hunting this weekend," I suggested casually as we waited on a corner for a traffic light to change.

"Don't you think apartment hunting is still a little premature, Beau? I don't even have a job here yet."

"You'll get one sooner or later. And I've been checking out the ads in *The Voice* lately just to see what's out there. I saw a bunch of Manhattan sublets that start in September, which would give me time to give notice so Valerie can find a new roommate. Then we can sublet until spring and move out to—"

"Whoa, wait a minute. Why would *you* have to give notice? I thought we were talking about an apartment for *me*. *You* already have a place."

"I do, but…" I took a deep breath and faced him. "I thought maybe we would move in together."

"You did?"

I nodded.

The light had changed, but neither of us moved. I was afraid to even let out the breath I was holding, much less take the plunge off the curb, and Mike appeared to be rooted to the spot in sheer horror.

This was not good.

This was also not what I was expecting.

"We never talked about moving in together, Beau."

"I know…but I just kind of figured we would."

"You just kind of figured that we would…what? Talk about doing it? Or you just kind of figured that we would do it?"

"I just kind of figured that we would talk about doing it," I lied, thinking that this wasn't going as well as it should be. "I figured since you were moving here, and you would need a place to live, it would make sense for us to get a place together."

"Oh," he said. Just, *oh.*

Rhymes with *no.*

And *go.* As in, *Go away and leave me alone, you clingy girlfriend you.*

"It's just that rents are so expensive, it's hard to make a go of it without a roommate."

"That's my point. In L.A., you can rent a—"

"And if you're going to have a roommate," I cut in, not caring that in L.A. you can rent a freaking oceanfront house for the price of a bagel with lox, "I'm the perfect candidate. I don't smoke, I don't hog the remote and I don't leave the toilet seat up."

Splat. Another cute quip fallen flat as seventies hair.

"You already have a roommate," Mike pointed out.

"I know, but I'd rather live with you. Valerie smokes, hogs the remote and leaves the toilet seat up."

"Valerie leaves the toilet seat up?"

"Only when she vomits," I conceded.

Still, he failed to crack a smile.

"The thing is, Beau, moving in together is a huge step."

"I know. But we've been going out forever, and…" *And*

I just assumed forever was in our future, as well. But I was suddenly afraid to tell him that, because I was afraid, for the first time, that he might not feel the same way.

"Living together is different. That's a huge commitment."

"I know."

"I just don't think I'm capable of that yet."

"Yet? So you will be…soon?"

He hesitated. "I don't know."

"You mean, you might not ever be ready?"

"I don't know, Beau!" He sounded exasperated.

No, this wasn't going as well as it could be. In fact, if it were going any worse, you might call it a breakup.

"I don't know what to say, Mike."

"I don't either. But I'm being honest."

We walked on in silence for a good five minutes.

I felt sick inside. All I wanted was to be home. Alone. So that I could cry in my bed.

But Mike was staying with me, and Valerie was probably there, and I knew I would be trapped once I got there.

About as trapped as I felt out here on the street with Mike.

The crowd had thinned now that we were getting away from the theater district. If we headed over to Eighth Avenue and up a few more blocks, we might even be able to catch a cab uptown. I said as much to Mike.

"You want to go right home? I thought you wanted to eat first."

"I'm not hungry anymore."

"Well, we can go get a drink and talk."

"About not moving in together?" I asked tartly.

He shrugged. "Whatever. Never mind. I'm beat. Let's get a cab and go back to your place and just go to sleep."

And we did.

nine

The present

I'm curled up on the couch in the family room watching David Letterman and eating lo-carb coffee-mocha ice cream straight out of the container when I hear a key in the back door.

"Beau?" Mike calls, his wing tips tapping across the ceramic tile in the kitchen. "You still up?"

"Down here," I call, and mute the volume on the television remote.

I hear a jangling sound as he tosses his keys on the counter and a thud as he drops his briefcase on the floor by the door. The refrigerator door opens and closes and he comes down, a bottle of Poland Spring in hand.

"Hi," I say, making room for him on the couch by my feet.

He plants a quick kiss on my forehead. I can smell the city on his clothes and liquor on his breath. Not a lot, and I actually kind of like the smell. Plus, it explains the kiss. He's always affectionate when he's had a drink or two.

"Sorry it's so late," he says, plopping down on the couch and twisting the plastic top off his water. "I missed the 9:52 train by three minutes and I had to wait an hour for the next one."

"That stinks." I watch David Letterman silently asking Demi Moore something that's making her squirm and laugh.

"Yeah. How are the boys?"

"Asleep, finally."

"Did they give you a hard time about going to bed?"

"Do they ever *not* give me a hard time about going to bed?"

He shrugs and guzzles some water. "What did you do all day?"

"Played the world's longest game of Candyland. Cleaned up a zillion spills. Changed diapers." *Answered an e-mail from the ex-love-of-my-life.* "Mikey had a playdate with Chelsea. After she left, we went to the park and played in the sandbox until Josh stole some kid's metal shovel and hit Mikey over the head with it."

He winces. "Ouch. Why is he so bad these days?"

"You mean naughty."

"No, I mean *bad*. Violence is bad. Poor Mikey. Do they even make metal sandbox shovels these days?"

"Apparently, they do. Either that or it was a valuable antique, which now has an indentation the shape of Mikey's skull."

"Great. Was he okay?"

"After the bleeding stopped, he was fine. Oh, and Tyler has another yeast infection. I called the doctor, and he called in a prescription. After we picked it up, we had dinner at McDonald's, then I took them over to the pool to cool them off before bed."

"That sounds fun."

I bite back a sarcastic remark. Whenever I mention going to the town pool, Mike seems to envision me lounging in the sun with a trashy novel and a piña colada while strapping cabana boys hover at my beck and call.

The reality is reminiscent of a female baboon I saw at the Bronx zoo when I was chaperoning Mikey's class trip last year. I felt for my primate counterpart. I really did. There she was, looking miserable in the hot sun while her newborn nursed voraciously and two other small baboons were draped around her, clinging and squirming.

So much for evolution. Take away the fur, give the older two baboons whiny voices in which to beg for more, more, more snack-bar crap, throw in last summer's out-dated tankini, a body of overchlorinated water that smells faintly of urine, and the town's entire noncommuting population splashing about, and there you have it: my daily pool experience.

"Yeah. Fun," I tell Mike, who apparently misses my ironic inflection, because he still looks pretty damn wistful.

He chugs down more Poland Spring and tells me about his evening, which sounds businesslike and boring, but beats wrestling three perpetually protesting kids into and out of car seats, fast-food restaurant booths and wet bathing suits.

"I'm going to bed," he says, stretching and yawning. "Are you coming?"

"I was going to finish watching Letterman," I say, dipping my spoon into the ice-cream container again. "Sting is going to be on."

"Can I have a taste?" Mike asks, eyeing my ice cream.

"You don't like this kind. It's lo-carb."

"You're right. I don't like that kind." He makes a face, then runs a hand over my bare lower leg. "But I can think of something I do like."

So can I. For example, watching *Late Night* when Sting is Dave's special musical guest.

"Come on…come to bed."

There's a TV in the bedroom, but I know that's not what he has in mind. Like I said, give him a few drinks and he turns into *Bachelor* Bob Guiney, the kissing fool.

Still, I resist. Sting is sexy.

And I'm not the least bit ready for bed, thanks to the large coffee I drank at McDonald's and the additional caffeine in the ice cream. After Mike does his thing and rolls over, I'll undoubtedly be left to lie awake and think.

Given the day's events, I would most likely think about the other Mike, and that's the last thing I want to do. I've checked my e-mail at least six times since this afternoon.

He hasn't written back yet.

Chances are, he won't.

Oh, who am I kidding?

He wrote to me in the first place and he asked me to write back. Sooner or later, he's going to reply to my reply.

And then what?

And then I'll be tempted to reply to his reply to my reply, that's what.

"Come on, Beau." Mike runs his hand up over my knee to my thigh. He's been around long enough to know his way around my erogenous zones better than I know my way around Super Stop and Shop. I can feel goose bumps rising on the back of my neck, and they aren't from a lo-carb coffee-mocha head freeze.

Yes, Sting is sexy, but Mike is sexy, too.

Okay, not as sexy as Sting, but my chances of bedding my favorite rock star are probably nil.

Okay, definitely nil.

My chances of bedding Mike are imminent if I move

now, but nil if I wait for Letterman to end. And now that I'm all hot and bothered, somebody is sure as hell going to get lucky tonight.

I contemplate waiting just a little while to join Mike. But waking my husband from a dead sleep after he's been drinking is about as likely as Sting showing up at our door, sans Trudy, to seduce me into an evening of tantric sex.

In other words, it ain't gonna happen.

I glance at the silent action on television as Mike's hand arrives provocatively at the leg band of my boxer shorts. Which are actually his boxer shorts—my version of summer pajamas. As his fingers make their well-choreographed rounds from outer to inner thigh, my stomach launches into its usual gymnastic routine despite my desire to find out why Demi Moore just gave Dave the finger or a thumbs-up—I couldn't tell which.

"Let's go," Mike says suggestively, wiggling his dark eyebrows.

"I guess I can TiVo Letterman," I concede, pressing a few quick buttons on the remote.

Have I mentioned that TiVo is the best invention ever?

Oh. Sorry. But it really is. Especially at moments like this.

Because the thing is, while I like sex as much as the next married mother of three, I have to admit that lately it isn't necessarily worth the time and/or effort. And unlike *Late Night with David Letterman,* sex these days is highly predictable, not as creative as it used to be, and over in fifteen minutes or less.

I hate that I'm at a place in my life when I actually have to weigh the benefits of romance versus post-prime-time viewing. I never thought I'd feel that way. There was a time when all Mike had to do was look at me, or graze my hand with his, and I was a primate in heat.

But the truth is, after a day of traipsing around town like

an attachment parenting baboon, the last thing I want is some-body else pawing at me or attached to my breasts—even if this brand of pawing and breast attachment is more pleasurable.

When it comes to defining pleasure, there's a lot to be said for the prospect of being undisturbed in a quiet house with a television remote, the entire length of the couch and the remaining half carton of melting ice cream all to myself.

Then again, sex with my husband might remind me why even the fond recollection of sex with somebody else is bad.

No, not bad.

Naughty.

Definitely naughty.

As I follow Mike up to our bedroom, I do my best to ban-ish the barrage of erotic memories that keep popping up.

He looks in on the boys one at a time while I put away my ice cream and brush my teeth. Then I lie on our brand-new king-size pillow-top mattress and watch him uncere-moniously strip off his suit, tie, shirt, T-shirt, boxers, socks.

He seems a little off balance as he hops on one foot and removes the opposite sock.

"How many drinks did you have tonight?" I ask him.

"I don't know. A few. Why?"

"Just wondering." I find myself wishing I'd had a glass or two of wine instead of lo-carb ice cream. Then maybe I'd feel a little more relaxed, and a little less anxious about that e-mail I sent earlier.

Not so much anxious, really, as guilty. If Mike knew…

But he doesn't know, and he'll never know.

If I get a reply, I'll just delete it immediately and forget all about the other Mike.

I'll stop thinking about the past, about what might have been.

Because that, of course, is what I keep wondering about.

What would have happened if I had made a different choice that summer? If I had married a different man?

I wouldn't have my boys…a thought so horrible that it should be enough to nip this thought process in the bud.

But it isn't.

I envision the other Mike standing there naked; I try to see him as he probably looks now. Is he graying? Gaining weight? Losing his hair?

I can't help seeing him in my mind's eye as a modern-day Dorian Gray, immune to the passage of time.

As I watch my husband walk naked toward the adjoining bathroom, I can't help noticing the slight paunch around his stomach, and, when he turns around, the hint of love handles just above his stark white buttocks.

I know every inch of his body; have seen him naked every day for years. I'm well aware that he's no longer a buff twentysomething with a six-pack and sculpted biceps. But rarely do I see him as a middle-aged man.

I see that now.

He doesn't bother to close the door.

Neither of us has; not in years. There's nothing either of us can do in there that the other hasn't seen or heard—or smelled—a thousand times before. Back in the beginning of our marriage, there was a certain thrill to sharing each other's most intimate moments, knowing that no part of our lives was too private to share.

Back then, I couldn't imagine keeping any secrets from the man I loved.

Now, I have a few.

Like, he doesn't know that I still have a Neiman Marcus credit card in my own name. We mutually agreed to cut up all our store cards years ago and use cash or American Express.

He doesn't know that I dented the fender of our old

Trailblazer when I backed into a stone wall in the Applebee's parking lot. When he spotted the damage, I feigned innocence and let him think somebody must have backed into me while I was parked somewhere.

He doesn't know that it isn't mandatory that both parents attend conferences at Josh's preschool; that our old washing machine could have been repaired instead of replaced with a shiny new front-loading model; that I lost one of the sapphire earrings he got me for Christmas a few years ago.

And he doesn't know that I heard from Mike today.

As I listen to the steady stream of urine hitting the toilet water in the next room, I find my arousal waning.

I can't help it. There's nothing sexy about pee, unless you have some sick fetish.

I wonder if the other Mike would shut the bathroom door if we were married.

I can't help that, either. The wondering.

Where would I be, right this very moment, if I had married the other Mike?

I'd still have my career, because my children are the reason I gave it up. I might even be an executive producer by now.

Or maybe I'd still be Ma Ingalls meets Olivia Walton meets Marian Cunningham. Maybe I'd still have my boys, only they'd have a different daddy.

But that's impossible. If they had a different daddy, they'd have half his genes. They wouldn't be who they are now. They'd be different.

I don't want different boys.

I don't want a different husband, either. Really, I don't.

The toilet flushes, the water runs, and Mike steps back into the bedroom. He's familiar and safe and comfortable, and I welcome him into our bed, shoving his fantasy counterpart out of it.

Mike turns out the lamp and slips in beside me. I hear him patting the mattress, as if he's feeling around for me.

"Where are you?" he asks.

"On my side."

"Way over there? I told you this bed would be too big."

He did tell me that.

But I told him there was no such thing as too big, and insisted that our queen-size bed was too small. As evidence, I offered the following:

Exhibit A: our nightly battle over the queen-size comforter—also too small;

Exhibit B: the boys' tendency to join us whenever they've had a bad dream, are sick, need to cuddle, or simply feel like they might be missing something;

Exhibit C: Mike's irksome habit of sleeping with one arm bent beneath his head and the protruding elbow jabbing my face every time one of us moves slightly.

In the end, Mike gave in and let me charge the king-size pillow-top at Sears' last one-day sale—no payments, no interest until the new year. It cost over two grand and we don't have a headboard for it yet, but I don't care. The last thing I want at night is somebody else crowding my personal space. I really need my space lately, even in my nonwaking hours.

But the whole point of my being in bed with Mike now is to be near him, so I scooch across the cushy new mattress and into his arms.

"That's better," Mike says, and kisses me.

"You taste like minty toothpaste."

He tastes like limes and stale gin.

He kisses me again, first on the lips, then in the hollow behind my ear, then just above my collarbone. I'm aroused again; he knows my body as well as I know his; knows what to do, where to touch me.

Our lovemaking is passionate; more so than usual. As he moves over me and then into me, I find myself closing my eyes and, for the first time in our marriage, pretending that he is somebody else.

The name I call out in a pivotal moment is the right one, but it isn't my husband whose sweaty body is climaxing into mine, and it isn't my husband's face that haunts my dreams when I finally fall asleep hours later, on the far side of the vast new mattress.

ten

The past

Cue *Mission Impossible* music:
   Duh-dah-da-da-duh-dah-da-da-duh-dah-da-da-duh-dah.
Badadah. Badadah. Badadah. Badadah...da-da-dah.
   Gaile and I had exactly half an hour remaining in which to locate a dozen wintergreen-flavored candy canes on the isle of Manhattan in the dog days of summer.
   Why, you ask, did we face such a daunting task?
   Because today's coveted guest on *J-Squared*, a female pop star who shall remain nameless, had stipulated in her contract that the greenroom be stocked with certain items.
   So there we were, lowly production assistants on a glorified scavenger hunt that had thus far taken us uptown, downtown, all around the town. We had little trouble locating the specific brands of bottled water and crudités dip.
   But so far, catering to our diva's other demands had

proven to be a tremendous pain in the ass. We had to go to a specific Mulberry Street bakery for white-chocolate toasted-almond biscotti and to a specific health-food store in the East Village for the homeopathic lozenges to protect her precious vocal cords.

We had found a box of stale candy canes in a discount bin in a NoHo drug store, but alas, they were peppermint. Now we were headed to a dollar store in Chelsea that was rumored to have received an assorted-flavors Christmas candy closeout shipment.

"Okay, which way is north?" Gaile asked, bending to adjust the strap of her high-heeled shoe as we emerged from the subway at Fourteenth Street.

I looked around for the reassuring sight of the twin towers of the World Trade Center, every New Yorker's trusty old anticompass. Wherever they were, that was south. Unless you were in Brooklyn, in which case you didn't need a compass or the World Trade Center to find your way around; you needed a full-blown guidebook. At least, I did.

All that mattered to me that summer was that I had mastered Manhattan, the only borough that counted. Nobody I knew had resorted to living in Brooklyn, or wanted to.

As we zigzagged our way uptown, our Oakley Frogskins shielding our eyes from the bright midday sun, I filled Gaile in on my conversation with commitment-phobe Mike before he got on his return flight to L.A. the night before.

"He said that even if he lands one of the jobs he interviewed for, he isn't sure he's going to take it," I told Gaile. "He said something about having to make sure they're offering the right 'package.'"

"Package? What the hell does that mean?"

"You know…salary, benefits, vacation days, perks."

"Oh, please. Who the hell is entitled to a 'package' the first year out of grad school?"

I explained to Gaile that things were different outside of our industry, where hordes of brilliant and ambitious new-comers were willing to sign on for slave labor at a pittance. In the real world—i.e., the high-tech computer world—entry-level applicants with master's degrees actually shopped themselves around.

"So it's beggars—you and me—versus choosers—Mike. He has the luxury of entertaining offers instead of jumping on the first one that comes in. Is that how it works?" Gaile asked, stopping to lean against a Batman movie poster on a bus-stop wall so she could once again adjust the strap of her left four-inch-heeled stiletto.

"Beggars and choosers. Yup, that pretty much sums it up," I agreed, thinking she didn't know the half of it. The half of it being that I had begged Mike to move in with me and he had pretty much chosen not to.

"My feet are killing me," Gaile announced, using Michael Keaton's masked face to push her weight off the bus-stop wall.

"Mine, too."

We resumed race-walking west toward Ninth Avenue.

"Look at me. I'm not dressed for this freaking marathon," she grumbled.

"Neither am I."

"At least you're wearing flats."

I glanced down at black high-tops. "Yeah, but at least you have bare arms and legs." I was wearing a belted microfi-ber tunic over spandex leggings.

"Nobody told you to dress like that," Gaile reminded me, looking cool and crisp in her sleeveless jungle-print dress.

"Your skin would probably breathe better if you mummified yourself in Saran Wrap, for God's sake."

"Well, I didn't plan on spending the day hiking around in the blazing heat," I pointed out. "The studio is, like, fifty degrees."

"Layers, honey," Gaile said in her infinite fashion wisdom. "It's all about layers. So, getting back to your man...if he doesn't get a worthy package in New York, then what?"

"Then I guess I'm supposed to move to the West Coast to be near him."

"Maybe Janelle has connections to get you a job out there."

Instant vision of becoming the next Marcy Carsey, sitcom producer extraordinaire.

Instant memory of Mike—the other Mike—the would-be future sitcom star.

For some reason, he had been popping in and out of my head ever since I'd met him last week. Probably because a face that good-looking was hard to forget. So was his enthusiasm for living in New York.

Too bad my Mike didn't share it.

"I don't want a job out there," I told Gaile. "I don't want to move. I want *him* to move. That makes more sense."

"See, that's the thing about you, Beau."

"What's the thing about me?"

"You're spoiled."

"Yeah, yeah, yeah. I'm spoiled. You've told me a hundred times. So has everyone else in the world."

She laughed. Then she said, "Someday, girlfriend, you're going to have a rude awakening."

"What do you mean?"

"Just that things aren't always going to go your way."

"Things don't *always* go my way."

"When don't they?"

"Now. With Mike."

"Well, if you love him, you might have to consider moving."

"Maybe I could *consider* it," I admitted reluctantly. "But it's so far away."

"So? You'd visit."

"I'd rather live here than there."

"You'd adapt."

"Yeah, sure. Next thing you know I'll have fake platinum hair, a fake tan, fake big boobs…"

"So? You'd look good with fake big boobs," said Gaile, who had authentically gigantic boobs herself.

"I can have fake big boobs right here in New York."

"Nah. Nobody does fake big boobs better than L.A."

"Then I'll stick with a flat chest. Sooner or later, the super-skinny waif look might be back in fashion."

"I wouldn't bet on it," she said, shaking her head. "We're over that. Healthy curves are here to stay."

We had arrived at the dollar store. Wouldn't you know it? They were fresh out of wintergreen candy canes.

"Ms. Diva is just going to have to make do with these," Gaile grumbled as we headed uptown on the number-one train ten minutes later, loaded down with plain old—and I mean that literally—peppermint candy canes and Wint-O-Green Lifesavers for good measure.

"What if she throws a fit? She'll probably get us both fired," I said, trying not to inhale the pungent body odor of the man whose armpit was adjacent to my nose as he clung to the next overhead strap.

The air-conditioning wasn't working in this car and the lights flickered for the first minute or two before going out for good. I could think of few things more unpleasant than being crammed into a hot, dark subway car with hundreds of overheated, smelly strangers, hurtling through rat-infested tunnels at high speed.

I mean, was this what I'd always wanted?

I don't think so.

Maybe I *should* consider L.A., I found myself thinking reluctantly when Gaile and I emerged on the street to find that the bright blue skies had given way to a torrential downpour.

Maybe there was something to be said for fresh air, sunshine and fake big boobs after all.

eleven

The present

"What we need," I tell my next-door neighbor Laura as we lounge in my yard soaking our feet in the plastic kiddie pool and licking rapidly melting red, white and blue ice pops, "is a thunderstorm. That would cool things off."

"Chelsea, put the hose down," Laura bellows at her daughter, who is chasing Josh around the yard, soaking him in spurts thanks to the many kinks in the hose.

To me, Laura says, "Screw the thunderstorm. What I need is to have these babies. I feel like Jiffy Pop that's about to burst open in this heat."

I want to reassure her, but the thing is, she *looks* exactly like an overheated Jiffy Pop, too.

We both stare at her tremendously swollen belly. Unfortunately, it's encased in a silvery metallic maternity bathing suit no self-respecting pregnant woman would be caught dead wearing out in public, though it comes in handy for sweltering days like this.

My mother-in-law gave it to me and I passed it along to Laura after Tyler was born, knowing I would never again— God willing—need maternity clothes. For good measure, I also gave her Ty's entire layette and a bunch of newborn toys he hasn't even outgrown yet. I feel a little guilty, but we have so much clutter lying around, he'll never miss it. And with twins, Laura is going to need everything *à deux*.

"Look at me," she wails. "I'm huge."

Yes, she is. I reach across the Parsons table between our chairs to pat her arm, which is slathered in thick white sunscreen. Being a fair-skinned, freckled redhead, Laura pretty much wears SPF 15 year-round. On a day like this, she ups it to 45, and will still be red and blotchy in an hour.

I, on the other hand, doused myself in Hawaiian Tropic oil with minimal SPF in an effort to get a little color. I've actually been trying to get a little color since Memorial Day, but whenever I have a spare five minutes to spend outside, it seems to be overcast, or too hot, or dusk, or time for one of my boys to need me inside, pronto.

But right now, the sky is blue, the kids are relatively entertained, the baby is down for a nap in the house, and I'm thinking life is good.

In fact, lying here next to Laura, it's easy for me to convince myself that I'm already somewhat tanned—and svelte to boot. That's probably mostly because compared to poor Laura, I am.

But don't let me fool you. In reality, I'm paler and puffier than a marshmallow. My legs and arms may be fairly toned, and I've managed to keep my butt and thighs to a minimum, but there's an ugly little fold of tummy between my belly button and my tankini bottom, and no amount of crunches will make it go away.

Maybe that's because the only crunches I've been doing these days are the Nestlé variety.

But I tried. Really, I did. In between my pregnancies for Josh and Tyler, I worked out religiously in a futile effort to get my pre-Mikey figure back. I was almost there, and oops! Along came Tyler.

But there's no chance of another *oops* now. Mike had a vasectomy in April, at my request. I was shocked that he didn't put up more of a fuss about it. I guess when he weighed a winceworthy snip-snip against the possibility of another round of endless sleepless nights, it was a no-brainer.

So, there are no remaining obstacles between me and my cellulite-free former bod. Unless you count another decade's worth of polishing off half-eaten peanut butter sandwiches and "neatening up" my boys' dripping chocolate ice-cream cones.

"How long do you think it'll take me to lose this baby weight?" Laura asks.

"I don't know…maybe a few months?" I lie.

"You really think so?"

Nope.

"Yep."

"I don't know…" She sighs. "Sometimes I think I'll never see a hundred and thirty-five again."

I want to remind her that even if she sees her former weight again, she won't be wearing it the same way she did the first time around. I mean, I'm back down to a hundred and twenty, but I could never wriggle back into the jeans I wore in high school. Everything about my body is permanently wider and lower and softer.

Laura shifts her weight, and her sunglasses topple off her head, landing on the grass beneath her seat.

"No!" she cries out in the utterly helpless tone I recognize all too well. I made that sound myself, whenever I was in my third trimester and dropped something.

"It's okay, I'll get them," I soothe in the *don't panic* tone of one who has walked a mile in her espadrilles (the only thing that will fit on her poor swollen feet these days).

"Thanks." Laura sighs and plunks the sunglasses back above her forehead, where they serve to keep wayward frizz out of her eyes. They're strictly for show; the one time she wore them, earlier in the summer for twenty minutes tops, she wound up looking like a raccoon for a week.

"You're welcome. Poor you."

"Yeah, poor me. Why do I always have to get pregnant in the fall?" Laura grumbles, ignoring—or perhaps not noticing—a sticky blue ice pop drip splashing onto her bare leg, where it blends in nicely with the varicose veins.

I try—and fail—to think of something encouraging to say.

She isn't in the mood for a pep talk. She rants on, "You'd think I would have learned my lesson after not one, but two third trimesters that lasted all summer. But no. Here I am, the village idiot, doing it once again, with twins, no less."

"I know. I'm sorry," I murmur.

"How come your babies were all born in the winter and spring, Beau? Did you plan it that way?"

"Not on purpose. It just worked out." I set my empty ice-pop stick on the table beside the cordless phone and the baby monitor.

"Yeah. Things always just work out for you, don't they?"

"Not always." Sometimes I get sick of people assuming I lead a charmed life. I mean, I have problems just like everybody else.

"Well," Laura says with a grunt as she shifts her weight in her chair, "if you ever consider trying for a girl, make sure you time it right again."

Okay, I'm *really* sick of people saying that. It's bad enough when my friends do it, but sometimes complete strangers will come up to me when I'm out with my three boys and ask me if I'm going to try for a girl. Josh even asked me once if I wished he were a girl so that I could have a daughter. And I'd be rich if I had a dollar for everyone who asked me if I was hoping for a girl when I was pregnant with Tyler.

Maybe it's the heat that makes me more irritated than usual with Laura's innocent comment. Or maybe it's PMS. In any case, I retort, "Are you kidding me? Who in their right mind would want four kids?"

"Trust me. I feel the same way," Laura says, watching Chelsea and Mikey screeching and pouring plastic cups of water over each other's heads. "Kirk had to talk me into three as it was, and that was where I drew the line. The thought of multiples never even crossed my mind, and now look."

I immediately feel guilty. "Yeah, but at least you get two for the price of one pregnancy and labor."

"Gee, what a bargain."

"Anyway, we can't have any more. Mike had a vasectomy, remember?"

"Yeah."

"Maybe Kirk can get one after the twins are born."

"He'd never agree to that."

"Why not?"

"Who knows? Maybe he thinks I'll get hit by a bus and his new wife will be young and childless. I guess Mike figures that if you get hit by a bus, his new wife will be beyond the childbearing years."

"If I get hit by a bus, Mike had better not have a new wife. I want him at my graveside daily, crying and carrying on."

"He probably would be. Unlike you."

"What do you mean?"

"Just that if Mike got hit by a bus, you wouldn't be alone for long."

"What, you think I'd be gallivanting around like some merry widow?" I can't help feeling a little insulted. And, okay, intrigued.

"I just can't see you staying single, Beau. You'd be remarried right away. Men are always checking you out. If you didn't have that wedding ring on, they'd be all over you like flies."

I have to laugh at that. The only thing I can imagine being all over me like flies is my kids. And, well, *flies,* since chances are at least one of my kids tends to smell like poop at any given time.

"Mommy, I'm done with this," Laura's son, Adam, announces, thrusting a melting ice pop into her free hand. "I'm all sticky. Can you clean me?"

"Clean yourself in the pool." Laura sticks his ice pop into her mouth to lick away the drips, then tends to her own. "You know, I'd much rather be double-fisted with frozen margaritas."

I laugh. "I'll smuggle you a pitcher of them in recovery."

"With salt?"

"With salt. And little paper umbrellas."

She laughs.

"I'm so not kidding."

"I know you aren't. Neither am I." She smiles at me.

"What are friends for if not to dull the aftermath of childbirth with tequila?"

"I hope you're not planning to pour it right on my episiotomy stitches, because the lime would probably sting."

"Sting? Sweetie, after birthing two babies, you think a little sting is going to bother you?"

We both laugh, and for some reason, in that moment of

female bonding, I find myself wanting to tell her about Mike. The other Mike. He's been in the back of my mind the past few days, ever since I sent that e-mail.

He hasn't written back. I was obsessive about checking my e-mail at first, but now I'm down to just a few times a day.

"What's wrong?" Laura asks.

"What do you mean?"

"You look upset."

"Upset? Me? Why would I be upset?"

"I don't know. One minute you were laughing, the next you weren't. Is something bothering you?"

Yes.

But where do I start?

I've never even mentioned Mike to Laura. Isn't that strange? She's somebody I see almost every day of my life, but I never realized until this moment that our interaction is all about the present: playdates, PTO meetings, soccer practice, leads on new babysitters.

The past just doesn't seem to come up. She's probably my closest friend in the world now, and yet I don't even know her maiden name. How very odd that is. Odd, and disconcerting.

I shake my head, gazing around at the frolicking kids, the baby monitor, the house, the SUV parked in the driveway.

This is my life now, and it's a life that has nothing to do with the person I once was. I've lost touch entirely with her. To Laura, and to my children, she never even existed.

"Mommy, Adam's washing his hands in the pool!" Chelsea shrieks.

"I told him to."

"Yuck! I'm getting out."

"At least nobody pooped in the pool this time," I comment, wriggling my toes in the shallow water, which now has a purplish ice-pop slick floating on the surface.

"Oh, ick. Remember that?"

We laugh about it, and I wonder why it is that any time I'm chatting with one of my fellow mommy friends, the conversation always gets steered around to bodily functions. Maybe I need to broaden my horizons, expand my circle of friends beyond the neighborhood and the PTO.

Not that I don't have other friends.

I think about Valerie, who is still living in New York but caught up in her job and the search for Mr. Right.

I think about Gordy, who is also still living in New York, but is currently doing summer stock in the Berkshires.

I think about Gaile, who's living in Beverly Hills, producing reality television programs for cable, and married to a casting director who has three kids from two ex-wives.

Thinking about Gaile leads naturally to thinking about e-mail, because that's how I found her again.

Thinking about e-mail leads naturally to thinking about Mike…

And no sooner does the thought of him cross my mind than the cordless-phone extension rings.

It's him, I think as I scramble to pick it up, not wanting it to wake Tyler just yet.

But of course it can't be him, because that would be far too coincidental. I mean, to think of him and have him call in that exact second?

What are the odds of that happening?

"Beau? Is that you?" a male voice asks. A voice so familiar that it's hard to believe I haven't heard it in fifteen years.

My heart stops.

Yes, it's me.

And yes…it's *him*.

twelve

The past

"Beau? Where the heck have you been?" Valerie called from our tiny kitchenette as I trudged into our apartment a few days after Mike returned to the West Coast.

"I went to see a movie with Gordy after work," I told her, dumping my shoulder bag on the floor. "I swear, it was my favorite movie ever."

Valerie said from the other room, "I thought *Say Anything* was your favorite movie ever."

"This is my new favorite movie ever. You have to see it, Val. It was called *When Harry Met Sally*. Meg Ryan was in it, and Billy Crystal."

"Mike's been trying to reach you. He called twice." Valerie emerged from the kitchen in an oversize T-shirt and black leggings that had a run in the knee. Her teased, product-lacquered hair towered vertically above her head as usual. She was carrying a can of Diet Coke and a bag of fat-free oat bran pretzels, which she offered to me.

I took a handful despite the fact that I wasn't even hungry, having devoured a large popcorn and the rest of Gordy's Sno-Caps at the movies.

"What did he say, Val?"

"He wants you to call him back. He said it was important. He has good news."

"Did he get a job offer?"

"I don't know." She handed me the cordless phone. "Call him. I'm dying to know. He sounded excited."

I finished crunching as I dialed. The phone rang once on the other end. I helped myself to a swig from Valerie's soda can and checked my watch after the second ring. It was only seven-thirty on the West Coast. Too early for him to be sleeping, too late to be out to dinner, according to him.

"Hello?"

"Mike! I just got home. What's your news?"

"I just got a job offer."

"Which one? The software place?"

"The TCP/IP research place."

"What TCP/IP research place? And what the heck is TCP/IP research?"

"It stands for Transmission Control Protocol/Internet Protocol," he said, as if that helped in the least. He might as well have been speaking in Swahili.

"I have no idea what you're talking about, Mike," I said, shrugging in response to Valerie's questioning look.

"Have you heard about the World Wide Web?"

"Oh! You mean that U.S.A. for Africa thing?"

"What?"

"You know," I said impatiently, "the video from a few

years ago with Michael Jackson and Bruce Springsteen and Tina Turner and all those other stars singing?"

"He met Michael Jackson?" Valerie croaked at my elbow. "Oh my God!"

I shushed her, shaking my head.

"That's 'We Are the World,' Beau," Mike was saying flatly.

"Right." I paused. "So this is something different?"

"Yeah. This is something different. You know Bradley?"

Bradley Masterson was his professor at school; the one he was helping with that research project.

"Of course I know Bradley." It was Bradley's fault Mike wasn't already back in New York. I hated Bradley.

"One of his colleagues is going to be working on something called the World Wide Web, which is a new concept in blah, blah, blah…a global hypertext database that could be blah, blah, blah…"

Okay, I admit it. I tuned him out, as I always did when he got too technical.

When he paused for breath, I said brightly, "Hey, that sounds great."

"Great?" Was it my imagination, or was he disdainful over my choice of adjectives? "This could be hugely excellent, Beau."

"So how was the package?" I was determined to show him that we were on the same page after all.

"It was rad."

Rad? First *dude,* now *rad.* Good Lord. The sooner I got him back to the East Coast, the sooner I could banish that annoying surfer lingo from his vocabulary. Anything was better than rad. Even the lackluster *great.* Even the Long Island–tainted *oh-awe-some.*

"So did you take the job?" I held my breath.

Valerie squealed in a high-pitched whisper, "He got a job?"

I nodded, holding her off with a raised hand as Mike said, "I wanted to talk to you first."

I laughed. "Take it. Definitely take it. When do you start? Maybe I can fly out and drive your stuff back with you."

Silence.

Not good silence punctuated by page-flipping as he checked his calendar for a suitable date. No, dead silence as he obviously tried to figure out how to break some horrible news to me.

I knew, before he spoke, what the horrible news had to be. I knew the job wasn't here.

"It's in L.A., isn't it, Mike." It wasn't a question.

"It's in L.A.?" Valerie echoed in dismay, hovering at my side. "Tell him that's out of the question."

Before I could do that, Mike shocked me by saying, "No, it's not in L.A."

"It's not?" My heart soared higher than the top of Valerie's hair. Of course it wasn't in L.A. Of course things were going to fall into place. They always did, didn't they? Why did I ever doubt it?

"What a relief," I said, feeling giddy. "For a second there, I thought for sure you were going to say that it—"

"It's in Silicon Valley."

Okay, I was no computer geek—not by a long shot— but even I knew that Silicon Valley was nowhere near Manhattan.

"Isn't that in California?" I asked Mike slowly.

"Yeah. But not L.A. It's in northern California. You'd love it up there."

No, I wouldn't. I wouldn't love it anywhere other than here, I thought stubbornly.

Then again…was he asking me to move with him?

"Maybe if I take the job, after I get settled you can come out and visit for a few days and I can show you around. Then down the road you might want to come out."

Maybe? Might? Down the road?

Could he be any more noncommittal? I wasn't necessarily hoping for a marriage proposal, but the least he could do was be a little less vague about our future.

"You're so quiet," he said.

"Yeah. Because I think you really want to take this job."

"Well, it could be a major waste of time. There's no way to tell. Or…"

"Or…?" I nudged when he fell silent.

"Or it could be the opportunity of a lifetime."

"Which do you think it is?" I asked, thinking he had just pretty much summed up how I felt about our relationship at that point. Major waste of time? Or opportunity of a lifetime?

"I don't know," he said. "I don't know what to do."

I noticed he wasn't asking me to tell him what he should do. Which was a shame, because I would. Gladly.

"I guess I'll sleep on it," he mused aloud.

"That's a good idea." Hopefully, while he was sleeping on it, he'd dream about me. And New York. And being with me in New York. Hopefully, he'd see that that was the way things were supposed to be.

As he went on about the job and technical computer stuff, I closed my eyes and tried to send *Beau-in-New-York* vibes to his subconscious.

When he paused for breath, I said brightly, "So how about those Yankees?"

"They suck," was the prompt response. "I'm a Mets fan, remember?"

"Oh, right. I forgot."

He went on and on about the Mets for a few minutes, which wasn't exactly fascinating but better than all that technical World Wide Web stuff. I couldn't imagine living with that on a full-time basis if he took the job.

We chatted for a few more minutes about baseball, and eventually, we hung up after exchanging our usual *I love you*'s. Mine was laced with more silent *Beau-in-New-York* vibes. His wasn't very reassuring.

I mean, if you love someone, you want to be with them. Right? If you love someone, you don't consider taking some stupid Tee-pee-something or other research job three thousand miles away.

I tossed the cordless phone onto the laminate countertop with a curse.

Valerie peered into my face. "Are you okay?"

"Do I look okay?" I burst into tears. "He wants to take a job in Silicon Valley."

"He wants *you* to move to Silicon Valley?"

"Did I *say* that?" I knew I was being bitchy. I also knew she understood. That was the great thing about Valerie. Not much fazed her.

"You mean he wants to move to Silicon Valley *without* you? Pretzel?" she asked almost as an afterthought, offering the bag.

"No, thanks." I sniffled and reached for the pack of cigarettes we kept on top of the microwave. I wasn't technically a smoker—mostly just when I was out drinking, or depressed.

I puffed away and vented my frustrations about Mike while Valerie crunched her way through the bag of pretzels, alternately offering consolation and salty pats on the shoulder.

Whenever Valerie was depressed, she ate.

Whenever *I* was depressed, Valerie ate.

"The worst thing about it," I said, lighting a new Salem Slim Light from the stub of my old Salem Slim Light, "is that that horrible 'We Are the World' song is now stuck in my head."

"I like that song."

"You would. You like New Kids on the Block and Richard Marx, too."

"What's wrong with that?"

I shot her a pointed look and an "Ew."

"I'm insulted," she said mildly, obviously not the least bit insulted.

The falsetto pop chorus to "We Are the World" sang in my head.

"Did he say when he has to let them know about the job?" Valerie asked.

"No."

I couldn't get that damn song out of my head.

"I can't take it anymore. I have to go turn on some music," I said abruptly, heading into our bedroom. "Anything is better than this."

In the bedroom, I headed straight for the boom box, which had been moved from the milk-crate bedside table to the desk, which was next to the wastebasket, which was beside a pale blue cardboard rectangle that lay on the floor.

It must have fallen out when Valerie tossed the trash the other day.

I reached down to grab it, realizing what it was in the instant before I picked it up and turned it over.

Mike.

Stylin' Mullet Mike from the airport.

"What's that?" Valerie asked, and I looked up to see her watching me from the doorway, an unlit cigarette in her hand.

"It's just a business card." I held it poised over the wastebasket again, but I couldn't quite bring myself to drop it in.

"Whose business card?"

"This guy's. I met him at the airport last week when I was waiting for Mike."

"Is he cute?" She leaned in and lit her cigarette from the one I was holding.

"Really cute."

"Available?"

"I guess."

"And you asked him for his number?"

"No! He sort of…forced it on me."

"Why don't I ever meet any really cute available guys who force their numbers on me?" she asked wistfully. "Do you know how lucky you are?"

"If I hear that one more time…" I shook my head. "I don't feel very lucky right now, okay, Val? My boyfriend wants to abandon me to live a million miles away. That isn't lucky."

"True." She waited a second, then said, "Come on, Beau. Don't just stand there holding that card. Either call this cute available guy or give me the card so I can call him."

"Call him!" I echoed. "Why would I call him? I have a boyfriend. And why would *you* call him?"

"Because I don't have a boyfriend. And desperate times call for desperate measures."

"You're not desperate, Val."

"Sure I am," she said cheerfully. "So are you going to call him?"

"No! And neither are you. I'm going to throw the card away, which is what I thought I did in the first place." I was still holding it over the garbage can, but I couldn't seem to make myself let go.

"What do you mean, you thought you did?"

"I threw it into the wastebasket last week. It must have fallen out when you dumped the garbage."

"Nothing fell out when I dumped the garbage. I always check the floor around it, ever since we had that mouse problem."

Yeah. That.

I shuddered just remembering the morning we woke up to a hear a horrible thumping, scratching sound. Turned out it was coming from a mouse gnawing its way through a sauce and grease–stained pizza box that had fallen from its perch atop the jammed garbage can in the kitchen.

"Of course it fell out of the wastebasket," I said impatiently.

"Don't be so sure. Maybe…"

"Maybe what? It magically reappeared?"

"Stranger things have happened," she said mysteriously.

"No, they haven't." I rolled my eyes.

"I think it's fate. Forget about me calling him. You need to call him, Beau."

"I'm not calling him."

I let go of the card and watched it flutter into the waste-basket again.

"Guess you don't believe in fate, Beau."

"Guess not."

Valerie shook her head. "I'm going to go order Chinese. You want some?"

"No, thanks."

I watched her leave the room.

I waited until I heard her on the phone with Dragon Panda before I plucked the pale blue card from the litter of lipstick-stained tissues.

I tucked it under my pillow, just in case…

Just in case, what? I asked myself.

I didn't know the answer. All I knew was that I just couldn't throw it away.

thirteen

The present

"God, you sound exactly the same," Mike's voice declares in my ear as, gripping the phone, I wrench my bare feet out of the kiddie pool and bolt from my chair.

"You, um, sound the same, too," I tell him, scurrying across the yard, leaving the kids and Laura and the baby monitor behind.

But he doesn't really sound the same. His voice is deeper, and he's got a different accent. A bit of a drawl, really.

I find myself feeling inexplicably betrayed. He's gone on to build a whole life without me; developed a whole new accent without me.

Well, what did you expect, Beau? Did you think he'd stay frozen in time, right where you abandoned him fifteen years ago?

"How did…"

"I get your number? You're listed," he says with a laugh. "You don't mind, do you?"

"No! Where…I…do…I mean, are you in Florida?" I manage to ask.

"Yeah. For a few years now."

"Really. What are you doing there?"

"Not much of anything, actually." His laugh is easy, his drawl decided.

"Oh. So you're not, um…" *Married* is what I want to say. "Working?" is what I say instead.

"Working?" He laughs again. More of a chuckle. "Nope, I'm not working. Not at the moment."

Terrific. He's unemployed, which he seems to find oddly amusing, and living in Florida. Probably in a run-down trailer park. Yet, I can't help myself. Once again, I find myself wondering whether he's married.

"How about you?" he's asking.

I absently watch Josh shoving Mikey's head underwater in the kiddie pool across the yard. "Me? Yes, I'm still married."

There's a pause, and then he says, "I meant are you working?"

"Oh! Sorry, I thought you…" I trail off, mortified.

"It's okay. Just…I mean, I knew that. You mentioned that you're still married in your e-mail. That's great."

"Yeah! It is! It's great!" I look skyward, mortified, and realize that the broken branch I asked Mike to remove from the oak tree last month is still dangling precariously overhead. It so figures. I step out from under it, just in case.

"And you have three kids?" Mike is asking.

"Yeah! Three kids! They're great!" And one is currently trying to drown the other as an oversize Laura struggles to play lifeguard. "Can you hang on for a second, Mike?"

"Sure."

I set the phone on the ground, making sure that it's out of earshot and beyond the range of falling branches, then stride back over to the pool.

"Mikey, are you okay?" I ask my sputtering firstborn, whom Laura has rescued from his brother's clutches. "Josh, get into time-out under that tree. Now. March!" To Laura, I say, "Thanks."

"No problem." She settles back into her chair.

"Listen, Laura, this is a hugely important phone call. I have to take it in the house. Can you please-please-please just make sure they stay alive for five minutes while I'm gone?"

"Sure. What's wrong? Is it Mike?"

"Yeah, it's Mike," I say with only a twinge of guilt because it's not a lie. "Everything's fine. I just need to talk inside, where it's quiet."

"Go."

"Thanks. I owe you a big favor."

"Where were you when I was looking for a surrogate?" she asks wryly, wrapping my shivering son in the nearest beach towel.

I rush back to the phone, grab it, and make a beeline for the house, accidentally trampling what's left of my prized stargazer lily bed in the process.

My heart is pounding. I can't believe I'm actually in the midst of a conversation with Mike after all these years.

In fact…what if he hung up?

Pressing the receiver to my ear as I walk, I hear the faint sound of music playing in the background. So he's still there. Thank God. Continuing the conversation is crucial. I don't know why it is, but it is.

I wait until I'm sealed into the cool, dim, quiet interior to say into the receiver, "Sorry about that. I'm back."

"Hi."

"Hi."

Somehow, the conversation just got more intimate. It's almost as if we're suddenly alone together at last.

"So...you're still married," he says again.

"Yeah." I wait. "To Mike," I repeat, when he doesn't speak.

"And you have three kids?"

"Three boys.

"That's great."

"Do you have kids?"

"No. I always wanted them, but..." He sighs. "You know how it goes. Some things just aren't meant to be."

Yeah.

I know how it goes.

Some things just aren't meant to be.

Like fatherhood.

And like...

Us.

I read sorrow into his silence and I wonder if that's what he's thinking.

Probably not. Our relationship is ancient history. I'm not self-centered enough to think that he's been pining away for me all these years.

Maybe he's just thinking it's unfair that I have three children and he doesn't have any. Maybe he's thinking about his beloved wife, and how the two of them have been through years of infertility treatments.

I always wanted them.

Wouldn't you think he'd have said "We always wanted them" if he were married?

I would think that. But then, I don't want him to be married. I don't want him to have a beloved wife. I want...

I want him to tell me he's spent the last fifteen years frozen in time, longing for me. Longing for what might have been. That's what I want.

And whatever Beau wants...

"I'm divorced, Beau," he says.

Just like that, my burning question is answered.

I'm divorced.

Yippee, I think.

"I'm sorry," I say, chiding my immature inner self. I mean, what kind of person is exalted to hear about another's misfortune?

A terrible person, that's what kind...

I look heavenward for forgiveness, absently noticing cobwebs wafting in the corner where the soffit meets the ceiling.

The kind of terrible person who is fantasizing about committing adultery with said misfortunate person.

There. It's out there. That's my fantasy. I am fantasizing about seeing Mike again and having an illicit affair with him. Obviously it can't happen, and not just because he's in Florida and I'm in New York.

There are plenty of other reasons.

Like that unsightly ridge of tummy fat beneath my belly button.

Oh, and the fact that I'm happily married and I wouldn't dream of cheating.

Okay, obviously I'd *dream* of it.

I just wouldn't *do* it.

No, sir.

I picture myself stepping into the Diane Lane role in that movie *Unfaithful,* a Westchester housewife sneaking around behind Richard Gere's back with a sensual French lover.

I could never do that.

I'm a Westchester housewife, yes.

But Mike isn't French.

And my husband isn't Richard Gere.

Speaking of which, who in their right mind would cheat on Richard Gere?

Still, the fantasy takes hold. I see myself wearing decadent, tummy-bulge-camouflaging lingerie, see Mike having his way with me on a rumpled bed in a SoHo loft lined with bookcases and exposed brick.

"Beau? Are you still there?"

Reality check. The accent in my ear is Southern, not Parisian.

If he knew what I was thinking...

"I'm still here," I say, wishing Tyler would wake up crying so I'd have an excuse to hang up.

"Listen, I don't know why I called you," he says suddenly, candidly. "I don't even know why I e-mailed you. I just...I guess when I found you, I had to get in touch. And when I got your e-mail back, it wasn't enough. I had to hear your voice."

"Well...here I am." I hate my chirpy, nervous laughter. I hate that I can't think of anything clever to say. I hate that I feel so giddy and girlie all of a sudden, like a twelve-year-old getting her first phone call from a boy.

There's an awkward pause.

I study the cobweb overhead. I have to remember to sweep it away before Mike spots it and wants to fire Melina.

"Beau?" Mike asks.

"Yes?" I ask, loving the sound of my name on his lips again after all these years, and thinking that *he* would never want to fire a poor immigrant cleaning lady over a stray cobweb or two.

"Do you want to hang up?"

"Hang up? No! Do you?" *Please don't want to hang up. Please.*

"No…I just don't know what else to say. I guess I never thought past the hearing-your-voice part."

I'm not the only one prone to nervous laughter.

"Well, how do I sound?" I ask.

"You sound great. How do I sound?"

"Like you've been living in the South for too long. Don't tell me you eat grits and have a Rebel flag on your car antenna."

"Hey, that's all stereotype. No fair."

"Do you?"

"Yes to the grits, no to the Rebel flag."

Down the hall, I hear Tyler stirring to consciousness in his crib. I will him back to sleep, not ready to return to motherhood just yet.

As though he's read my mind, Mike says, "Tell me about your kids, Beau."

I do. I tell him about earnest, sensitive Mikey; mischievous, full-of-fun Josh; sweet and lovable Tyler. Talking about my children relaxes me. The tension dissipates, on both ends of the line, and Mike seems genuinely interested in my boys.

"So you're a stay-at-home mom?"

"Yup, that's me."

"I'm having trouble picturing that. I really thought you might be a producer by now. Any regrets?"

"Nope. Not really." Not about leaving work, anyway. Just about…

Leaving him?

No. I love Mike. *My* Mike. Till-death-do-us-part Mike. I know I made the right choice. Really, I do.

I guess what I regret is ending my other relationship the way that I did. I mean, I basically turned my back and ran away. And suddenly, after all these years, it feels like unfinished business.

"What about you?" I ask, attempting once again to shut

out our troubled past—along with Tyler's increasingly urgent whimpers. "Are you in between jobs?"

"You could say that," he says, almost sounding coy. "I'm not sure what I want to do next, so I'm taking my time with it."

"What did you—oh, crap." Tyler has let out an earsplitting shriek from his crib. "Hang on."

I drop the phone and run down the hall to the nursery, where my indignant baby lets me know he's had it with this nap stuff. He's soaked through his diaper and ravenous with hunger.

Guilt surges through me.

Clutching my crying child in my arms, I return to the phone and say with firm reluctance, "I've got to go, Mike."

"Is that Tyler crying?"

"Yeah, that's him." I'm impressed that he remembers his name.

"Okay, well…it was great talking to you, Beau."

"You, too."

I hang on, bouncing inconsolable Tyler slightly on my hip, wishing he would quiet down so that I could prolong the conversation. It's not that I have anything specific to say, just that I'm not quite ready to let go again. Yet.

"Listen, I'll e-mail you. Okay?"

I grin, relieved. "Yes. That would be great."

And that's how it begins. Again.

fourteen

The past

I was fifteen minutes late getting to La Margarita on Bleecker Street.

Not because I got hung up at work, or couldn't get a cab, or had subway trouble.

No, I was late because I wasn't sure I could go through with this.

I had made the date with cute Mike from the airport—well, not a date, exactly, so I'll call it an appointment—impulsively last night.

Twenty-four hours and much soul-searching later, my impulse was to call it off. When I tried to reach him from the studio earlier to offer some lame excuse, the phone just rang and rang. No answering machine, so I couldn't even leave a message.

What kind of person didn't have an answering machine? This was 1989, for God's sake, not the Dark Ages.

I considered standing him up, but Valerie wouldn't let me. She said the least I could do was show up.

She also pointed out helpfully that it wasn't necessarily a date. It was just a New Yorker being friendly to a newcomer. That the New Yorker happened to be involved with somebody else and that the newcomer happened to be an incredibly attractive bachelor was moot, according to Valerie.

"You know you're not going to cheat on Mike," she told me when I called her from the office to remind her I'd be home late. "There's nothing wrong with going out and having a little fun with a platonic male friend."

"He's not even my friend, Valerie. He's just some guy I met."

"Well, he might become your friend. And you can never have too many of those."

No, you couldn't. Everybody needed friends, I told myself.

But I couldn't help thinking about Harry and Sally in that movie I'd just seen. Harry claimed that it was impossible for a man and a woman to be "just friends." And by the end of the movie, that theory was proven.

Okay, granted, it was just a movie. I mean, I saw *Batman* last week and I don't exactly anticipate any leotarded Caped Crusader sightings here in Gotham in the near future.

"Besides," Valerie went on, "you and Mike are having trouble. For all you know, he might dump you and move to San Francisco. It's good to keep your options open."

"Valerie! Mike is not going to dump me."

She was silent. I knew she was wearing that tight-lipped, raised-eyebrowed *you never know* expression of hers.

So here I was, and there was my possible future platonic

friend, sitting at a table by the window munching tortilla chips and salsa.

"Beau!"

He really looked happy to see me. Or maybe it was more relieved.

He stood and clasped both of my hands in his, then pulled out a chair for me. "I was worried you weren't going to show."

"Why would you think that?" I asked airily, sinking into the chair, telling myself that my weak knees had nothing to do with those awesome dimples of his, or the fact that we were practically holding hands.

"You're late," he said, letting my fingers slip from his grasp all too soon. "And I'm paranoid."

He was paranoid? He thought I was going to stand him up? Thank God for Valerie, who wouldn't let me. The last thing I'd want to do was stand up a sweet, gorgeous guy like this.

Not that this was a date.

Because it wasn't.

It was an *appointment.*

The thing about the phrase *stand up* is that it implies a date.

I hoped he didn't think that was what this was. Maybe I should tell him that it wasn't.

"I, um, got stuck on the N train," I lied, because he was still waiting for an explanation. "Why were you so paranoid?"

"Because when I told you to call me if it didn't work out with your boyfriend—"

"Or if I was casting a sitcom—"

"Or if you were casting a sitcom, right…well, I never expected to hear from you again. And when I did, it happened so fast I think I convinced myself the call must have been my imagination."

"Oh…well, obviously, it wasn't, so you can relax now." I smiled, hoping he couldn't tell how nervous I was, and hoping he didn't think this was a date. Maybe I could pretend that I was casting a sitcom.

My mind raced with possibilities as Mike said, looking somewhat sheepish, "You know, I don't normally react this way to a woman on a first date."

First date?

So this *was* a date. Dammit.

You know, this was all Valerie's fault.

If she hadn't told me to call him, I wouldn't have gotten the idea in the first place.

"I guess it's just that you're so beautiful," he went on, sounding crazily sincere. "The second I saw you sitting there in the airport, I wanted to talk to you. And then you said you had a boyfriend, and I figured that was it. I was positive you had gone home and thrown my card into the garbage."

"Why would I do that?" I asked, kind of shrilly.

"Because you have a boyfriend."

"Oh. Right."

Him again.

You know, this whole thing was more Mike's fault than Valerie's. Mike, and that stupid Silicon Valley job offer of his. He had called me at least three times since he first told me about it, and every time, he claimed to be wavering on whether to accept it. He didn't ask for my advice; he almost acted as though any input I gave him was strictly incidental.

Last night was the last straw, when he accused me of sounding like I didn't want him to take this great opportunity. When I admitted that he was right, I didn't want him to take it because I wanted him to come to New York, he blew up at me. He told me I was being clingy and unreasonable.

I hung up on him.

Then, without thinking things through, I spontaneously dug out the business card and dialed the number on it. I told myself that the would-be sitcom star probably wouldn't even remember me, but he did.

Meeting tonight for a drink was his idea.

Meeting here, at La Margarita, was mine. They had two-for-one happy-hour drinks, a bonus since I was broke and I figured we'd be going dutch, since it couldn't possibly be a date, since I had a boyfriend.

An added bonus: I had never been to La Margarita with said boyfriend. He had an inexplicable aversion to Mexican food. You'd think he'd have gotten over that, living in the Southwest, but he hadn't.

This Mike, however, claimed to love Mexican. The waiter appeared before the boyfriend angle of the conversation could develop any further. We both ordered frozen margaritas and chicken chimichangas with refried beans.

"Gotta love a girl who knows how to eat," Mike said with an approving laugh. "Can I tell you how glad I am that you didn't order some fat-free salad?"

"Me? I never order fat-free if I can help it."

"Good for you."

I got the feeling there was a fat-free woman in his past, but I didn't know how to ask without prying.

Our drinks were on the table in record time, another reason I adored the place.

"Cheers," Mike said, raising his glass.

"What are we drinking to?"

"New York. The greatest city in the world."

Wow. Was that perfect or was that perfect? I grinned. "To New York."

We sipped our drinks and smiled at each other.

There went those dimples again. Sigh.

Not wanting to blatantly check him out, I casually noted his black T-shirt tucked into a great pair of orange baggy pants.

He was hot, definitely, and an awesome dresser.

"So, anyway, why *did* you call me?" he asked, in a strictly no-bullshit manner that caught me off guard.

"I don't know, exactly," I answered honestly. I added, "I'm not casting a sitcom for Janelle, if that's what you were thinking."

"Damn." He snapped his fingers. "Then I guess giving you my head shot and résumé is out of the question?"

"You brought your head shot and résumé?"

He burst out laughing. "I was kidding. Do you think I'm that much of a loser?"

"Hey, you never know." Actually, I didn't think he was a loser at all. I merely *wished* he was a loser, so it would be easier for me to call it a night before the sun actually set.

"So if you're not going to give me my shot at stardom…why did you call?" he asked again, obviously unwilling to let me off the hook.

"I don't know…I guess because you were new in town, and I figured you might be kind of…lonely."

"That was nice of you." Dimple time.

I have to say, he certainly didn't *seem* lonely. He seemed like the kind of guy who radiated confidence and charm… the kind of guy anyone would want to be around.

Okay, so maybe that was why I called him. Maybe I simply couldn't resist his charisma.

Or maybe I was just royally pissed off at my boyfriend and this was my retaliation.

Who knew?

After a pair of margaritas, who cared?

Mike was easy to talk to, and I was having fun. That was all that mattered.

He told me about his Midwestern childhood and his college years at a Big Ten school where he played football and studied acting.

"That's unusual, isn't it?" I asked, trying not to slurp the last of my second drink. "Being in theater and sports?"

I was thinking of Gordy, who had a bachelor of fine arts and an aversion to any nonsexual activity that involved sweating and white sneakers.

"Yeah, well, I was a communications major and I had to take a drama class to fill a requirement freshman year. Next thing I knew, I had a knee injury and a minor in theater arts."

"What happened? You fell off the stage?"

He smirked. "No, the injury was from football. I was sidelined my last year of school, which gave me time to focus on the acting stuff."

"So you came to New York to be a star?"

"Doesn't everyone?" He grinned. "Actually, I came to New York because I had to get the hell out of the Midwest."

"Why?"

"Have you ever been to the Midwest?" he asked dryly.

I shook my head. "Is it that horrible?"

"Worse."

I laugh at his expression. "So it was just too…what? Dull? Conservative? Quiet?"

"All of that, and less. Plus…" He hesitated.

"Plus, what?"

"Plus, I went through a bad breakup. I was engaged to my college girlfriend, and…it just didn't work out."

There it was: the info I'd been tempted to sniff out earlier. I wondered if she was the one who ordered fat-free salads.

"You dumped her?" I asked, figuring no woman in her right mind would dump a guy like him.

"Other way around."

"Really." I tried not to act stunned. Of course, I knew that women weren't the only ones who got dumped. I mean, look at poor Lloyd Dobler in *Say Anything,* my former favorite movie of all time. He gave the beautiful Diane Court his heart and she gave him a pen.

Then again, after Lloyd professed his undying love and superior upper-body strength hoisting a Peter-Gabriel-blast-ing-boom-box for hours on end, Diane had a change of heart. Who wouldn't?

And who wouldn't offer a second chance to the appealing jiltee sitting across from me?

"It was a few weeks before the wedding," Mike told me after a prolonged sip of his drink.

"Ouch."

"Yeah."

"So…" He drained what was left of his drink. "I had to get the hell out of Dodge."

"To get away from her."

"Basically. So here I am. And I hate to break it to you, but this is my first date since the separation. Boy, does it feel good to be over *that* hurdle."

I took a deep breath. It was now or never. Never was preferable, but I couldn't stand the guilt for another second.

"Mike," I said gingerly, "I hate to break it to *you,* but…"

"But what?"

"But you aren't exactly over that hurdle yet."

"What do you mean?"

"I mean, this isn't really a *date,* per se."

"It isn't?"

"No."

He laughed. "What is it? Don't tell me it's an audition after all, because I really didn't bring my head shot or résumé, and I sure as hell didn't prepare a monologue. Although I feel like I just gave one."

I managed a small, tequila-fueled laugh. "It isn't an audition. It's just…dinner and drinks."

Too many drinks, at that. Was it getting warm in here, or was it just me? I felt flushed.

"Dinner and drinks is my favorite kind of date."

The dimples made an appearance again, dammit. Whew…I was definitely warm, and he was definitely hot.

"Yeah," I told him, "but dinner and drinks doesn't always have to be a date, you know? Sometimes it can just be…dinner and drinks."

"If that's what you want," he said with a shrug.

"That's what I want."

There was just one teensy problem with that.

A platonic dinner and drinks appointment *wasn't* what I wanted. All at once, La Margarita was the Garden of Eden, and I had a fierce hankering for forbidden fruit.

"Sorry if I read you wrong," said the forbidden fruit.

"No problem," said Eve, staring into his bottomless black eyes, thinking that she always got what she wanted, and what she wanted right now was…

Stop it. Bad Eve!

He squirmed a little. "Do you want to leave?"

"No! Do you?"

"No. But I should warn you…I don't know if I can do the platonic thing with you. I felt like there was something there, you know?"

"You mean like…?" I couldn't think of a word that didn't sound ridiculously corny.

Sparks…an attraction…a bond…

I just couldn't bring myself to say any of those things without cringing.

"You know…like sparks," he said.

He wasn't cringing.

"You felt sparks?" I asked, hating that I felt them, too. Big, scary sparks.

"Yeah."

We stared at each other for a second, and it was weird, but there was definitely a connection. It wasn't awkward, and it should have been.

I wasn't moved to flee, and I should have been.

An odd little sensation darted from my stomach to my lower back; the ultraresponsive region where I always feel the initial shivers of desire.

He exhaled, broke the gaze, shook his head. "How long have you been together?"

"What?"

"You and your boyfriend."

"Oh." Suddenly, I couldn't remember. That definitely wasn't a good sign. "Um, awhile."

"Months?"

"Yes. Er, years, actually."

"Years? That's…that is…great."

I sensed from his tone and the look on his face that what he really wanted to say was that it sucked, and all at once, I wanted to tell him that I felt the same way.

I wanted to point out that if I didn't have a boyfriend, we could be a couple, and wouldn't that be fun?

What the hell are you thinking, Beau? demanded the part of my brain that was irritatingly immune to tequila and temptation, and stored preachy tidbits from Sunday sermons to spout at every moral impasse. *This is wrong. Keep your mouth shut. Do you hear me? Do not say anything you'll regret later.*

"My boyfriend and I are kind of having a crisis," said my voice, fueled by the part of my brain that soaked up tequila, thrived on temptation and relied on past issues of *Cosmo* for ethical guidance.

He leaned forward, clearly intrigued. "What kind of crisis?"

He was so close I could smell the cilantro and lime on his breath, and I found myself wondering how it would taste on his lips. I heard myself mumbling some convoluted explanation about Mike's job offer out West, and my wanting to stay in the East, but the whole time I was blabbing I was wondering what it would be like to lean across the table and kiss him.

"So he's a plastic surgeon?" Mike asked.

"Who?" I looked around.

"Your boyfriend."

"A plastic surgeon?" I frowned. "No, he just got a master's in computer science."

Mike nodded, but he still looked confused. "And he's living in a teepee?"

I wondered if he'd had a couple of extra drinks before I arrived. "A teepee?" I echoed. "He doesn't live in a teepee. He lives in a condo in Long Beach. But he wants to move to Silicon Valley to take this job, so—"

"Wait a minute…were you talking about Silicon Valley?" A slow smile was spreading over his face.

"Yes. Why?"

"I thought you meant Silicon…you know…"

"No… What?"

"You know…"

"I really don't know."

He was laughing now, shaking his head. "Boob jobs."

"Boob jobs?"

"Yeah, you know…silicon implants…boob jobs…plastic surgeon."

"Oh!" I started laughing, too.

"But what about the teepee?"

"What about it?" I giggled, picturing Mike living in a teepee wearing surgical scrubs.

"I don't know…I thought you said something about a teepee."

Teepee…

Teepee…

Lightbulb moment.

"TCP/IP," I announced, and screamed with laughter.

I guess you had to be there.

But trust me, I wasn't the only one who was laughing.

When at last we stopped cracking each other up with various comments about boob jobs and teepees, it took us a few seconds to recover. You know how, after a really good laugh you wipe your eyes and shake your head and make those little sighing sounds? Well, we were both doing that, and grinning at each other, and it was then that I realized I was having a better time with this new Mike than I'd had at any point last week with my Mike.

In fact, I was having such a good time that I found myself wishing that this Mike were my Mike and the other Mike were…well, old Mike.

That was why, when he walked me to the subway, I asked him if he wanted to hang out again sometime.

And that was why, when he asked me if it could be a date next time, I hesitated only for a second before I said yes.

fifteen

The present

It's been six days since Mike and I started e-mailing each other regularly.

Maybe *often* is a more apt way to describe it.

I guess *constantly* would be even better.

Or worse, depending on how you look at it.

Worse in the sense that I am a married mother of three and I really have no business whatsoever carrying on an electronic flirtation with an old flame.

The key word being *electronic*.

Because really, the whole thing is harmless, if you think about it. It isn't as though anything can come of it, what with fifteen years and a thousand miles lying between us.

I keep telling myself that what I've been doing with Mike is the postmillennial equivalent of a seventies housewife batting her eyes at the Maytag repairman.

Less provocative than that, even.

It certainly isn't as though we're exchanging steamy missives laced with longing and innuendo.

All right, it's not exactly like we're exchanging recipes, either.

There might be a slight undercurrent of longing and innuendo, but believe me, it's totally innocuous. Here's a sample:

Subject: Good Morning
Date: August 4, 7:53 Eastern Standard Time
From: HappyNappy64@websync.net
To: Beauandco@websync.net
Hey, guess what? I dreamed about you last night.

Subject: Good Morning
Date: August 4, 8:44 Eastern Standard Time
From: Beauandco@websync.net
To: HappyNappy64@websync.net
Uh-oh. What was it about? Did you wake up screaming? Was it a nightmare?

Subject: Good Morning
Date: August 4, 8:46 Eastern Standard Time
From: HappyNappy64@websync.net
To: Beauandco@websync.net
LOL No! I woke up wishing I could go back to sleep and finish the dream.

Subject: Good Morning
Date: August 4, 8:47 Eastern Standard Time
From: Beauandco@websync.net
To: HappyNappy64@websync.net
So why didn't you? It's not like you have to go to work or anything.

Subject: Good Morning
Date: August 4, 8:48 Eastern Standard Time
From: HappyNappy64@websync.net
To: Beauandco@websync.net

No, but it's not like we're both single or anything, either. If we were, I wouldn't just be seeing you in my dreams. <eg>

Naturally, being new to this cyber-shorthand stuff, I have no clue what <eg> means. I'm dying to know, but I refuse to come right out and ask. Not only am I reluctant to have him make fun of me, the way he did when I asked him what LOL meant, but I guess I'm afraid of what <eg> might mean.

The possibilities that have run through my head aren't exactly harmless.

What if <eg> means erotic grope? Or, I don't know…ecstatic groan?

I can't help feeling that nobody other than my husband should really be groaning in ecstasy over me. Not even over the Internet, or in a dream. Not even if it's somebody with whom I have shared many an ecstatic groan in person.

It might not be so bad if my relationship with Mike in the past hadn't been simultaneous with my relationship with my husband. You know, if Mike were simply somebody with whom I'd had a meaningless fling long before I met the man I was destined to marry.

But I was seeing both Mikes at the same time before everything blew up in my face and I was forced to choose. If Mike—*my* Mike, aka father-of-my-children Mike—knew that I had struck up a correspondence with the man who almost stole me away from him…

No. He isn't going to know. There's no way he'll ever find out. I'm certainly not going to tell him. I'm not going to tell anybody.

Except one person.

The one person I have always turned to when things get dicey.

As far as I'm concerned, things took a turn for dicey at <eg>. So here I am, taking advantage of the fact that all three boys are safely captivated by a *Blue's Clues* video, flipping through my address book in search of a telephone number I've never quite managed to memorize.

That's because I don't dial it nearly as often as I should. Especially considering that it's not even long-distance.

"Good morning, Valerie Kenmore's office."

"Is she there, please?"

"Who's calling?" Valerie's secretary asks crisply, as though she is a pivotal player in *The Life and Times of Valerie Kenmore,* and I am a mere extra.

"It's Beau."

"Beau...?" Clearly, she expects a last name.

"Just Beau," I say, piqued. I mean, come on. The world is hardly populated by hordes of women named Beau. "She'll know."

She does.

Take *that,* snotty secretary!

Two seconds after she puts me on hold there's a click, and Valerie's voice exclaims, "Hey, stranger! How's it going?"

She sounds so pleasantly surprised to hear from me that I instantly feel bad that I never think to call her just to chat.

Guilt, in case you haven't noticed, is my specialty these days.

"Everything is great," I say. "How about with you?"

"Same old thing. Although, I just got back from Denver."

"Business?"

"Vacation."

See, this is what I mean. There was a time in my life when I would have been privy to Val's vacation plans. As a matter of fact, there was a time in my life when Val and I took annual vacations together.

Without fail, every spring, the two of us would jet off to some spa or resort for a long weekend. I swore, when I got married, that it wasn't going to change. I promised her we would still do our girls' weekend every year, no matter what. And, even though it was hard for me to leave Mike for three whole days, I always kept that promise...

Until Mikey came along.

If leaving Mike was hard, leaving his precious newborn namesake was impossible. That first year, I invited Val up from the city to spend a weekend at our house instead. She grumbled, but she came.

We gossiped, we shopped, we sat up late watching chick flicks and drinking wine—same things we had done a thousand times as roommates and on our getaway weekends.

But it wasn't the same. For one thing, we no longer knew the same people; gossip isn't nearly as scintillating when it's about a total stranger.

Plus, I had to bring Mikey shopping because he was nursing and a militant La Leche League lady had brainwashed me regarding the evils of pumping breast milk into bottles. So my girls' weekend with Valerie was a threesome. A cumbersome threesome, at that. You can't take the stroller on escalators at the mall, so we had to keep waiting for elevators. The stroller didn't fit in changing rooms, so we had to take turns trying things on. And I hadn't lost all my baby weight, so unfortunately for Val, I was more interested in browsing through the racks at Baby Gap than Neiman Marcus.

The evenings were even more challenging. Mikey's rigorous wee-hour-feeding schedule had left me so zapped that I couldn't keep my eyes open past the opening credits of even the most compelling chick flick, especially after two sips of wine—which was all I was allowed to have, lest my tainted breast milk transform my suckling offspring into a drunkard.

The following year, when I invited Valerie to join me in mommyland again, she was prepared with an excuse. Thus, the pattern was broken. I think we were both relieved.

In the past, our friendship had worked despite our major differences. Valerie was overweight and underemployed and perpetually lovelorn; I was thin and career-driven and had a steady boyfriend (or two at once). But somehow, the two of us shared acres of common ground.

These days, the chasm between us is considerably more vast than the mere fifty-minute Metronorth ride that separates my suburban raised ranch and her East Side co-op.

She's a workaholic marketing manager; still single, still struggling with her weight, still searching for Mr. Right even as her biological clock prepares to toll its final hour. She's also still the first to admit—without resentment, which has always amazed me—that she desperately wants what I have.

Sometimes, I look at her solitary life with a shudder and I think, *There, but for the grace of God…*

But once in a while, especially lately, I look at her solitary life and I think I wouldn't mind trading places with her for a day. Maybe two.

If I were Valerie, and single, I would be able to sleep late on weekend mornings. I would always have the remote control to myself. And I would probably know what <eg> means.

"Val, what does <eg> mean?" I ask, because preamble is largely unnecessary with Val, which is one of the reasons I love her.

"E.g. stands for the Latin phrase *exempli gratia,* which means *for example,*" she says promptly.

"No, not that e.g. I know that one. I'm talking about the

kind of <eg> with those greater-than/less-than signs around it. The kind people use in e-mail."

"You mean an emoticon?"

"A what?"

She laughs. "An emoticon. You know…like a little smiley face made out of a colon and a parenthesis."

Yes, I think. Like :)

"The emoticon <eg> stands for evil grin," Val informs me. "Why?"

Evil grin.

Evil grin?

What a relief. Evil grin is far more innocent than erotic grope.

Then again, when I think about what Mike wrote—it's not like we're both single or anything…if we were, I wouldn't just be seeing you in my dreams—and I picture his handsome face wearing an evil grin while typing that—there's nothing innocent about it.

"So spill it, Beau. Who is grinning evilly at you?"

"You're never going to believe this."

"Try me."

"Mike."

"Mike?" Clearly disappointed, she says, "I thought it was going to be something juicy."

"Oh, it's juicy."

"I hate to break it to you, but exchanging e-mails with one's husband isn't exactly juicy."

"Who said I'm exchanging e-mails with my husband?"

Silence.

Then, "You mean, *Mike,* Mike?"

"I mean *Mike,* Mike."

"Oh, my God."

"I know. He found me."

"I didn't even know you were hiding."

"I wasn't. I just…we lost touch after that last summer. You know how it is. I had no idea whatever happened to him, and then, bam. He Googled me."

She snickers. "Scandalous! So where is he?"

"Florida."

"Good. I was hoping you weren't going to say New York."

"Why?"

"Because if he was in New York, you might be tempted to see him, and that would be…well, wrong. Thou shalt not Google thy neighbor's wife." She snickers again.

"I'm glad you find this so amusing."

"I can't help it. Is he married?"

"Divorced."

"So he's available."

"Yes, but—"

"Mommy, I want French toast," Mikey announces, appearing in the doorway.

"In a second, sweetie. Go back and watch *Blue*."

"But I saw this one before, Mommy. It's the one where Mr. Salt and Mrs. Pepper take baby Paprika to—"

"Mikey, please. This is a very important conversation." He doesn't budge, so I add, "If you go in the other room right now, I'll give you chocolate."

"Okay."

I give him a handful of Hershey's Kisses I keep in the top of the plate cupboard for bribery. "Half of these are for your brother."

"Which brother?"

"Josh. Do *not* give Tyler any candy. Do you hear me?"

"Yes, Mommy."

"Are you going to give Tyler any candy?" I ask, because that's how these things work.

"No, Mommy."

"Are you going to share half your candy with Josh?"

"Yes, Mommy."

"And are you going to make sure Josh doesn't put his chocolate into his pockets for later?"

"Yes, Mommy."

"Okay, go." To Valerie, I say, "Sorry."

"Chocolate in his pockets for later?" she asks, laughing.

"It's a habit he's picked up lately. He stashes food away like a little squirrel. Which isn't so bad when it's not chocolate and ninety degrees out."

"I don't know how you do it."

"Do what?"

"This whole Mommy thing. It's so stressful."

She doesn't know the half of it.

"Get back to the Mike thing," she urges. "He's available?"

"He's available. But I'm not, and he knows it. So don't worry."

"Beau, be careful."

"I am being careful. I'm not stupid."

"No, but you are vulnerable when it comes to him. He had such a hold on you back when you were dating him."

I squirm, remembering all too clearly my fierce attraction to Mike. Remembering what it was like to lie in his arms, to be kissed by him, loved by him…

"I was young," I tell Valerie, pouring myself another cup of coffee.

"No kidding."

"I'm older and wiser now."

"We're all older," she says, "but the wiser thing…well, I'm not so sure about that."

"What's that supposed to mean?"

"That no matter how old a person is, she isn't always

in control of her emotions when it comes to the opposite sex."

"Are we talking about me, or you, Val?"

"Both." She tells me about her latest failed romance, with
a man she didn't realize was married. "Oldest story in the
book," she says. "I wish I could say that I broke it off the minute I found out he had a wife and kids."

"But you didn't?"

"No. I never broke it off, period. He dumped me."

"I'm sorry." But not really. Of course I'm not sorry that
her married lover cut her loose.

"So am I. Still."

"Val…"

"I know, Beau. But I was crazy about him. So crazy about
him that I managed to overlook all the things that were
wrong about our relationship, and all the people I was po-
tentially hurting. Including myself."

"Point taken. Don't worry. I'm not going to get involved
with Mike again. I love Mike. *My* Mike. I wouldn't do anything behind his back."

"You did once before."

"That was different. We weren't married. We didn't have
three children and a life together."

"Just be careful," she says again. "You can't trust yourself
around him."

"I'm not around him. We're just e-mailing."

"You're playing with fire."

"Oh, come on, Val." I laugh. Nervously.

"I'm serious, Beau."

"I'm fine, Valerie. Trust me."

Silence. Clearly, she doesn't trust me.

Time to change the subject to something a little less vol-
atile. "Tell me about your trip to Denver," I suggest.

She does.

As she talks, I check on the boys, making sure there are no signs of chocolate in the drool on Tyler's chin, then retrieving silver foil Hershey's Kiss wrappers from the floor, the crevices between the couch cushions, the soil around the potted ficus tree.

Then I head down the hall and make the beds, wipe the gobs of turquoise toothpaste out of the sinks, empty the bathroom wastebaskets Melina forgot to empty yesterday.

The whole time Valerie is chattering about her trip and I'm going about my mundane morning routine, I find myself battling intrusive, titillating memories of a dark-haired, dark-eyed Mike who isn't the dark-haired, dark-eyed Mike I married.

"I have to get to a meeting," Valerie says reluctantly at last, as, back in the kitchen, I start the French toast for the boys' breakfast.

"I should go, too. I have to get…dressed."

"Lucky you," she says with a wistful laugh. "I'd kill to stay in my pajamas past seven some morning."

"Come up to visit us soon and I promise you can," I tell her.

"Maybe I will." But she won't. "Or you can come down to the city, Beau, for lunch and a matinee."

"Maybe I will." But I won't.

Despite our best intentions, Val and I will never have that day-to-day kind of friendship again. I feel a pang of loss every time I talk to her. Loss, yet also a touch of reassurance, because we still know each other inside and out in the ways that really count.

We hang up with the promise to reconnect in person before the summer is over.

I slap a pat of butter on the griddle and set it on the burner, thinking about Mike.

The *wrong* Mike.

Valerie is right. I never did have any willpower where he was concerned. Despite my best intentions, one glance from him, or the slightest touch, would have me back in his arms again.

The best thing to do, I decide, whisking milk into eggs in a bowl, is to ignore his e-mails from here on in. I'll just delete them without reading. He'll get the message.

The phone rings as I'm flipping the first four slices of egg-soaked bread.

It's Mike.

The *right* Mike.

"What are you doing?"

"Making breakfast for the boys. What are you doing?"

"Wishing I were anywhere other than here. The train was late and only one elevator is working in my building. It's going to be a bad day. I can tell already. Maybe I can get out of here early tonight."

"That would be great," I say, knowing he won't. He never does.

"Thank God there are only two more weeks until vacation. I really need it this year."

"Yeah." I sit down at the table and sip my lukewarm coffee. "But I wish we were going away, Mike."

"I know you do, Beau. But there's too much to do around the house, and..."

And he just wants to be home, because he so rarely is. I know that. Suddenly, I'm so sick of the same-old, same-old everything that it's all I can do not to scream.

I desperately need a change of scenery. So desperately that I can't help making a last-ditch attempt to sway him.

"If we went to the Cape or somewhere for even just part of the week, Mike, I could hire a mother's helper when we got back and you and I could work on the house stuff together."

"Not this year," he says, though he does sound contrite. "I know you're bored, Beau."

"I'm not bored."

"Yes, you are."

"You're right. I am."

He laughs. Not a mean laugh; more of a sympathetic chuckle.

"It's just hard," I say, "being at home with the kids all the time. And I know it's hard for you to be at work all the time."

"Yeah. But I like to get away once in a while, too. Listen, maybe you and I can go somewhere romantic for a long weekend for our anniversary this fall."

"Really?" I try to sound enthusiastic, but our anniversary isn't until October.

"Sure. We'll talk about it. Hang in there, Babs."

"I'm hanging in there," I say with a sigh. I really should tell him someday how much I hate when he calls me Babs.

"I love you," he adds. "I'll see you tonight. Oh, and one more thing—"

"Hmm?"

"Melina."

"Mike…do we have to get into this now?"

"Beau, when I got into the shower this morning, the drain was filled with hair. And I'm not as upset that I'm losing it as I am that she's not cleaning it out. Wasn't she there yesterday?"

"Yes. I guess she forgot to do our shower."

"And our sink. There was a big gob of dried toothpaste in it."

I sigh.

"We have to talk to her, Beau."

"I know. I will."

"You need to call her and tell her that if she wants to come next week, she's got to get her act together."

"I can't call her, Mike."

"Why not?"

"She told me her phone got disconnected again. She hasn't even been able to talk to her kids in Guatemala in weeks."

"Oh, come on, Beau. With what we're paying her, she can afford to fly to Guatemala every week to see them in person."

"No, she can't. She's poor, Mike."

"She has you brainwashed, Beau. Why are you so protective of her?"

"I don't know," I tell him with a sigh.

But I do know, and he wouldn't understand. It's that mutual maternal thing, that constant sense of empathy for a fellow female. I really hate that she's here scrubbing our toilet and her children are in another country.

All right, maybe it's been awhile since she actually *scrubbed* our toilet. After she left yesterday, I spotted a stray poop stain in the bowl in the hall bathroom and cleaned it myself before Mike got home.

Too bad I didn't check the sink and shower drain in the master bath as well.

"If you don't talk to her, Beau, I will."

"No, I'll do it. When she comes next week, I'll talk to her in person. But she doesn't speak English, remember?"

"Then how did she tell you about her kids in Guatemala and her disconnected phone?"

"She knows a few words, and she uses sign language. We can communicate that way most of the time. I'm just going to have to figure out how to tell her she needs to make a little more effort."

"No, not a little more effort. *Mucho* effort."

"Right. *Mucho* effort." I shake my head. Why does everything have to be so complicated? "I really hate stuff like this, Mike."

"I know you do. You're too nonconfrontational, Beau. You need to learn how to deal with things head-on. Listen, I have to take another call. See you tonight."

"See you tonight."

I hang up and hoist my nonconfrontational self from the table. As I turn back to the stove, I realize that the neglected French toast is sending up a cloud of black smoke.

"Shit!"

"Mommy, you said a bad word," a small voice promptly announces from the next room.

I rush over to the stove. In my haste to lift the griddle from the burner, I scorch the side of my hand on the open gas flame.

"Shit!" I exclaim again, wincing in pain.

"Mommy! You said the bad word again!" Josh scolds.

"Mommy's very sorry," I call, biting back an even badder word as I run my stinging hand under cold water.

"*Shit* is a bad word," Josh informs me, materializing in the kitchen.

"I know it's a bad word, Josh, and you shouldn't say it either."

"Well, I was just telling you what you said, Mommy."

I clench my teeth. "Mommy knows what she said, Josh. Mommy couldn't help it. Mommy got hurt."

Another set of footsteps patter into the kitchen immediately. I look up to see that my firstborn has joined his little brother in the doorway, still clad in his baseball print Skivvy Doodles with a fierce case of bedhead. His big dark eyes, so like his daddy's, are worried.

"What happened to you, Mommy? Are you okay?"

I turn off the water and wrap my blistering hand in a dish towel. "I'm fine, sweetie. I just got burned."

"Were you playing with matches?"

I smile and kiss the spiky patch of hair on top of Mikey's head, and then the identical one on Josh's. "No, I wasn't playing with matches."

"Good. Because that's naughty."

"And dangerous, too," Josh adds solemnly.

"You're right, boys. It is naughty *and* dangerous."

So, I think ruefully, scraping the charred toast into the garbage can, *is playing with fire.*

sixteen

The past

As luck would have it, before Mike could accept the job in Silicon Valley, the software company in Manhattan called him for a third interview. They flew him back to New York the first week in August and put him up at a hotel in the East Fifties, near their office.

It wasn't a luxury hotel like the Plaza or the Waldorf, just one of those Manhattan East Suite places. Still, I was impressed. Like I said, in my industry, entry-level applicants are lucky if they're allowed to keep a pen after an interview. They certainly aren't put up in hotel suites complete with kitchenettes *and* coffeemakers.

Naturally, I was staying with Mike while he was here. His idea, not mine. Not that I protested. But I didn't dare suggest it myself, lest he inform me he wasn't ready for a commitment like that.

Ironically, Mike called and told me about the interview the morning after my non-date with Other Mike at La Margarita. He sounded so upbeat about the software place and so excited to see me that I instantly realized I'd made a big mistake the night before. I wouldn't be seeing Other Mike again. No way was I going to jeopardize my longtime relationship for a few laughs and a great pair of dimples.

I told myself he probably wouldn't even call me again, anyway. But when he did—twice—I screened his calls. My Mike was back in town, maybe for good, and that was all that mattered.

"You know what we should do tomorrow?" I asked him as we lounged in bed watching *The Tonight Show* the night he arrived.

"No, what should we do?" He nuzzled my neck. We were both naked, limbs lazily entwined under the covers. Naturally, we had made a beeline for the hotel from the airport.

"I should call in sick to work, and we should stay here all day, in bed," I said, raking my fingers through his short, dark hair.

"Can't. I have my interview in the morning, remember?"

"Oh, yeah." I stifled a yawn.

"Sleepy?" he asked with a smile.

"A little."

"I wish I were. It's barely nine o'clock my time."

His time.

My time.

That our body clocks were no longer in sync really bothered me. We used to fall asleep together and wake together, but not anymore. Now, whenever he was here visiting, I heard him prowling around long after I was drifting in and out of consciousness. Then, when at last I was feeling refreshed and wide awake by the light of day, it was impossible to rouse him for breakfast before noon.

"You know," I said, stifling another yawn, "I can still call in sick tomorrow morning and wait here for you. And when you finish your interview, you can come right back here and we can celebrate."

He laughed. "Celebrate what?"

"That you got the job. You're going to, you know."

"How do you know?"

"I'm psychic." I pressed my lips to his bare chest, then laid my head against it.

He tightened his arms around me. "Oh, yeah? Well, go ahead and tell me what else is going to happen, then. What does my future hold?"

I grabbed his hand and pretended to examine his palm. "Hmm, let's see. You're going to live happily ever after."

"Where?"

"In New York," I said decidedly, tempted to add, with me.

I bit back that last part, though, knowing I didn't dare. He might be back in town and considering taking a job here, but that didn't mean he'd changed his mind about our moving in together.

"I don't know, Beau," he said, and his voice was no longer teasing. "The research job out West still sounds pretty good. And I might not get an offer tomorrow."

"You will," I said with a confidence that didn't quite resonate. "They don't fly you back for another interview and put you up in a hotel if they're not serious about you."

"Well, what if I screw up the interview tomorrow?"

I pulled back to look up into his uncertain gaze. "You won't," I said, running a fingertip down his cheek. "You're great, Mike, and they'll want you…"

Just as much as I do.

He kissed me, on the lips this time, tenderly. "I hope they do. But if they don't—"

"They will."

"But if they don't," he repeated, "we'll have to talk, Beau."

I frowned. "About your moving up to San Francisco. I know."

He nodded. "It wouldn't have to be forever. And it wouldn't mean our relationship has to change. We've been separated for as long as we've known each other. We've always managed to make it work."

"This is different."

"How?"

"It's much farther away. And before, we always knew there was an end in sight. We always knew we'd be together for the whole summer, every summer."

"True."

"We were supposed to be together *this* summer," I reminded him.

"I know. But this thing with Bradley has been an incredible experience, Beau. I know you don't understand a whole lot about technology, but this project we're working on has the power to change the world. And the research job in Silicon Valley is the same type of thing."

"You said it might also be a big waste of time."

"Right," he admitted. "There's no way of knowing. But listen…you have to trust me. You know I'm crazy about you."

My heart skipped a beat, the way it always did when he looked at me that way and said something like that.

"I'm crazy about you, too," I said softly.

"I'm not going to let go of everything we have together just because I'm living across the country. You'll come out to visit. And maybe you'll love it so much you'll want to move out there, too."

"What if I don't?"

"Maybe I'll want to come back East."

"What if you don't?"

"We'll work it out. You're overthinking everything, and you're getting way ahead, anyway. Maybe the job in New York will come through."

"It'll come through," I said again, firmly, almost daring to believe that I could make it happen by sheer will.

"And if it doesn't come through, we'll work things out."

I sighed. "I can't stand the thought of living apart again, Mike."

"I know. Believe me, Beau, it doesn't sound great to me, either. I don't like being away from you. I keep thinking about all the things we could be doing together…and I get worried that you're going to find somebody else."

My heart stopped.

"Why would you worry about that?" I asked slowly, wondering if he could possibly know what I had done.

Not that what I had done was so wrong. I had drinks and dinner with another guy. So what? It wasn't even a date. We didn't even kiss.

But you wanted to, I reminded myself. *You wanted him to kiss you. If he had tried, you would have let him.*

Good thing he hadn't tried.

My definition of cheating was kissing somebody else. If there was no kissing, there was no cheating.

And anyway, I reminded myself, Mike was just speaking hypothetically. Still…

"You know I would never cheat on you!" I told him vehemently. Maybe too vehemently, because he scowled.

Before he could question me, I went on, "Even when we were supposed to be allowed to see other people, I never did."

Okay, it was a white lie.

The first few years of our relationship, when we left summer camp and went back to our separate lives, we always told each other that we were free to date. We thought it was the mature thing to do. We just promised we wouldn't talk about it unless one of us met somebody we liked better.

I assumed he never did, and I never did, either.

But I did date. I went to movies and dances with other guys. I saw some of them more than once, and I kissed more than a few. But Mike was always there, in the back of my mind. He had my heart from the moment we met, and I was pretty certain I had his.

I mean, when something works as well as our relationship always had, you didn't tamper with it. Why would you? My trying to recapture with somebody else what Mike and I already had together would make about as much sense as some wannabe superstar remaking a great old song like, say, "American Pie." Or an aspiring Hitchcock remaking an awesome movie like *Psycho*.

When the original was a classic, nobody else was ever going to come along and make it better. Period.

"Beau," Mike said now, his breath warm against my bare shoulder, "we're going to make this work. Trust me. No matter what happens."

I wanted to believe that. I wanted to trust him. I wanted us to go on being *us*.

"But…" I took a deep breath. "You don't even want to live with me, Mike. You said you're not ready for that."

I could feel the tension tightening his body as I spoke. I wished I could take back the words, but they were out there.

"Please don't push me on that, Beau."

"I'm not pushing you. I'm just stating a fact."

He said nothing.

"Mike, I'm not saying we should move in together right away—"

"You're not? Because it sounds like that's exactly what you're saying."

"No, I'm not."

"Sure you are. And I just don't get it. What's the rush, Beau?"

"There's no rush. But I guess I just don't get it, either. Why are you dragging your feet?"

"I'm not dragging my feet. I'm just not in any hurry to make more than one huge decision right now that could impact the rest of my life. One thing at a time. I have to figure out my career before I can even think about anything else."

"But the decision about your career isn't entirely separate from the decision about us."

"Sure it is."

"No, it isn't. Not when where you live is going to impact our relationship."

"It doesn't have to."

"Yes, it does. If you're living thousands of miles away, our relationship is impacted."

"You won't be happy if I'm living anywhere other than under the same roof with you."

"That's not true, Mike." I pulled myself away abruptly and sat up to face him. "You're not listening. I just want to know whether there's a possibility of it down the road, or if we're both just wasting time."

"I'm just wasting your time? You think this relationship is wasting your time?"

"No! I didn't say that. I—"

"You—"

"Wait, Mike. Just listen. We've been together for—"

"I know how long we've been together, Beau."

"Please don't interrupt me. All I'm saying is that after all these years, it's time to sink or swim, Mike."

Gazing up at me from his white hotel pillow, he just blinked and said, "Wow."

Yeah. *Wow*.

I think I just gave him an ultimatum.

An inadvertent ultimatum, at that.

Oops.

"I'm tired," Mike said, and rolled over, turning his back on me.

But I knew he wasn't really tired. It was only nine o'clock his time.

His time.

My time.

Obviously, like I said, when it came to the time thing, we were definitely not in sync.

seventeen

The present

Typical weeknight dinner hour at our house: Somebody left the television blasting a Nickelodeon cartoon downstairs; the older boys are at the half-set table fighting over who gets which vinyl-coated place mat; I'm balancing a fussy Tyler on one hip while stirring the fake orange cheese powder into the overcooked Scooby-Doo–shaped macaroni in a pot on the stove.

Don't get me wrong, I'm a decent cook when I actually *cook*. But I'm not about to go to the trouble and expense necessary to concoct my famous veal saltimbocca or chicken chausseur for three finicky kids who prefer simple carbs and synthetic cheese from a sixty-nine-cent box.

On the rare occasions Mike is actually home for dinner on a weeknight, I will occasionally surprise him with a home-cooked meal from scratch. And occasionally, I will give him simple carbs and synthetic cheese from a sixty-nine-cent box. He knows better than to complain. I have often reminded him that he's as capable as I am of opening a cookbook and throwing together a fabulous meal—something he has yet to do.

In the midst of the chaos, the front door opens and closes, an incident so unprecedented that everybody but Sponge-Bob SquarePants falls silent for a moment.

Then Josh exclaims, "Daddy's home!"

My eyes immediately go to the stove clock. It's not even six-thirty yet.

"Daddy's not home, Josh."

Yet I hear footsteps and the jangling of keys in the front hall. Either Daddy is indeed home, or a stranger just broke in to our house. A stranger who has his own set of keys.

To tell you the truth, both scenarios seem equally outlandish. True, Mike said he'd be home early tonight, but I wasn't born yesterday. If I believed his promises, I'd also expect Mikey's framed school picture from last September to be hung in its appointed position above the mantel any second now.

Still, the boys have abandoned their seats at the kitchen table and are making a beeline for the next room, where I can hear Mike laughing and greeting them.

Will wonders never cease?

Leaving the macaroni and cheese behind, I tote Tyler into the front hall, where Mike is already stripping off his tie.

"You really are home early."

"I really am home early."

"I can't believe it."

"I told you I would be. What's for dinner?" he asks, bending to press a kiss on my cheek, then on Tyler's.

"Now that you're here, takeout."

He laughs. "No problem."

No problem? He hates takeout almost as much as he hates boxed macaroni and cheese.

"You're in a good mood tonight," I say as the baby stretches his arms up toward his daddy.

"I'm always in a good mood."

I snort at that.

"Hey," he says, but he's still smiling.

I'm surprised when Mike takes the beckoning Tyler from me without being nudged to. Usually, he'd rather change his clothes, wash up and spend fifteen minutes on the toilet before he's ready to take on one of the boys...let alone three.

I watch in disbelief as he plunks himself down on the couch, balancing Tyler in the crook of his arm and cradling Josh on the opposite knee, with Mikey sandwiched in between.

"So what's up?"

"What do you mean?"

"You're home early and you're in a great mood. Did you get a raise?" I ask, lowering myself into a wingback chair.

"Nope."

"A promotion?"

"Uh-uh."

"You won the lottery and quit your job?"

He laughs.

I notice an incredible amount of dust on the end table and, come to think of it, in the air. It's clearly visible in the late-day sunlight streaming in through the front window.

Darn that Melina, anyway. She must have skipped the living room, too.

"What's the lottery?" Josh wants to know.

"It's a big waste of money," Mikey tells him. "That's what Grandma tells Grandpa when he talks about it."

"Well, I didn't win the lottery or quit my job," Mike informs all of us. "I just felt like coming home early to see my family for a change. Not that I don't feel like doing that every night."

"So why is tonight special?" I ask him, because I get the feeling that it is. He never comes home in a wonderful mood. Hopefully he won't notice the dust. Or if he does, he won't threaten, again, to fire Melina.

Mike informs me, "I have a surprise for you and the boys."

Said boys erupt in cheers and queries.

"A surprise! Yay!"

"I love surprises!"

"What kind of surprise?"

"Is it candy?"

"Can I have the biggest piece?"

"When can we have it?"

"You can have it in a few days," Mike says, laughing and throwing up his hands.

"Why do we have to wait, Daddy?" Mikey protests.

"Yeah, no fair. I didn't even break Mommy's favorite pink teacup this afternoon."

"Yes, you did, Josh. Daddy, he did!"

"Not on purpose," he tells his big brother. "It was an accident. Right, Mommy?"

I sigh. "It was an accident. What's the surprise, Mike?"

"You know how you've been saying you need to get away?"

My breath catches in my throat. "Yes…"

"Well, you're going to get away."

I squeal and leap up to hug him as the boys launch into a happy dance. "We're going to the Cape?"

"Not the Cape…"

"Where?"

He reaches into his jacket pocket and pulls out a folded sheet of white paper, handing it to me across Mikey's and Tyler's bouncing heads.

"What does it say, Mommy?"

"Hang on, Mikey, I'm reading…." It's a computer-gener-ated receipt for plane tickets purchased online this after-noon. Four tickets from New York to Tampa, Florida.

Florida.

My first thought, God help me, is that Happy Nappy Mike lives somewhere in Florida. I don't know exactly where. I never asked.

Florida is a huge state.

He could be hours from Tampa. He could be out in Key West, for all I know, or on the panhandle, or…

Or he could be in Tampa.

"We're going to Florida?" I ask, looking up at Mike's grin-ning face.

"Yup." He looks pleased. If he ever knew…

But he doesn't know.

"That's awesome," I say, trying to muster enthusiasm as the boys jump around cheering.

"My parents bought the tickets. They insisted. When I called my mother from the office this afternoon to ask her if they were up for a couple of houseguests next week, she gave me her credit-card number and said the tickets are on them. They can't wait to see the boys. And you, too, of course."

"That's…that's…great." I glance down at the itinerary again, then say, "Oh, Mike, we need to get a seat for Tyler, too. It's dangerous just to hold him on our laps the whole way. We can pay for it ourselves, and—"

"He's already got a seat."

"No, he doesn't. There are only four tickets."

"Right. For you and the boys."

Thud.

"You're not going?" I am incredulous. I haven't traveled

without him in years. I picture myself alone on a plane with three young children and am overwhelmed.

"I can't go, Beau. My vacation isn't until the following week, remember?"

"But…the boys and I are going to Florida without you?"

Florida.

Where Mike lives.

"I thought you'd be happy about it." The twinkle in his dark eyes is fading faster than the August sunlight beyond the picture window.

"I was happy…when I thought it was going to be a family vacation. Not your shipping me and the kids off to your mother's for a week."

I'll admit, I shouldn't have said that.

I love my mother-in-law.

And Mike clearly believes he's doing me a favor.

But I can't help it. I'm just…

Shocked.

And…

Afraid.

Afraid that I might be tempted to look up an old friend while I'm down there.

"I'm sorry," I tell Mike before he can speak. "I'd just…I'd rather go to the Cape. With you."

"Cape Canaveral?" shouts Mikey, who studied the space program in school this year. "That's in Florida. Can we ride on a rocket ship, Mommy?"

"Cape Cod," I say, still watching Mike's face.

"What's Cape Cod?" Josh asks.

"Is it in Florida, Mommy?"

"No, Mikey. It's in Massachusetts."

"I want to go to Florida. Daddy said we're going to Florida. I want to see Grandma and Grandpa and ride on a rocket ship. Why don't you want to go to Florida, Mommy?"

"It's not that I don't want to go to Florida," I say, mostly to my ominously silent husband. "But me and the kids alone...I'd miss you, Mike. We all would."

"I want to ride on the rocket ship, too," Josh announces. "And I want to get cotton candy. Okay?"

"I thought this would make you happy," Mike tells me, shaking his head, his expression softening. "You said you wanted to get away to the beach."

"I know, but...I don't always have to get what I want."

Yes, you do. You always have. You're spoiled rotten.

"Well, you aren't getting exactly what you want, Beau. I'm not about to send you to the Cape alone with the boys. My parents will help you with the kids. You can have some time to yourself. It'll be good for you, Beau."

"No, it won't," I say, alarmed at what I might be tempted to do with time to myself in Florida. "It won't be good for me, Mike. It isn't fair for me to be off in Florida having...time to myself...while you're up here, working."

He puts an arm around my shoulders. "You deserve it. You never get a break from the kids. Go to Florida. Let my mother baby-sit. She loves it. And you can go shopping or whatever it is that would make you happy."

"I *am* happy," I say, my eyes filling with tears.

I hate myself. I hate that I've been e-mailing back and forth with Mike. I hate that I've been thinking about him the way that I have.

Most of all, I hate what I did that summer fifteen years ago.

"Why do you think I'm not happy?" I ask Mike, struggling not to blink. If I blink, the tears will fall, and I can't let him see that I'm crying.

"Hey...why are you crying?"

Yeah. I blinked.

"I'm just...I'm so happy. They're tears of happiness. I love you so much, Mike." I bury my head in his shoulder, awash in tears and guilt and regret.

He laughs. "I love you, too. So go to Florida with the boys and have some fun. You deserve it."

No, I don't. I don't deserve it...

And I don't deserve him.

eighteen

The past

When the phone rang the morning after Mike flew back to Los Angeles, I picked it up without thinking.

"Beau! There you are!"

My heart sank. "Oh! Hi, Mike!"

Yeah. *That* Mike.

I tossed aside the issue of *People* magazine I'd been reading, with its huge cover photo of Rebecca Schaeffer, the *My Sister Sam* actress who had been murdered a few weeks earlier by a crazed fan.

"Wow," Mike said. "I can't believe you answered. I expected to get your machine. Or your roommate."

"Why did you think that?" I asked, my mind racing.

Dammit. Why did I have to go and answer the phone?

I should have screened the call. I should have realized it

might be him. Valerie had said he'd left a few messages while I was staying in the hotel the last two nights.

"When you didn't return my calls, I got paranoid," he said. "In fact, I wasn't even going to bother calling you back again, but something made me give it one last shot."

"Oh…well…"

"You wish I hadn't called, right?"

Talk about awkward.

"No," I protested, determined to put an end to this… this…this whatever was going on between us. I was going to be detached, no-nonsense, firm. "Actually, I'm glad you called."

"Why? You have a thing for stalkers?"

All right, I laughed. I laughed despite the article I'd just been reading in *People* magazine. I couldn't help it. The guy was amusing.

"Yeah," I said, "stalkers are definitely my type."

"Great. So let's get together and I can stalk you in person. When are you free this week?"

I wasn't free this week…or ever.

That was exactly what I wanted to say.

So why didn't I?

Why did I hedge and tell him vaguely that I was going to be kind of busy at work this week?

That left the door open for him to suggest that we get together today, since it was Saturday. Or tomorrow, since it was Sunday.

I couldn't think of an excuse. I swear, I tried…but I couldn't come up with anything.

All right, maybe I shouldn't have been grasping for an excuse. Maybe I should have come right out and told him to bug off.

But didn't I at least owe him an in-person explanation as to why I could never see him again?

I told myself that I did.

I told myself that agreeing to meet him for a glass of wine tonight was no big deal.

Not even if a glass of wine on a Saturday night sounded suspiciously like a date.

But I knew it wouldn't be a date. It would merely be my telling him—over a glass of wine on a Saturday night—exactly why he wasn't allowed to see me, or call me, or stalk me, in the future.

Shortly after we hung up, Valerie came home lugging two Key Food shopping bags. I met her at the door and blurted out, "I just did a really, really crazy thing."

"You threw water balloons out the window on people's heads as they walked by down on the street?"

"What? No!"

"Oh. Because I was thinking we should do that later. People would thank us. It's a freaking heat wave out there. Look at me."

I looked at her. She was flushed, her face shiny with sweat, her hair plastered to her head in a frighteningly limp do.

"You need a cold drink," I said. "And I need to tell you what I did."

"What did you do?" She followed me into the kitchen, which was barely big enough for both of us, the groceries and the open refrigerator door.

"I just told Mike I'd go out with him tonight." At her blank look, I clarified. "Mike. The guy I met at the airport."

"Business-card Mike? Cute, available Mike?"

"That's the one."

"This is so not fair," she said, shaking her head as she

sidestepped past me to reach for a glass. "I haven't had a date in months. You have a boyfriend *and* a date."

"Do you not see why that's a problem, Valerie?"

She turned on the cold water. "I'd kill to have a problem like that."

I have to admit, I was getting a little sick of her downplaying all of my troubles. It wasn't as though my life was perfect. I had plenty of problems—excess weight and a lackluster love life just happened not to be among them. Sometimes Valerie acted as though those were the only two issues that warranted sympathy.

Still, she was my only available sounding board, so I told her what had happened with Mike just now on the phone.

"I'd show up in your place if I didn't have to work tonight," she said, sounding half-serious.

"You're working on a Saturday night?"

"I'm baby-sitting. How pathetic is that?"

Pretty pathetic, I had to admit. My problems suddenly didn't seem quite as pressing.

Valerie, ever the good sport, suggested, "Maybe you should call him back and tell him you can't go, then."

"What would I say?"

"You'd say 'something suddenly came up.' It worked for Marcia Brady."

"No, it didn't. It backfired on her, remember? Doug dumped her when he saw her bruised nose."

"Are you sure?"

I gave her a look. "It's Brady trivia, Valerie."

Meaning, I was the Grand Poobah of seventies sitcoms.

Valerie shrugged. "Well, I guess you'll have to just go on this date then, won't you?"

I guessed that I would.

The truth was, I secretly wanted to. There was nothing

worse than staying home alone on a summertime Saturday night. I knew that for a fact, as I had done it one too many times lately.

So Mike and I met at a piano bar on Second Avenue in the East Fifties, according to plan. My plan. That neighborhood was no-man's land—not on my turf, not on his. We'd be forced to go our separate ways in order to get home at the end of the evening. There would be no awkward sharing of cabs.

Plus, a piano bar meant that if conversation lagged after I told Mike that he seemed to have the wrong idea about us, we could focus on other things. Like chiming in on a rousing if off-key rendition of "My Favorite Things."

The whole way over to the piano bar, I forced myself to think about Mike. *My* Mike. I made an effort to relive the moments we'd shared over the past few days.

The unexpected laughs, the unexpected tenderness.

The "proper goodbye" he always insisted on—a well-worn euphemism for the lovemaking that would have to last until we were together again.

The way he'd wistfully kissed me "one last time" about a dozen times at the airport and told me that he loved me.

I blocked out our one argument, the one we'd had in bed that first night before we went to sleep. I could chalk that up to jet lag on his part; to being overtired and cranky on mine. By the light of day, things were back to normal between us, and as long as we carefully avoided the topic of our future—which we did from that point on—we got along fine.

"I promise you we'll work things out," he'd said at the airport, just before he walked down the jetway. "Just trust me, Beau. Okay?"

I did trust him. Really, I did. I knew in my heart that he wasn't going to throw away everything we had for some stupid research job out West.

His third interview with the software place in New York had gone really well. All we had to do now was wait to hear from them. If they offered the job—and I had to think that they would—he wouldn't refuse it. I knew in my heart that he wouldn't.

Even though he hadn't come right out and said it.

So if I listened to my heart, and I fully intended to do that, it was pretty clear that my future was with Mike. All we had to do was work out the details.

Oh, and all I had to do was cut this other Mike loose. I decided to think of him as a pesky fly that kept buzzing around.

But when I saw him waiting for me at the bar, he didn't look like a pesky fly.

He looked like Johnny Depp. Better than Johnny Depp, even. I swear my knees went weak.

Don't get me wrong. My Mike was good-looking, too. But this Mike had something else. Some extra…I don't know. Some extra *something*. Maybe it was sex appeal. Maybe it was bad-boy magnetism. Maybe it was just that he was off-limits and I knew it.

Whatever the case, the second I spotted him, I knew I was in trouble.

He was Johnny Depp.

He was Lloyd Dobler hoisting a boom box and I was the helplessly smitten Diane Court.

He was trouble with a capital T that rhymes with B that stands for Beau. And Betrothed. Which I was not. Which meant that I was technically free to share a glass of wine with anyone I pleased.

Still, I should have insisted that we sit at the bar. The bar was big and crowded and impersonal.

But I didn't insist. That's probably because I was far too

busy reminding myself that I wasn't doing anything wrong—and all right, admiring his ass—to notice that he was leading me into temptation, by way of the darkest corner in the joint.

We sat at a table for two that was secluded and cozy and bathed in candlelight.

Blame it on the candlelight.

Blame it on the wine.

Or blame it on the fact that I had no willpower whatsoever when it came to those dimples.

When he leaned forward and kissed me halfway through the evening, I let him.

In fact, I kissed him back.

Looking back now on that night, I don't remember what we talked about, specifically. Only that it wasn't about my not seeing him again.

I'm pleased to report that I didn't go home with him after the wine—not just one glass, but three.

Nor did I allow him to come home with me.

Not that night.

But I kissed him.

Not just once.

I kissed him so many times I lost count, beginning at the table and ending on the street just before I went home in a cab.

Looking back at that night, what strikes me now is that a kiss can be so profound when you're twenty-four. More profound than anything—except, perhaps, for childbirth—can ever be, later in life.

A kiss, one kiss, can change everything in an instant.

That was how it started with us. In the moment Mike's lips touched mine, everything changed. I know it sounds crazy, but I knew in that moment that nothing about my life would ever be the same.

I, Beau, the golden girl who had been born under a lucky star and always got what she wanted, had come to a major crossroads.

I was torn between two men for the first time in my life. But I never dreamed that it wouldn't be the last.

nineteen

The present

I wasn't going to tell Mike that I was coming down to
Florida.

Yeah. Just like I wasn't going to answer the phone back in
the summer of '89. Or meet business-card Mike to go out
for a glass of wine on a steamy summer Saturday night. Or
kiss somebody who wasn't my boyfriend. Or—

But I'm getting ahead of myself.

The point is, I can't always be trusted to do the right
thing. Not even now, as a responsible adult.

Which, if you haven't figured it out by now, is my way of
admitting that I do wind up mentioning to Mike, via e-mail,
that I just so happen to be flying down to Florida with the
kids for a few days next week.

I'd be lying if I told you that I have any intention of leaving it at that.

I won't pretend that I'm surprised when he e-mails me immediately, asking if we can see each other for lunch or something.

It's the *or something* that scares the hell out of me.

I'll be in staying in Clearwater Beach. Where do you live? I type, with hands trembling so badly it takes me three tries to hit the question mark.

I'm in West Palm Beach, comes the quick reply. I can drive over to see you.

Isn't that a little out of your way? I return, reminding myself that I can hardly go around inviting strange men to show up on my in-laws' doorstep. Even if I tell them he's an old friend, they might be suspicious. And they'll probably feel compelled to mention it to Mike.

I shudder at the thought of my husband calling to check on me and the kids, and his mother saying, "Beau? No, she's not here. She went out on a date."

Still…

It's not out of my way, Mike insists. I don't have anything else to do. How should I get in touch with you? Do you have a cell phone?

Of course I do. Doesn't everyone?

But I can't bring myself to give him the number. That would feel duplicitous, even if I'm not technically doing anything wrong.

Unless you consider e-mailing an old boyfriend—and, all right, making plans to meet—*wrong*.

I have to draw the line at giving him my cell-phone number, though. Maybe because my husband is working so damn hard to make enough money to pay all of our bills, including that one.

I'll be hard to reach while I'm down there, I write back to

Mike. Why don't you just tell me when and where to meet you and I'll see you then?

That makes the most sense. Never mind that it smacks of *An Affair to Remember.*

This isn't an affair. Remember?

Me, too. Only sometimes, I forget.

All right, Mike responds after a few nerve-racking moments of waiting. I'll see you on Tuesday at noon in the garden level at the bottom of the grand staircase at the Don CeSar.

The grand staircase?

Forget *An Affair to Remember.*

This is starting to remind me of *Titanic.*

Hoping that isn't an omen, I respond, What is the Don CeSar?

You've never heard of the Don?

Never.

LOL Trust me. You'll find it. See you Tuesday.

I do find it, and sooner than Tuesday…thanks to Google.

It isn't a restaurant, as I'd assumed.

No, the Don CeSar is a *hotel.*

Not just any hotel.

A sprawling, world-class resort hotel. It's also pink.

Trust me. You'll find it.

Yes, I found it.

But I don't trust him.

Or maybe I don't trust myself.

★ ★ ★

At the airport, Mike kisses me and the boys goodbye about twenty times each.

"I hate that we're going without you," I tell him, watching him take a tissue from his pocket to mop a mixture of Zwieback crumbs and drool from Tyler's chin.

"I hate that you're going without me, too," he says, looking around for someplace to deposit the tissue.

I take it from him and tuck it into the pocket of my khaki shorts, saying, "Maybe we shouldn't go."

The sharp-eared boys at my feet cry out in dismay.

"Don't worry, you're going," Mike assures them. "You're going to have a great time."

He directs that last part mostly to me.

"I know we will," I tell him. "It's just…"

It's just that you're pretty much delivering me to the doorstep of the man who almost stole me away from you.

"I know what it is. Come on, Babs. Don't feel guilty about leaving the kids with my parents and going off by yourself. You deserve a break. I want you to have fun. Go shopping, go to lunch, treat yourself to a massage…."

A massage.

The word triggers an erotic memory.

I have to remind myself that he means a massage from a professional masseuse, not from an old lover.

"I'm thirsty," Josh whines. "I want juice."

"You'll get something to drink on the plane."

"Juice?"

"Whatever you want."

"I want juice."

"You can have juice. All right, you all have to get down to the gate now," Mike says, checking his watch.

"I hate all these stupid airport restrictions," I tell him. "I wish you could come to the gate with us."

"Mom, you said *stupid*," Mikey pipes up at my elbow.

"That's a bad word," Josh chimes in. "But *shit* is a badder one. Mommy said *shit* the other day."

"Joshua!" Mike says sternly.

"I didn't say it. Mommy did. I was just—"

"Listen to me." Mike squats so that he's at eye level with the two older boys. "You are both going to behave yourselves on this trip. You aren't going to give Mommy a hard time. Do you understand?"

"Yes, Daddy," they say in unison.

"This is Mommy's vacation, too. Do you understand?"

Another simultaneous "Yes, Daddy," followed by a tacked-on "I'm thirsty" from Josh.

"You can get something to drink on the plane," I remind him, digging through my purse to make sure I have the Benadryl that should knock all three kids out by the time we're ready to board.

Mike plants more kisses on the boys' cheeks, then stands and looks at me. "You're good to go, Babs. Have a great time."

I nod, unable to speak. I want to tell him that I love him, that he's the best husband and daddy in the world, but I can't force the words past the sudden lump of emotion in my throat.

The next thing I know, I'm juggling three kids, an umbrella stroller and too many carry-on bags through security. Mikey is frightened by the in-depth search and the metal-detecting wands, Josh is proclaiming his thirst to me, the security guards and our fellow travelers and Tyler is crying uncontrollably.

It takes a good five minutes for me to reassemble our bags,

get my belt and jewelry and everyone's shoes back on, and locate a pacifier to stick into Tyler's mouth.

When at last I turn to wave a final goodbye at Mike, who was watching from the other side of the glass partition, I can't find him in the crowd.

I search for what feels like a long time, until the boys begin tugging at my arms.

With a sigh, I turn away and propel my herd toward the gate.

"I'm thirsty," Josh informs me for the millionth time.

"Why are you so thirsty?"

"I think it was all that popcorn."

"All *what* popcorn?"

He looks at me as though I've just asked him what his name is. "The popcorn from my pockets, Mom."

"He put popcorn in his pockets before we left home so he could have a snack in the car," Mikey says helpfully.

"Yeah, only I didn't remember to put juice in my pockets and now I'm thirsty."

Through clenched teeth, I say, "When we get on the plane you can get—"

"I bet they have juice in there." Josh points.

I look in that direction and spot the airport bar, where unencumbered adults are sipping cocktails.

Instant memory trigger, so intense that I stop short to stare.

The place has been remodeled, probably more than once in the past fifteen years. But an airport bar is an airport bar, and this one has tremendous significance for me.

"Can we get juice in there?" Josh persists.

"No!" I say sharply—so sharply that a startled Tyler spits out his pacifier and begins howling.

"What's wrong, Mommy?" Mikey asks, sounding worried.

"Nothing, sweetie…come on, let's get on the plane. They

have lots of juice on the plane," I add as Josh opens his mouth to protest.

I've been an unofficial single mom for less than ten minutes and already I know that it would never be an option.

There is no way…absolutely no way…that I'm going to put my marriage at risk by having anything more than lunch with Mike in Florida.

If I'm the least bit tempted, all I have to do is walk away.

It isn't that simple, Beau. You couldn't walk away fifteen years ago.

Yes, I could. Ultimately, I did.

But not without a struggle.

Well, everything is different now. I'm married. I didn't take those vows lightly. For better for worse, for richer for poorer, till death do us part.

The safest thing for me to do is just not show up to meet Mike at the Don CeSar.

Safe, yes.

But also rude.

No, I have to go.

We'll just have a nice, platonic lunch and go our separate ways, I promise myself. *Lunch, and nothing more.*

No matter what.

twenty

The past

"What, exactly, are you doing, Beau?" Gaile demanded, materializing in the especially small kitchenette adjacent to the J-squared soundstage, where a show was in progress.

"I'm making a pot of tea for Rob and Fab," I told her, pouring steaming water over the special blend of exotic herbs Milli Vanilli's road manager had given me a few minutes earlier, just before they went onstage to perform. "It helps to keep them from straining their voices."

"Not that," Gaile said impatiently. "When I checked to make sure everyone in the audience was wearing their sombreros, I spotted him sitting up front in one of the reserved seats."

"Oh."

No use pretending I didn't know what she was talking about, or that she had mistaken a sombrero-clad stranger for

Mike. I had introduced her to him last week when he met me outside the studio after work, and Gaile prided herself on never forgetting a face.

"I gave him one of my comp tickets," I said with a shrug, arranging the contents of an individual pack of Chips Ahoy! cookies on a plate for Janelle, who always demanded something sweet and chocolaty after her shows.

"Why?"

"He's crazy about Milli Vanilli."

Not.

In reality, Mike was here because he was crazy about me, and all right, the feeling was mutual. It had been two weeks since our first illicit kiss, and we had spent every spare moment together.

"You told me just the other day that you weren't going to see him anymore," Gaile reminded me, shaking her head. "You said you felt guilty about Mike. Your boyfriend Mike...or did you forget he exists?"

"I didn't forget." I stirred the tea vigorously to keep my hands busy and avoid stealing a cookie from the plate. I had a hard time resisting anything chocolate, but shrewd Janelle would undoubtedly notice a cookie was missing. "I really was going to stop seeing Mike. I just...couldn't."

"You're not being fair, Beau."

"To whom?"

"To anyone. Including yourself. Somebody's going to get hurt."

I wanted to tell her that it was none of her business, but Gaile wasn't the type to back down. When she had an opinion, she voiced it. That was one of the things I loved about her...most of the time. The rest of the time, she was just a royal pain in the ass.

I listened to her go on and on for a few minutes about how

I wasn't being a responsible adult and it was time to grow up and do the right thing—as if the right thing were obvious. Which it wasn't.

When at last she paused for breath, I said, "You know, you sound just like Dear Abby. Maybe you should ditch this production-assistant stuff and start writing a syndicated advice column."

Ignoring that, she said, "Somebody has to shake some sense into you, Beau. This is wrong."

"I know," I said lamely. "I can't help it. I keep telling myself that I have to break it off with Mike, but—"

"Which Mike?"

The truth was, I no longer knew.

But for Gaile's sake, I said, "This one?"

She nodded her approval.

"I really like him, Gaile."

"Then you need to break up with the other Mike."

"I can't do that. We've been together forever. I love him. He's just…not here."

And he might never be here. The offer from the software company had yet to come through, but they assured him that he was still on their shortlist. Just yesterday he had called and told me that he couldn't hold off on making a decision about the California research job for much longer.

I begged him to give it another few days.

Then we said *I love you* and hung up.

Then I went out for Mexican food with Mike.

My guilt lasted as long as the guacamole did. By the time we were sharing a bowl of fried ice cream for dessert, my boyfriend in California was the furthest thing from my mind.

Whenever the thought of him did manage to intrude, I reminded myself that I wasn't necessarily cheating on him. My current and revised definition of cheating involved sex, and I hadn't had sex with the new Mike. In fact, I had never had sex with anyone other than the old Mike.

I said as much to Gaile, who seemed unimpressed by that news.

"It's only a matter of time before you sleep with him," she said with the unflappable conviction of Willard Scott predicting thundershowers.

"Why do you say that?"

"Because you have no self-control whatsoever, Beau."

"Sure I do," I protested, popping one of Janelle's Chips Ahoys! into my mouth whole without thinking.

Oops.

"And anyway," I went on, "don't you think a person should sleep with more than one person in their lifetime? Let's say I'm going to marry California Mike. What if I wake up someday in the next century and wonder what I'm missing? Wouldn't it be better to get it out of my system now, while I'm still free?"

"Sure it would be…if you were free. You seem to have a way of forgetting that you're not."

She was right. The more time I spent with Mike, the more amazed I was that I could put myself in the moment with such little effort. Maybe I was born with a genetic scruple deficiency.

Or maybe, I thought as I fitted the lid onto the porcelain teapot and set it on a tray, I was just a spoiled brat who was used to getting her own way and to hell with everyone else's feelings.

"Listen, Beau," Gaile said, "you say that you're in love with one Mike but you only like the other. That should make your decision a little easier, shouldn't it?"

I shook my head. "I could probably fall in love with this Mike too, if I let myself."

"Does he know you're in a serious relationship with somebody else?"

I hesitated. "Sort of."

"Beau…"

"All right, not really. I told him we were having problems. Which we are."

"So it's okay with Mike for you to see other people?"

"With my Mike? Not exactly."

"Stop calling him 'my' Mike. It's too confusing when you're going around acting like they're both *your* Mike."

She had a point.

"Let me get this straight. New York Mike thinks you've broken up with California Mike?"

"More or less."

"And California Mike thinks you're still in an exclusive relationship?"

"Yeah."

Gaile shook her head. "Beau, you need to tell California Mike that you want to see other people. And you need to tell New York Mike that you haven't broken up with California Mike. You can't have your cake and eat it too."

"Now you sound like my grandmother."

"Then she must be a wise woman."

"Yeah, she is."

And I sure as hell didn't get this deficient-scruple gene from her. I couldn't imagine my grandma Alice sneaking around with another Herman behind Grandpa's back, even before they were married…and even if there *were* actually another semi-appealing Herman in town.

Grandma Alice and Grandpa Herman were one of those

rare senior-citizen couples who still kissed each other hello and goodbye, held hands walking and laughed at each other's jokes even though they'd heard them a thousand times.

I wanted to be just like them someday, still madly in love.

I just didn't know with whom.

"The thing is," I told Gaile, "what if I break things off with this Mike and then the other Mike decides to take the job out West? Where does that leave me?"

"You can always move out West with him—"

"He doesn't want me to move in with him," I reminded her, since she, of course, knew that whole story.

"Well, not *in* with him, necessarily. Just near him. Or you can start seeing this Mike again."

"He's not going to hang around waiting for me, Gaile. He's an awesome guy. Some other girl will snap him up in a heartbeat."

She shrugged. "Then maybe it isn't meant to be."

"Maybe it is."

"Then maybe you and California Mike aren't meant to be."

"Maybe we're not." I swallow hard. "But I always thought we were. I've been in love with him since we were both basically kids."

"That doesn't mean it's going to last forever."

From the soundstage, I could hear the final strains of "Girl You Know It's True."

With a sigh, I picked up the tray and headed toward the guests' dressing room, telling Gaile I'd talk to her about everything later.

"Hang in there, Beau," she said, running after me and giving me a quick hug. "I don't mean to be so harsh with you. I just think you need to make a choice."

"I know. And I will. I promise."

After delivering the vocal cord–soothing tea to Rob and Fab and congratulating them on the wonderful performance I hadn't seen, I met Mike in the lobby, where the rest of the studio audience was still milling around.

He was wearing his *J-squared* straw sombrero and toting a freebie cassette tape of Milli Vanilli's latest album.

"How was the show?"

"It was great," he said after greeting me with a quick kiss.

"Really?"

"No. It was pretty horrible. Janelle kept forgetting the first guest's name, and I could swear the musical act was lip-synched."

"Sorry."

"Don't be—it was fun anyway. Thanks for the ticket. And I get to keep the sombrero. How do I look?"

"Like you should be holding a margarita," I said with a laugh.

"I wish. How long before you get off work?"

"At least a couple of hours. We have a staff meeting."

"Well, I've got two tickets to the Yankee–Red Sox game tonight. What do you say?"

I knew what Gaile would say I should say.

I also knew what my boyfriend would say, and it wasn't just that the Yankees sucked.

"I don't know…." I said slowly, thinking that even in that doofy sombrero, he looked hot. It was getting harder and harder to see him and not be tempted to take things even further than they had already gone. "It's a work night, and I have to be up early…."

"Yeah, but it's the Yankees. They're one of Major League Baseball's greatest teams of all time."

"Don't they stink?"

"Well, yeah," he admitted. "This year. But they're going

to be great again. And you can say you saw them play in person at Yankee Stadium. It's historic."

"I know…."

"You said the other night that you'd never been to a Major League game before."

"I haven't."

I hadn't done a lot of things, including sleeping with somebody other than my boyfriend.

But, I reminded my inner self, that didn't mean I should do them.

Looking up into Mike's dark eyes, I told my inner self to take a hike.

"Come to the game with me, Beau." Mike ran a fingertip down my jaw.

"I don't know…."

What was my problem? It was just a game.

"Oh, all right," I said.

We'll just have a nice platonic night out at the game and go our separate ways, I promised myself. *Just a game, and nothing more.*

No matter what.

twenty-one

The present

The Don CeSar is a flamingo-colored palace, far grander—and pinker—in person than it appeared in the pictures I found on the Internet last week.

What is Mike doing taking me to lunch in a place like this when he doesn't even have a job?

Is he trying to impress me?

Does he expect me to pick up the tab?

Maybe he does, since I more or less informed him that I was coming to Florida, which might seem like I was inviting him to lunch...even though, technically, he was the one who did the inviting.

If he does expect me to pay, and I do, how will I explain the credit-card charges to my husband when we get the bill? The cash in my wallet probably won't even cover one cocktail in a place like this.

And if ever I needed a cocktail—or six—it's now.

After valet parking my father-in-law's white Caprice Classic, I stroll into the lush lobby, prop my sunglasses above my forehead and do my best not to gape.

I live close enough to Manhattan that I've been in some incredibly elegant places. But this…

Well, this is so exotic, so distinctively Floridian, that I am momentarily awed.

Potted palms and fresh flowers galore. Pastel walls, luxurious mahogany woodwork and Italian-crystal chandeliers. A dazzling view of the placid blue waters of Boca Ciega bay. A grand piano, at which is seated a pianist who's playing something old and jaunty that makes me feel like Daisy Buchanan in a flapper dress.

All I can think, gazing around at the atmospheric backdrop reminiscent of a romantic bygone era, is what on earth am I doing here? I should be home in suburban New York, crawling around under a sticky high chair picking up stray Cocoa Puffs.

I close my eyes, certain that when I open them that's exactly where I'll find myself.

Instead, I open them to find a concerned staff member asking in a friendly drawl, "Are you feeling all right, ma'am? You look a little faint."

"Oh, I'm…I'm fine." I look around, shaking my head a little.

"Can I help you find something?" she asks, the smiling image of southern hospitality.

"I…uh…the…the ladies' room," I stammer, and she points me in the right direction.

Actually, I just said that for lack of anything better to say. But by the time I get into a stall, I'm such a nervous wreck that I have to pee yet again. I went twice within the past half hour before leaving my in-laws' house, which led Mike's mother to ask me if I have a bladder infection.

I assured her that I didn't, but she scribbled *cranberry juice* on her shopping list anyway.

"Just to be safe," she told me. "Now, you go off to your shopping at Westshore, and don't worry about the boys. They'll be fine with me and Granddad."

I hate that I had to lie to her about where I was going; hate that she was such a saint about baby-sitting; hate that she keeps insisting that I borrow their second car during our stay instead of renting one.

I want somebody to tell me that I have no business going off by myself in the middle of a Tuesday afternoon a thousand miles from home.

But nobody has.

Everybody, including Mike when he called earlier from the office, and my boys when I kissed them goodbye, has been urging me to have fun and not worry about anything.

So here I am, all dressed up with someplace to go, almost wishing I were back home in my mommy clothes.

I gaze at myself in the mirror in the ladies' lounge, taking in the makeup, the clothes, the hair.

I look great.

Dammit.

My skin is sun-kissed from all day yesterday on the beach, but not burnt; my green eyes look bigger and wider set than usual thanks to dark liner and mascara. The coral-colored sleeveless summer shift accentuates my long, bare, newly tanned arms and legs and minimizes the hint of post-baby bulge beneath my belly button. My normally straight brown hair, streaked a little lighter from the sun and chlorine, is hanging loose down my back in waves courtesy of the soft water at my in-laws' house.

Basically, I don't look anything like my mommy self.

No, I look like a woman who might be up to something. Something…

Naughty.

I frown into the woman's eyes, telling her that she'd better behave. She frowns back at me, but only for a moment.

Then she checks her watch, reaches into her purse to turn off her cell phone and turns her back on the mirror.

Tramp.

It's all I can do to force myself to walk, not run, out of the bathroom.

Part of me wants to scurry back out to my father-in-law's Caprice Classic, but the rest of me wants to make a mad dash for the grand staircase and hurtle myself into Mike's arms.

"Can I help you find something, ma'am?" asks yet another solicitous, overly friendly staff member.

"Yes, you can." I smile back at him.

Ask him how to get back to valet parking.

"Can you please tell me where I can find…"

Valet parking.

Say it.

Say it!

"…the grand staircase?"

I know, but I can't help it.

I want to see him.

I *need* to see him.

Seeing him will put to rest any doubt I ever had that I made the right choice.

Yes, I'm doing this for my husband's sake. For my marriage's sake.

Really.

I might have been a giddy, weak-willed young girl the last time I saw Mike, but I'm a grown-up woman now.

Never mind that I'm so jittery with anticipation I feel like a giddy, weak-willed young girl.

As I stroll toward the grand staircase, I remind myself sternly that my future will contain no hurtling into anybody's arms unless they're my husband's, at the airport back in New York.

I'll have a quick, congenial lunch with an old pal and then I'll hop in my big white old-man-mobile and go back to the retirement community from whence I came. Period.

There will be no flirting. No touching. No wine, no appetizers, no dessert. Nothing that will prolong this…this… *reunion.*

I round the corner, and there it is.

The fabled grand staircase.

It takes me a moment to realize that the attractive middle-aged man standing at the foot of it is Mike.

Oh, my God.

Oh, my *God.*

It's really him.

And he hasn't spotted me yet, meaning I can gawk without inhibition.

He looks good.

Really good.

Really good in a middle-aged way, like Richard Gere and Harrison Ford look really good in a middle-aged way; as opposed to having looked really good when they were fifteen years younger.

To my surprise, I'm…well, surprised. Surprised that he's aged.

I guess I forgot, momentarily, that the Mike I'm meeting today isn't the Mike from my past. Somehow I forgot that he, too, has grown older. Somehow, that makes him seem safer.

I find myself relaxing, just a bit, as I look him over.

There's gray in Mike's dark hair, but he's got a full head of it. He's tanned and clean-shaven and in good shape, with only the slightest hint of paunch sticking out beneath his pink— yes, pink—Ralph Lauren polo shirt above the belt of his khaki pants.

So much has happened to him since we last met. He's been married, divorced; employed, unemployed. Yet he certainly doesn't look any the worse for wear. In fact, he looks more relaxed and far better dressed than you'd expect of somebody who's jobless.

I force my legs to move, carrying me toward him.

He turns his head and spots me. "Beau?"

"Hi."

"Oh, my God."

He's walking, and I'm walking, and we're walking… straight into each other's arms.

I don't hurtle myself, exactly.

No, but I do put my arms around his neck and squeeze, and I do notice that he smells great—like salt air and limes.

"I can't believe you're really here," he says, his voice close to my ear. Then he pulls back and holds me at arm's length, saying, "Let me look at you."

I do, and it gives me another chance to look at him, up close this time. I can see a faint network of wrinkles around his eyes and the corners of his mouth, from the sun or from laughing or maybe just from age.

I decide that I like those wrinkles. He wears them well.

"You look gorgeous," he says, shaking his head. "Three kids and fifteen years, and you look even better than you did the last time I saw you. How is that possible?"

I laugh. It isn't my laugh, but an unfamiliar, giddy one— more of a giggle, really. I can't help it. The years have fallen away and I am a giddy, giggly girl.

"I was getting really worried while I was waiting for you," he confides, leading the way to wherever it is that we're going. It doesn't matter to me. It should, but it doesn't. He could be bringing me to his lair to have his way with me for all I care.

"Why were you worried?" I ask. "I wasn't late, was I?"

"No, I was early. And you were right on time. But I convinced myself that you weren't going to show up."

"Why wouldn't I show up?" I ask, and laugh. At what, I don't know. But there's that giddiness again, spilling out of me with reckless abandon that should set off warning signals in my brain, but doesn't.

"Because you're married with three kids," Mike says simply, and the giddiness evaporates just like that.

"Oh…I…well, of course I'm married with three kids, but that doesn't mean we can't have lunch."

We are just here for lunch, aren't we?

I don't say it aloud, but I must have conveyed the question in my gaze because he touches my arm and says pointedly, "I know we can have lunch, Beau. I just wasn't sure you'd want to have lunch with me after all…after everything."

"You mean everything that happened when we broke up?" Might as well get it out there for discussion.

We're still walking, but more slowly.

He nods. "That was ugly, wasn't it?"

"It was. And it was my fault. I'm sorry."

"So am I."

We stare at each other.

Then he says, "How about a drink?"

"You read my mind," I say with a laugh. Not a giddy laugh this time, but a nervous one.

Moments later, we're in the Maritana Grill, the Don Ce-Sar's legendary four-diamond restaurant. Mike doesn't tell me that it's legendary or four diamond; I read that on the Internet. So I'm impressed when the congenial maître d' greets him by name and even more impressed that Mike made a reservation…and that we're given the best table in the room.

I've already violated my no-flirting and no-touching rules, so when he immediately orders a bottle of wine from the extensive list, I don't protest.

As I watch him swirl it in his glass, taste it, and offer his approval, I realize he seems somewhat accustomed to the good life. Can he possibly be wealthy?

"What is it that you did, exactly, before you lost your job?" I ask him when we're alone again, with full glasses poised for a toast.

"I didn't lose my job."

"Oh! I thought you did."

"No."

"Didn't you say you were unemployed?"

"By choice," he says simply.

"Oh!" I say again, wondering exactly how wealthy he is. I can't think of a polite way to inquire, so I ask instead, "What are we drinking to?"

"To getting reacquainted."

"To getting reacquainted," I echo, and clink my glass against his.

I sip the wine. I can feel it going straight to my head.

My stomach is empty; I didn't dare eat the shredded wheat and whole-grain toast my mother-in-law put out for breakfast again this morning.

I ate it yesterday, along with a cup of coffee, and regretted it shortly afterward when I found myself doubled over with cramps and rushing to find a bathroom on the beach.

My in-laws, who ingest all that fiber along with prune juice and Metamucil every morning to keep themselves "regular," were actually worried that I might have picked up some kind of "bug" on the plane.

"Are you okay?" Mike asks, watching me.

"I'm fine. Why?"

"You looked like you were thinking about something."

"I was, but…"

But it was poop, and you're not one of my mommy friends, so I'm not going to bring it up.

At least that thought momentarily killed the romantic ambience. For me, anyway.

I tell myself that if I find myself getting too caught up in the moment at any time during lunch, I'll just force myself to think about poop.

"I can't believe you drove all the way over here just to meet me for lunch and you just have to turn around and drive all the way back," I tell him.

"I don't."

"You don't?" I repeat. "You don't what?"

"Have to turn around and drive all the way back. I got a room."

At last, the alarm bells are going off in my head, and it's about damn time.

"You got a *room?*" I echo.

"Well, not a room, exactly. It's more of a suite."

"A suite?" I've become Polly the Parrot, dammit, but I can't help it. I'm flabbergasted. By everything. The place, seeing him, learning that for him this is more than just lunch.

But I already knew that, didn't I? Lunch, for me, is polishing off somebody's peanut-butter-and-grape-jelly-on-white-bread. On a good day, it's the kids sitting still long enough for me to order and eat a turkey wrap and iced tea at the IHOP. It isn't…

Valet parking, reservations, fine wine.

And it sure as hell doesn't lead to a suite in the most elegant hotel I've ever seen.

"It's my favorite suite in the place," Mike goes on conversationally after a sip of wine. "The presidential one. I didn't think it would be available on such short notice, but they'd had a cancellation."

"The presidential suite?" I ask weakly, because he's waiting for me to say something and I have yet to find words of my own.

"Yes. You should see it. It's really something."

No, I shouldn't. I should definitely not see his suite.

I should see myself to valet parking, that's what I should—

"Have you decided on appetizers yet, folks?" the waiter asks.

Mike looks at me.

I glance helplessly at the menu in my hand. I haven't even glimpsed anything that's on it yet.

"Would you like me to order for us?" Mike asks.

"Oh…sure."

Without further ado, he rattles off a list that begins with seared ahi and ends with beluga caviar. This, from a man who once refused to try sushi.

When the amiably chatty waiter has collected our menus and disappeared again, I say, "Everyone is so friendly here."

"Looks like you're not in New York anymore, Dorothy."

"New Yorkers are friendly," I protest.

He just gives me a look.

"What? They are," I insist.

"Southerners are friendlier."

"Is that why you're here?"

"Partly."

Now that I've opened that door, I can't help asking, "So what did you do, exactly, before you quit working?"

"I was in business with a few other guys, but we sold it," he says vaguely. "Tell me about your life."

I nearly spit out my wine. "Tell you about my *life?* You mean…all of it?"

"Just the last fifteen years. You married Mike…when?"

"Um…" Almost fifteen years ago. Not long after the Mike I'm having lunch with and I had our explosive last night together and went our separate ways.

But I don't want to talk about that, so I say, "Wait, you forgot to tell me about your job."

"You don't want to hear about that."

"Sure I do."

"No, you don't, any more than I want to hear about you marrying somebody else."

Taken aback, I look into his eyes. In them, I see someone who was deeply hurt and maybe never got over it.

"Let's save all that for later and talk about something else now," he suggests.

"Like what?"

"Like those fish." He gestures at the enormous aquarium nearby.

I laugh.

But he's serious. We talk about the fish. Then we talk about the food. Then we talk about Florida.

It sounds crazy, but it's a good conversation. We laugh a lot, just like the old days.

Too soon, the waiter arrives to clear away the remains of my profiterole with chocolate gelato and chilled white Godiva liqueur and Mike's chocolate mascarpone tower with cinnamon cream.

"Oh, my God," I say with a groan as we stand to make our way out of the restaurant. "I've never eaten so much in my life."

"Yes, you have."

I look at him, startled first by his tone, and then by the fondly reminiscing expression on his face.

"You always had a huge appetite," he tells me. "I never met another woman who could eat the way you did."

"What about your wife?" I blurt, because I have to say something to jar him out of the past.

That certainly does the trick. A shadow slides across his features. "I don't really want to talk about her."

"How long have you been divorced?"

"A year."

"I'm sorry."

"Don't be. I'm better off, and so is she. Come on, let's go for a walk on the beach."

A walk on the beach?

I thought we were done. I thought lunch was it. I thought I was about to head home.

Caught off guard, I can only allow myself to be led out onto one of the wide piazzas. The humid August heat radiates in shimmering ribbons off the wooden boardwalk and the powdery white sand crowded with midday sunbathers.

"Let's take off our shoes," Mike suggests, bending over to remove his tasseled off-white leather moccasins.

Florida shoes, I think, and picture my husband in his polished black wing tips. I can't imagine him in moccasins, much less a pink shirt.

"Coming?" Mike asks.

"Won't the sand be too hot?"

"Not if we walk in the water. Come on."

I hesitate.

I've seen too many romantic movies where the couple walks barefoot along the beach.

I should tell him I have to get going.

I should thank him for lunch and promise to e-mail.

I should…

"Come on, Beau," he urges again.

I should think about poop, I tell myself, noting the dangerous spark in his eyes.

But somehow, I can't.

The only thoughts I can summon involve Mike—this Mike, not my husband—and our past.

God, I was crazy about him back then. And he was crazy about me.

I was so certain we were going to wind up together….

"Beau?" he asks.

"All right," I say, and quickly cast off my sandals—along with my reservations.

twenty-two

The past

I finally did it. I slept with Mike. Not the night of the Yankees game.

The next night.

And the night after that.

And yes, the night after that.

Once I started, I just couldn't seem to stop. And there was no way that I could further broaden my definition of cheating. Believe me, I tried. There was just no way around it. Having sex with somebody other than your boyfriend was definitely cheating.

I knew that what we were doing was wrong, but to his credit, Mike didn't. Not at first. He didn't know until I confessed to him that I was supposedly in a monogamous relationship with somebody else.

I confessed this in the wee hours as we were lying naked

in each other's arms in his twin bed in his Chinatown apartment.

"I thought you broke up," he said, pulling back a little. I couldn't see his face in the dark, but he sounded dismayed.

"I never said that."

"I guess I just assumed it. You said he was staying in California to do that teepee thing and you didn't want to move out there."

"Oh." I guess I did say that, or at least imply it. "Well…we didn't break up."

"You mean you're cheating on your boyfriend?"

"Sort of."

"Sort of?"

"All right. Yes. Yes, I'm cheating."

"So I'm the Other Man."

Why did he have to label it that way?

He was silent for a long time. I wondered what he was thinking about.

And I wondered about California Mike. He had left me a message on my home answering machine that he was flying back to New York tomorrow, which was why I found it necessary to bring up the subject just now, with this Mike.

I didn't know whether the original Mike was coming back from California to get the rest of his stuff from his parents' house and move it out West, or to accept the job in New York and find a place to live here.

The reason I didn't know was that I got his message secondhand from Valerie when she met me in the lobby at work this morning to drop off the change of clothes I'd requested. I hadn't been home to our apartment in several days.

Valerie, unlike Gaile, didn't judge me or lecture me. She just delivered my clothes, and Mike's message, with her usual efficient wistfulness. Clearly, she wished she were the one juggling two men; that she were carrying her own underwear around town in a Strawberries shopping bag.

"How did Mike sound on the answering machine?" I asked her.

"Like he was in a hurry."

"Not like he was suspicious or anything?"

"Nope."

"Did he want me to call him back?"

"He didn't say to. And he said not to meet him at the airport. He's taking a cab to our apartment."

"When?"

"Sometime tomorrow night. That's all I know."

That meant I would have to go home after work, instead of meeting New York Mike again as I had planned. I felt a pang at the thought of being apart for more than a night. I had become addicted to him in the space of a few days.

"Did I ever tell you that my fiancé cheated on me?" he asked abruptly now, bringing me back to the present.

"No."

"That's why we split up."

"I didn't know that." I stroked his hair. "I'm sorry."

He seemed to flinch at my touch. He repositioned his weight, as though he was trying to put some space between us, but that wasn't possible in a twin bed.

Needing to reassure him, I began, "Mike—"

"I probably should have known better than to get involved with somebody so soon," he cut in bitterly.

"Oh, Mike, come on. Don't—"

"Just so you know, I don't think I can handle being dumped again on the heels of what I went through last spring."

"You mean dumped by me?"

"What else would I mean?"

"But…I'm not going to dump you, Mike."

There was a pause.

"You're not?"

"No," I promised, even as I asked myself what the hell I thought I was doing.

"Then you're going to dump him?"

"Yes."

"You are? Really?"

"Yes," I said again, shocked by my own decisive response…and yet knowing, somehow, that it was the right thing to say. And do.

I was going to break up with Mike.

Of course I was.

It had been a long time coming, I realized.

Why did it take me so long to see that? We were already living separate lives. We didn't want the same thing. Apparently, we didn't even want to be in the same city. We were only hanging on because we had spent so many years together…but never *really* together.

All at once, I'd had it with a long-distance relationship. I was sick of bittersweet farewells, of counting down calendar days, of a huge monthly AT&T bill, of only buying and receiving birthday and holiday gifts that could be easily packaged and mailed.

It was almost a relief to see our relationship's many shortcomings with sudden clarity. Surely Mike saw them, as well.

So.

This was it.

I would set him free to pursue the job in Silicon Valley, and he would set me free to pursue…

Well, Mike. This Mike. *He* was everything I wanted.

And he was *here*.

"Are you sure you want to break up with him?" he whispered in the dark.

"I'm positive. I want to be with you." Day in and day out. I was ready for that. I was ready for permanence.

"And I want to be with you, Beau. I know that it's probably happening way too fast—"

"Not too fast," I protested, though I wasn't sure of that. Was it possible for a whirlwind romance to turn into something worthwhile?

"And anyway," he said, "this feels right."

"It does to me, too. I…I think I'm…"

He kissed me. "I know what you're going to say."

I kissed him back. "How do you know?"

"Because I think I am, too."

"You think you're what?" I held my breath.

"In love with you."

I expelled the breath, along with the last of my misgivings and the words that had been running through my head for days. "I think I'm in love with you, too, Mike."

As I settled my head against his bare chest and drifted off to sleep, I told myself that this couldn't be wrong. I had never felt so safe, so secure, in all my life. Neither of us was going anywhere. We had all the time in the world to be together.

Yes.

This was right.

Everything was settled.

The moment Mike the First got to town tomorrow, I was going to break up with him…if he didn't break up with me first.

I wouldn't be surprised if he did.

In fact, so convinced was I that our relationship was over that it never occurred to me that he might put up a fight…or that in less than twenty-four hours, I would seriously doubt the emotion I felt with such conviction right now.

twenty-three

The present

We walk on the beach for a long time.

Not holding hands.

Not arm in arm.

Just…walking.

And talking.

About the past.

Not the past we didn't share—meaning, the last fifteen years we've spent apart.

No, we talk about the past we *did* share. Our past.

There are more than enough great memories to keep us laughing…at least, for a while.

Then things get serious.

They get serious when Mike asks me, point-blank, "So Beau…do you have any regrets about the way things turned out in the end?"

"Regrets?" I echo, feeling as though I've just stepped into a pit of quicksand. "Regrets about what?"

As if I don't know.

"About marrying somebody else."

I open my mouth to answer, but he doesn't let me.

"And about you and me going our separate ways after that summer."

Going our separate ways. He makes it sound so benign. As though it were a mutual decision, when, in fact, I was the one who made it. I was the one who told him I loved him, then pushed him away.

"Do *you?*" I ask, mired in guilt.

"Have regrets? Yes."

"Oh." Somehow, I didn't expect such a straightforward answer.

Maybe I thought he was going to tell me how it was the best thing for both of us. Maybe I thought he was going to thank me for setting him free to…to follow his dreams. To marry somebody else, to live leisurely ever after in Florida, to wear white moccasins and pink shirts.

"I never got over you, Beau." He stops walking and turns to face me, grabbing hold of my upper arms with his hands and forcing me to stop, to turn, to face him.

"Mike…"

"I'm serious. I've spent fifteen years wondering what would have happened if you and I had stayed together."

"No, you haven't." I shake my head, reeling. "You got married. You must have loved your wife."

"I did," he admits. "In the beginning. But not the way I loved you, back then."

"That's because we were young."

"Maybe partly. But it was also because we were pretty damned good together. You know we were. It wasn't just me."

What I see in his eyes is more unsettling than the smell of rain that suddenly permeates the salt air.

I force myself to look away, to gaze at the sky, where thunderclouds loom; at the incoming tide, no longer blue and calm but gray and foamy.

He's waiting.

And whether I admit it or not, he knows.

But I admit it. I owe him that. I owe him more than that, probably.

"No," I say slowly, looking at Mike again at last. "It wasn't just you. But—"

"You can't tell me you haven't wondered what would have happened if you'd chosen me instead of him, Beau."

"I haven't," I lie, twisting a bit to the right and then to the left. His grasp on my arms doesn't flinch. He's got a hold on me that's impossible to shake off.

No, it isn't, I tell myself. *You could pull away if you really wanted to. You don't want to.*

"You're saying that you're happily married?" he asks.

"Of course I'm happily married."

"And you don't have a single regret?"

I can't find my voice. My thoughts are reeling.

"Why are you here with me, Beau?"

All I can think is that he *knows.* He knows that there's a part of me that's never gotten over him, either.

But I don't dare admit that. I don't owe him *that.* Admitting to him that my feelings are unresolved would open the door to something I'm not ready to face.

Thunder rumbles ominously in the distance; a hot wind kicks up the surf.

My God. This is surreal. I feel as though I've stumbled onto a movie set. My life—my real life—is not this dramatic. My life is my children, my husband, my cobweb-and-crumb-strewn house that needs another bathroom under the stairs.

"We have to get back," I tell Mike, my panic surging like the mounting tide. "It's going to storm."

"Wait, Beau…"

"No…I have to go…."

"First just tell me why you're here. Just tell me why you're here with me, and we'll go back."

"I don't know why I'm here with you, Mike," I say. "But I do know that I shouldn't be. I have to—"

"No, you don't have to go."

"Yes, I do. It's going to storm." Again, I make the effort to slip out of his grasp.

Not enough effort.

"Go ahead. Tell me that you never want to see me again," he says. "If that's really how you feel, then tell me."

"Why do I have to say it again? I've already told you that once in my life."

"But here you are."

I swallow hard. He's right. Here I am.

"I'm not in Florida to see you" is my feeble protest. "I'm visiting my in-laws."

"You didn't have to tell me you were coming. I would never have known."

I open my mouth to argue, but I can't. I can't because he's right.

"You didn't have to write back to me when I e-mailed you. You could have deleted it."

"I know, but—"

"Why did you write back, Beau? Why did you tell me you were coming to Florida?"

"I don't know."

"Well, I do. It was because you wanted to see me. You can't say that's not true."

"I *did* want to see you," I admit, "but that's all. Just see you. Not…"

"Not what?" He's leaning closer. Dangerously close.

"Don't," I say, but this time I don't even try to slip out of his grasp.

I close my eyes, hating myself for the way that I feel. I'm ashamed to admit it, but I don't want him to let go. I don't want him to stop leaning closer. I don't want—

His lips brush against mine.

My eyes fly open.

"No," I say. "Don't."

He does it again.

I can feel myself responding even as my hands come up against his chest and push. Hard.

"Beau…"

"No."

"I'm sorry."

My heart is pounding. I've never kissed anybody other than my husband…not since he became my husband.

I knew what Mike was going to do. It was wrong; I knew it was wrong, and yet…

I let him.

I let him because I have no self-control. I'm spoiled, I'm weak, I'm a giddy girl masquerading as a responsible wife and mother.

I hate myself, and I hate him.

I take off running.

"Beau, wait!"

No. I won't wait. I'm running down the beach with my sandals in my hand, not caring about the shells and pebbles that hurt my feet or the rain that's begun to fall or the lightning that strikes all around me.

I'm running, running away from him, running away from my shameful self. Running away from temptation, from what might have been.

And what am I running toward?

Toward a white Caprice Classic and three small jet-lagged children, toward a husband whose idea of a vacation is to install a toilet, toward a maid who leaves the cleaning to me, and friends whose lives revolve around teething and diapers and third markdowns at Baby Gap.

Yet I keep running. I want to look back, but I don't. I can't. I'm afraid I'll see that he's chasing after me...or that he isn't.

twenty-four

The past

"There he is," Valerie said when the door buzzed loudly that evening.

I stopped pacing and looked at her, then at the security panel. It wasn't as though I hadn't been expecting him. It wasn't as though I hadn't spent the entire day wanting to get this over with so that I could move on unencumbered.

So why, now that he was here, was I caught off guard? Why wasn't I ready for what lay ahead?

"Are you going to buzz him up or do you want me to do it?" Valerie asked, already strapping her overnight bag across her shoulder. She was going to Gordy's so that Mike and I could have some time alone.

"You do it," I said, clenching and unclenching my fists, taking deep breaths.

She did, pressing the button on the panel and saying, "Come on up, Mike."

"How do I look?"

"Gorgeous, as always," she said, glancing over my outfit: pleated pink pants, a high-collared blouse with a brooch at the collar, and a gray bolero jacket with shoulder pads.

"I mean, do I look nervous?"

"A little." She gave me a quick squeeze. "You can do this, Beau."

"Are you sure?"

"It's the right thing to do. You said it yourself."

"But are you sure?" I asked again.

"Are you?"

"Valerie! That's not supposed to be your answer. You're supposed to tell me that I should break up with him and follow my heart."

"Well, you definitely should."

"You don't look convinced."

"Neither do you."

I paced across the room again, feeling trapped. "I promised Mike I would do this," I said, more to myself than to my roommate. "I promised him I would be with him."

"Is that the only reason you're doing it? Because you told him you would? Or because you want to?"

"I want to." I said it with far less conviction than I actually felt at the moment.

Valerie gave me another hug and reached for the door. "I love you, sweetie. I know you'll make the right decision."

"I thought I already did," I said, but she was gone.

And, moments later, he was there.

He stepped over the threshold and swept me into a bear hug. "I'm so totally glad to see you."

It wasn't at all what I expected.

I had somehow convinced myself that because my feelings had changed in the past few weeks since we'd seen each other, his had, too. But one look at Mike's face told me he wasn't here to break up with me…and that he sure as hell didn't see it coming on my end.

"What are you doing here?" I asked, prolonging the hug so that I could bury my face in his shoulder once more and not be forced to focus on the unsettling expression on his face.

"I'm taking the job. I wanted to tell you in person."

"Which job?" I asked, pulling back, looking up again reluctantly, seeing something in his eyes that had never been there before.

"The one in New York. The dude called me a few days ago. They came through, Beau. They really did."

New York.

He was moving to New York.

"They offered you more money than the research thing in Silicon Valley?" I asked, incredulous, my heart racing.

"No."

"Better benefits?"

"No. But it's a decent package. And the thing that counts is that it's here."

I shook my head, stunned. "I can't believe it. You said you didn't want—"

"I know what I said. I didn't want to live here. I still don't. But I realized that if I wasn't willing to compromise, I was going to lose you. And I can't lose you, Beau. I love you."

"I love you, too." I swiped a hand across my teary eyes, overwhelmed. "But I never expected you to give up a job that you really, really wanted."

"It's a job," he said with a shrug. "Who even knows if it would have been worthwhile? Beau, what's wrong? Aren't you happy?"

I realized that I was still shaking my head. I forced myself to stop, to smile, to tell him, "Of course I'm happy."

"You're happy, but…"

"But are you sure this is what you want?"

"I'm positive."

And he really did look secure in his decision. Clearly, he was doing this for me. He loved me enough to give up his dreams for me.

And I loved him, too. I really did. I couldn't turn my feelings off just like that. Now that he was here, standing in front of me…

Well, I still loved him.

But did I love him enough to give up Mike?

"So what do you say? Do you want to go apartment hunting with me in Jersey?"

"You mean…to help you find a place?"

"A place that can be big enough for two down the road. Not right away, but maybe after I get settled in…"

"You're saying you'll be willing to live together?"

"I'm saying I'll be willing to give it a shot."

He kissed me. His kiss was tender and passionate, comfortably familiar. I lost myself in it, and when at last we came up for air, I heard myself whisper, "I can't believe this is happening."

He laughed. "Neither can I. This is excellent."

"What made you change your mind?"

"Being away from you, Beau. I went back out there to my apartment and it felt lonely. I realized that if I moved up north I'd be just as lonely there. I'd have a great job, but I'd still be lonely. I'd still miss you. And I'm really, really sick of missing you. It totally sucks."

"I feel the same way." I also felt that he had been living precariously close to the San Fernando Valley long enough.

But a few weeks back on the East Coast would banish the *totallys* and *dudes* from his vocab.

"Other than summer camp, we've never had the chance to live in the same place and have a normal relationship."

"I know we haven't."

But what about Mike? a voice screamed inside my head. *You promised Mike…*

You promised him something you had no business promising.

How could I have convinced myself it was possible to fall in love with somebody overnight? I had read enough magazine articles to know that whirlwind romances couldn't last; that what I felt for the other Mike had to be mere infatuation, not full-blown love.

"We've got a lot to talk about, Beau. A lot of planning to do."

Despite my qualms, anticipation bubbled up inside of me, frothy and promising as wedding champagne.

Mike and I had a past together, and we could have a future together, if that was what I really wanted.

Maybe you had to have one to have the other.

But maybe not.

Maybe what I had with the other Mike in the here and now could blossom into full-blown love.

What did I want?

Which Mike did I want?

God help me, I didn't know.

"What are you thinking about, Beau?"

"I'm thinking that this is all happening so fast."

"Really? I'm thinking that it's about time."

Before I let this go any further, I should be honest about what I had done. I should tell him that I had feelings for somebody else.

"Unless," he said, and I saw a question in his eyes.

I pulled his face down to mine again and kissed it way.

I was afraid of what he was going to ask me.

Afraid of what I wasn't going to be able to say. At least, not yet. Not tonight.

The decision I thought I had made evaporated, leaving me more torn than ever.

I knew only one thing for certain. "I've missed you so much, Mike."

"I've missed you, too. I never want us to be apart like that again."

twenty-five

The present

"I never want us to be apart like that again."

"I don't either," I tell my husband fervently, allowing him to pull me close, crushing poor little Tyler, who is balanced on my hip.

That our flight was delayed for a few hours—and turbulent—feels suspiciously like poetic justice. I mean, all I've wanted since I ran away from Mike on the beach was to be back home where I belong.

Now that I'm here, I'm positive that I'll be able to get back to normal at last. For the last few days, in foreign surroundings, without my husband's constant presence to ground me, I haven't been able to shake the eerie feeling that I'm living somebody else's life—that nothing is familiar.

I've felt this way once before…that summer.

But that's well in the past; now, thank God, so is Florida. It's time to go back to the real world.

In the real world, there is no nagging sense of unfinished business.

At least, there had better not be.

"The house was way too quiet without all of you," Mike says, releasing me from his fierce embrace at last. He takes my carry-on bags and swings Joshua up onto his shoulders, adding, "And now I bet Grandma's house will be too quiet, too."

"Oh, I don't think she'll mind," I tell him, deftly unfolding the umbrella stroller and strapping Tyler into it.

"Grandma's head was hurting really bad last night," Mikey informs Mike, holding tightly to his hand as we start toward the baggage-claim carousel downstairs. "And so was Grandpa's. Josh was being loud."

"I wasn't being loud," Josh protests—loudly—from his lofty perch. "It was the fire truck."

"Fire truck?" Mike looks at me. "What fire truck?"

"The very loud one your father insisted on buying Josh at Toys 'R' Us the first minute after we got there."

"It has a real siren, Daddy. And a bell."

"Did you leave it at Grandma and Grandpa's house to play with next time you visit?"

"You bet he did," I say with a laugh.

"Grandma and Grandpa wanted him to bring it home," Mikey reports, "but Mommy said no."

"They kept saying yes," Josh put in, "but Mommy kept saying no. And Mommy won."

Mike laughs. "Good for Mommy."

"Hey, Dad, did you know that Grandpa knows even badder words than Mommy does?" Josh asked. "Grandpa said a lot of bad words about my new fire truck last night to

Grandma after we were supposed to be sleeping. I heard him say *damn*. And he said *hell,* too. And then he said—"

"That's enough, Josh," Mike cuts in, and sets him on his feet again as we reached the baggage claim. He looks at me. "Did they drive you crazy?"

"The kids?"

"My parents."

"Oh…" I shrug. "They were wonderful. Really. Your mother just kept thinking I was sick, or that the kids were sick, or that your father was sick. Has she always been like that?"

He laughs. "Hell, yes."

"Daddy, you said a bad word," Mikey pipes up. "Did you learn that one from Grandpa?"

"Maybe he learned it from Mommy," Josh puts in. "Mommy said *hell* when the car trunk closed on her finger this morning."

"The car trunk closed on your finger? Are you okay?" Mike asks, so concerned that I feel guilty.

About everything.

Not that I didn't feel guilty before now.

I've been swamped in guilt, in fact, ever since that kiss on the beach on Tuesday afternoon. I've done my best to forget it ever happened, but I haven't been able to.

At least I haven't had to see or hear from Mike again since I abandoned him on the beach. He didn't know where I was staying; he didn't have my cell-phone number. For a while I was mortally afraid that he would call my home phone and tell Mike what had happened.

Clearly, he hadn't. I mean, Mike is acting totally normal.

And the other Mike would have nothing to gain, really, by blowing the whistle on me.

Nothing other than revenge.

Which, when you come right down to it, I wouldn't blame him for wanting.

Especially now.

If I try hard enough, I can almost forgive myself for being a fickle female fifteen years ago. But I can't forgive myself for what I did this past week.

I suppose I can't expect Mike to forgive me for that either. He clearly had the wrong idea about…lunch.

"How was the beach?" Mike asks, jarring me back to the present.

"The *beach?*" I echo, my mind racing wildly.

Can he possibly know? Is this a veiled attempt to get me to confess?

"Did the boys have fun with their boogie boards?"

"Daddy! How did you know Grandpa bought us boogie boards?" Mikey asks as relief courses through me.

"He told me on the phone. Did you like them?"

"We loved them," Josh says, bouncing around with the enthusiasm of an energetic child who has been strapped into seat 7E for three and a half hours. "Did you ever ride a boogie board, Daddy?"

"No, I never did."

"You should try it sometime. Maybe if you come to Florida with us next Easter, you can try it then."

"Florida? Next Easter?" Mike looks at me.

I shake my head. "Your parents want to fly us down, but I told them I didn't think you can get away."

And I can't go to Florida with you, Mike. I can't go to Florida ever again.

"Maybe I *can* get away," he says thoughtfully, catching me as off guard as the baggage carousel that suddenly buzzes and lurches into rumbling rotation. "When does Easter fall this year? March? Or April?"

"I don't know, but if you want to take a vacation then, let's go someplace we've never been before. Maybe the Caribbean, or…Mexico."

"You want to go to Mexico?"

"I bet they have great chimichangas."

He laughs. "I haven't heard you talk about chimichangas in years."

"That's because I had an aversion to deep-fried food every time I was pregnant, and I was trying to lose the baby weight whenever I wasn't. Hey—there's one of our bags." I point as a black nylon duffel approaches on the conveyer belt.

"Are you sure?"

"Positive. I tied red ribbons around the handles of our stuff so that we could tell them apart."

Apparently, I'm not the only one who thought of that clever trick.

A dozen mistaken red-ribbon-bedecked black bags, twenty minutes, and a hefty short-term parking fee later, we're on our way home.

All three boys fall asleep in the back seat before we reach the Whitestone Bridge.

"So how was it, really?" Mike asks, slowing the SUV as we approach the EZ Pass Only toll lane, backed up with Saturday-afternoon traffic heading north from the beaches.

"What do you mean?" My heart is pounding. What is he asking me, really?

"A week with my parents. Did they drive you up the wall?"

"Oh…" *That.*

Thank God. I exhale.

You know, I really have to stop thinking he knows that I saw Mike.

Kissed Mike.

After all, it's the *kissing,* and not the *seeing,* that's problematic. If I had merely had a simple lunch with him—say, a turkey wrap and an iced tea in IHOP—then parted ways, I wouldn't feel as if I were keeping a shameful secret from my husband.

Heck, I could even mention it casually in passing, just to get everything out in the open: *Oh, by the way, Mike, you'll never guess who I ran into in Clearwater Beach last Tuesday....*

Oh, who am I kidding?

I didn't *run* into him.

And anyway, I wouldn't have told Mike about Mike even if lunch had just been lunch.

"Your parents were great," I say, noticing the silence and realizing it's still my turn to speak. "Really. They kept insisting on taking care of the boys for me, even when I was right there with nothing else to do." Like go around kissing old lovers. "I swear I haven't changed a diaper in a week."

"I'm glad."

We fall into a comfortable silence.

Comfortable, I assume for him.

I won't breathe easily until...

Well, sometimes I wonder if I'll ever breathe easily again.

But at least I'm home.

I turn to look at the Manhattan skyline out the driver's-side window, remembering what it was like when the city itself was home; when I couldn't imagine that any other place ever could be.

What would it be like to live there now?

People do it.

Families do it.

If we lived in the city, Mike would spend a lot more time at home with us instead of on his commute. We could rent a place and leave leaky faucets and repairs to the super....

Mike interrupts my fantasy with, "You're so quiet. What are you thinking about?"

"Oh, I don't know. Just that it might be better to live in the city than up in the suburbs."

"Are you crazy? We can't live in the city. Where would we put our cars? All our crap? All our kids?"

"All our kids?" I echo with a snort. "This isn't *Cheaper by the Dozen,* Mike. There are only three of them."

"Three kids who are all used to having their own rooms. Do you know what a four-bedroom apartment in Manhattan costs?"

No, I don't know, but yes, I can imagine. I know what Gordy paid for his no-bedroom, aka studio, in Hell's Kitchen. It's the same place Valerie and I once considered a dump located in no-man's-land. Who would have guessed that his building would one day go co-op, or that the western reaches of midtown would command top dollar?

"Why would you want to live in the city when we have a beautiful house in Westchester, Beau? I mean, come on! Do you know how many families living in the city would gladly trade places with us?"

No, I don't know, and no, I can't imagine.

Our house is in Westchester. But it's far from beautiful. I consider telling him that, but I don't want to come across as discontented.

"We can't move to the city," he says again.

"I know we can't. Never mind."

He's right. I know he's right.

"Why would we want to live in the city?" he asks, persistent as a new Madonna album, still shaking his head.

"We wouldn't want to live in the city. Just drop it. It was a thought, that's all. You asked what I was thinking, and I told you."

"It just seems like that came out of left field."

"Yeah. It did. So never mind. Um, that line is shorter, Mike." I motion at the other Easy Pass Only lane; the one we're not in.

"It's okay. This one is moving too."

"That one is moving faster."

"This one will catch up."

Irked, I watch car after car slip through the adjacent toll while our line crawls along.

"So I'm glad my parents took good care of you and the boys," Mike says, picking up where we left off a few minutes ago, as though the rest of the conversation never happened.

"Yeah. They really did."

More comfortable/uncomfortable silence.

More creeping along.

I'm about to once again urge the maddeningly relaxed Mike to switch lanes, when he glances over at me and asks, "So you feel better, then?"

"Better?" Confused, I assume he's talking about the bridge traffic. But that doesn't make sense since I won't feel better about that unless he moves into the shorter lane, which he hasn't. "Do I feel better about what?"

"About everything."

"What do you mean 'everything'?"

"Just…you know."

"No. I don't. What?"

"You've been so unhappy lately. I just thought this break would be—"

"I haven't been unhappy," I protest, as déjà vu settles in. "Why would you say that? I told you before I left that I'm not unhappy."

"Maybe *unhappy* is the wrong word. I guess I mean that you've been so…tense. Or, I don't know, restless."

"Restless?"

Restless as in bored with our marriage?

God help me.

"I am *not* restless, Mike. I don't know what you're—"

"Why are you getting so worked up? All I said was—"

"You said I was miserable."

"No, I didn't. I said you were restless."

"And tense. And unhappy." Which, in my opinion, adds up to miserable.

"Well, you have been. Is that why you want to move to the city all of a sudden?"

"I don't want to move to the city," I snarl. "I was just wondering what it would be like."

"Well, it would suck." Mike brakes as the stream of cars in front of us slows to a stop once again.

"Why are you still in this lane? There's obviously something wrong up at the toll. Can't you just move over?"

"What's your rush? You couldn't wait to get away last week. Now you can't wait to get back home?"

"I never said I couldn't wait to get away last week."

"Well, it was obvious, Beau. And that's fine. Just don't…" He trails off, falling into silence that's all around uncomfortable now.

"Don't what?" I ask, needing to push him. I don't know why I can't let this go, but that isn't an option.

"Don't pretend everything was great before you left," he says. "Please don't pretend you were happy, because I know damn well that you weren't."

I shake my head, staring out the window at a long black limousine with tinted windows as it glides effortlessly past us toward the tolls.

Don't pretend you were happy.

If Mike and I were alone together in the car, I might admit

that I wasn't. Yes, I might admit that, along with God knows what else.

Suddenly, I'm sick of it.

Sick of everything.

The guilt.

The past.

The present.

Marriage.

The suburbs.

Mike.

I guess, deep down, I just can't believe that this is it.

That this is my life.

The life I chose.

"Listen, I'm off this week, remember?" Mike says suddenly. "You and I can spend some time together. I can help with the kids. It'll be good for you."

"Why does everybody think I can't take care of the kids?"

It isn't what I meant to say when I opened my mouth, but somehow, it's what spills out, along with, "Oh, and putting in a toilet isn't my idea of quality time, just so you know."

And, "I don't know why you're suddenly so worried about what's good for me."

And, "If you're not going to switch lanes, we're going to be on this bridge for an hour."

If he would only speak, I could shut up.

But he doesn't.

The silence in the car has gone from uncomfortable to foreboding.

I'm afraid to look over at him—afraid of the expression I might find on his face.

Suddenly, he guns the engine and jerks the wheel.

I cry out as our SUV swerves into the next lane, cutting off a pickup truck whose driver hits the horn long and hard.

"What are you doing?" I ask Mike, glancing over my shoulder at the boys, still reassuringly strapped into their seats, still somehow asleep.

"I'm switching lanes. Are you happy now?"

No.

I'm not happy now.

But I don't bother to tell him.

He already knows.

twenty-six

The past

"Hey," Gaile whispered, poking me in the side. "At least try to look awake."

I stifled a tremendous yawn and said under my breath, "I *am* awake. I'm just thinking."

That, after all was the whole point of this endless meeting, according to Janelle. She wanted us to try to come up with some fun, gimmicky theme-week ideas for her show, which was slipping in the ratings as Arsenio picked up steam.

So far, nothing anybody had suggested had managed to banish the pout from Janelle's beautiful face, although Gaile had come close with a suggestion that we do a week of cliff-hanger endings: a send-up of sorts to Janelle's soap-opera career.

"Ooh, I like that," she said. "Like what kind of cliffhangers?"

Gaile admitted that she hadn't thought that far ahead.

A few of the producers kicked the concept around half-heartedly while Janelle sent Gaile for a fresh mug of coffee, probably as punishment for hatching an idea that wasn't fully formed.

At least she tried.

I was operating on maybe an hour's worth of REM sleep. The most creative idea that had drifted into my mind thus far was to do an entire week of shows about the effects of sleep deprivation on a person's career.

Or on a person's love life.

I didn't have the strength to deal with mine, that was for sure.

I had been in a turmoil ever since Mike got into town last night and dropped his bombshell about moving back to New York. That, of course, was part of the reason I hadn't slept.

The other reason had to do with sex.

I know…

So sue me. I couldn't help it. A few kisses, the promise of a future together, and I was tumbling into bed with him before you can say Mike….

But which Mike?

I was more confused than ever this morning when I dashed off to work, leaving the original Mike snoozing on my pillow.

It didn't help that he had called me twice during the course of the day to see what our plans were for tonight—or that the other Mike had done the same thing. Three times.

Or maybe the other Mike had called me twice and the Mike in my apartment had called three times.

I couldn't quite tell them apart on those pink message slips that Anita, the receptionist, kept leaving in my slot. Too bad we didn't have mini answering machines at our desks. Now *there* was an idea.

Anita was so irritated about my letting all my personal calls bounce back out to her that I didn't dare ask her which Mike had called more often. In fact, for all I knew, one Mike could have called me five times while the other one blew me off completely…or four times and—

The math was dizzying. And I didn't have a head for numbers even on a well-rested day. The point is, my life was crawling with Mikes with whom I had tentative evening plans, and I didn't dare answer my phone.

"Beau," Pat, one of the senior producers, said abruptly, jarring me out of my speculation over whether I could somehow convince one of the Mikes that I was hospitalized with something highly contagious for at least a few days.

"Yes?" I tried not to look startled. I didn't even know Pat knew my name, although I was pretty sure I had once caught her giving me dirty looks in the ladies' room when I sprayed my hair.

Gaile said she was probably just wincing from the aerosol fumes, but I really thought she didn't like me. She reminded me of one of those girls in high school who hate the cheerleaders just because they're cheerleaders.

Yes, I was a cheerleader.

Ten to one, Pat wasn't.

"You've been awfully quiet," she said. "Don't you have any ideas?"

"I…deas?" I sipped lukewarm coffee from the disposable cup in front of me, stalling so that lightning would have a chance to strike. "I do have a couple of ideas, but I didn't want to, um, interrupt."

"Well, you have the floor now," she said, steepling her fingers under her double chin.

Wench.

I thought desperately for a moment, then blurted the first

thing that came to mind. "What about if we do a whole theme week about...regular people?"

The room was silent.

I snuck a peek at Gaile.

She sent me the kind of look the lifeboat occupants on the *Titanic* must have given the poor saps left up on deck.

But I plunged ahead with my regular-people idea because everyone was waiting.

Waiting, and secretly wondering how long it would take for human resources to replace me.

"We could, uh, have a camera crew follow someone—or maybe a couple of people—around for an entire week. You know, just to see how they interact with each other and what they do in their daily lives."

"Who would these people be?" Janelle asked, looking confused—but also a little intrigued.

Buoyed by the fact that I had actually captured her notoriously scant attention span, I forged on. "They could be roommates, or, um, a married couple. Or maybe total strangers we could throw together, just to see what happens."

"Like what?" Pat wanted to know. "What would happen?"

"We don't know. That's the point. Just day-to-day stuff."

"That would never work," Pat said, really getting on my overcaffeinated nerves. "And the budget would be huge. We'd have to bring in casting people to hire the actors, and scriptwriters—"

"There wouldn't be any scripts," I cut in. "And there wouldn't be actors. It would be real. You know. Real people having real conversations. Real arguments. Maybe real romance. Whatever. The whole point would be to capture regular people's lives."

"Why would anybody want to watch regular people on television?" one of the talent managers asked. "People want to see celebrities. That's the whole point of the entertainment industry."

"I have to agree with that," said Janelle the celebrity, fluffing her red mane.

"Haven't any of you seen that show *Cops?*" I asked, frustrated that they didn't get it. Granted, it was a half-assed idea, but the more I tried to convince them that it could work, the more convinced I was that it was brilliant.

"Cops?" Janelle echoed. "What's that?"

"It's a new show on Fox. Camera crews follow real cops around with cameras."

"That'll never last," Pat said, and everyone agreed.

"Doesn't anybody else have any ideas?" Janelle asked plaintively, looking around the room.

"How about wacky-sidekick week?" somebody suggested.

Talk about lame.

"Wacky-sidekick week? I love it!"

And they were off, brainstorming, leaving me to shift my attention back to the Mikes.

Clearly, I couldn't go on juggling them forever. Especially now that Mike was back in town to stay.

Something had to give…and soon….

twenty-seven

The present

If hugging my husband at the airport made me remember
all the reasons I chose to be with him, the argument in the
car was a reminder of all the reasons I almost didn't.

When we get home from the airport, I'm tempted to go
straight to the computer.

But I swear it's out of curiosity more than anything else.
I just have to know if there are any messages from Happy-
Nappy64, or if he's been permanently deleted from my life.

I can't quite bring myself to wish for that…nor do I dare
wish for anything different.

Anything different would be wrong.

No, it would be more serious than wrong. It would be
adultery.

I have many shortcomings, but I refuse to let that become
one of them. It's one thing to juggle two men when you're

young and single. It's another thing altogether when you've taken vows to be faithful to one person for the rest of your life, and when the future happiness of three children depends on your doing just that.

And anyway, I love Mike. Even when he's being a complete asshole the way he was when he switched lanes on the bridge.

I have complete-asshole tendencies myself, in case you haven't noticed.

Yeah, I thought you might have.

So anyway, if there's an e-mail from HappyNappy64, it might be enough closure for me just to know that he cared enough to write. I might even delete the message and move on.

Or I might read it and reply.

Not that I would say anything provocative. I can just accept his apology for kissing me on the beach, and wish him well. Case closed.

But e-mail will have to wait. There are hungry kids to feed, mail to open, laundry to unpack and start.

To his credit, Mike takes over with the boys as soon as they're done eating their canned, microwaved Chef Boyardee. He promises Mikey and Josh a trip to the town pool if they run and get their bathing suits on quickly.

He looks at me, as if to ask if that's all right.

"Go ahead," I tell him from beneath Tyler's high chair, where I'm picking up soggy bits of the graham cracker he just ate—along with a petrified Cheerio or two. Ew.

"Didn't Melina come this week?" I make the mistake of asking Mike as I spot a stray—and green-speckled—piece of Wonder Bread crust under the table.

"Oh, she came. And I'd be willing to bet she stayed all of an hour, since there was nobody around to keep an eye on her. When I got home that night, she hadn't even flushed the pee I left in the hall bathroom toilet."

"How do you know you left pee in the hall bathroom toilet?"

"Because I left it on purpose. To prove a point."

"The point being that she refuses to flush other people's urine?"

"The point being that you can't clean a toilet without flushing it."

I sigh, crawling out from under the table. I'm disgusted by what was under there, but just as disgusted by Mike's un-flushed urine.

"She has to go, Beau," he says firmly. "If you don't tell her this week that she's fired, I will."

"We can't just fire her, Mike."

"I can."

"She has kids to feed in Guatemala. We have to give her time to find another job."

I swear, this argument is as stale as the cereal strewn under Tyler's high chair. But after the confrontation in the car, it's almost a relief to be back on familiar ground.

"If we had told her she was fired back when I wanted to," Mike says grumpily, "she would already have another job. I'm serious, Beau. She has to go. I'm going to—"

"I'll do it," I cut in, depositing the moldy crust, the old Cheerios and the graham cracker sludge into the garbage can. "I'll fire her. Okay? Just let me do it."

"Why? Are you afraid I might be too mean?"

"I know you will be."

"How? It's not like I speak a word of Spanish."

"Your gestures and your tone will be mean. I can do it nicely."

Stacking the boys' plastic bowls and collecting their crumpled, sauce-stained napkins from the table, he says, "Whatever. As long as she's gone by the end of the week."

"How about the middle of next week?"

"This week."

Silently, I decide that next week will be soon enough. That poor woman is going to be so upset when she loses a large chunk of her weekly income.

Maybe I can squeeze an extra week or two of severance pay for her from what I saved on groceries while we were gone last week....

"Hey, do you want to come swimming with me and the boys?" Mike asks, brightening a bit now that the Melina issue is apparently settled. "I bet the pool won't be crowded on a Saturday night."

I bet it will. The pool is always, always crowded.

"No, thanks," I say. "I'll stay here. I want to let Tyler relax a little bit after all this traveling."

"Okay." He doesn't sound the least bit suspicious.

Well, why would he be? I'm allowed to stay home without him. I do it all the time.

And even if he caught me checking my e-mail...

So what? There's no law against checking e-mail.

You know, I might be overthinking this whole thing.

I warn Mike, "Just don't go into the deep end with the boys. And make sure you check the pockets of Josh's bathing suit for food before he gets into the pool. Oh, and make sure he goes potty."

"Josh! Go potty," he calls obediently as he runs water into the saucy bowls in the sink.

"You have to make him go again when you get to the pool."

"I thought you said the bathrooms there are disgusting."

"They are." I press the latches that release the tray on Tyler's high chair and lift it off. "But if you don't make him go at the last possible moment, he'll pee in the pool."

"Well, nobody will know the difference, will they?" This is coming from a man who pees and doesn't flush on purpose. So why am I surprised?

"That's disgusting," I tell him.

"Oh, come on, Beau. You don't think every kid in town isn't peeing in that pool?"

"That doesn't mean it's okay for ours to do it." Hoisting Tyler onto my hip, I realize he stinks. For a second, I'm tempted to ask Mike to change him.

Then guilt seeps in and I decide to do it myself.

By the time I've got Tyler cleaned up and the diaper hermetically sealed in Diaper Genie, Josh and Mikey are calling goodbye from the back door as it slams closed.

Alone at last.

Well, sort of.

"What do you say, Ty-Ty?" I ask my gurgling son. "Do you want to go in your Exersaucer?"

Tyler informs me that he does.

Either that, or he's just babbling gibberish.

But I carry him down to the family room and deposit him in his Exersaucer.

After lining up an array of rattles, blocks and stuffed animals on the plastic tray that surrounds him, I say cheerfully, "There you go, little guy. That will keep you busy for a while, right?"

He happily agrees that it will.

I settle in at the computer a few feet away.

During the few minutes it takes to boot up, Tyler manages to toss overboard every toy I placed on his tray.

"Okay, sweetie, you're going to have to hang on to these this time," I say, crawling around on the floor to retrieve them. "You know Mama doesn't want to do this again."

Obviously, he thinks Mama does, because a toy tugboat and a set of plastic keys are sailing through the air again before I've even returned to my seat.

"Aaah," says Tyler, which can be translated into *I want my toy tugboat and my plastic keys.*

"Just a second." I click on the Internet-server icon.

"Aaah, aaah," says Tyler more urgently, waving a plush hammer over his head, which means *I want my toy tugboat and my plastic keys now, or the hammer goes too.*

I type in my password, then bend over and scramble for the tugboat, the keys, and yes, the hammer as the computer whirs and clicks through the sign-on process.

"There. Keep your toys on your tray this time, bub."

"Blee-blah," says Tyler.

Translation: *Yeah, right.*

Returning to my seat, I immediately see that I've got mail.

Well, of course I do. I haven't checked in a week. My box is probably stuffed with spam.

It is.

But a quick visual scan down the list reveals that there are a couple of "real" e-mails as well. One from Gaile, three from Valerie, one from my oldest brother…

And one from HappyNappy64.

twenty-eight

The past

I spotted Business Card Mike the second I stepped out of
the air-conditioned building onto the blast-furnace street
after work that night.

Oh, no.

What was he doing here?

That much was obvious. He was waiting for me.

Well, maybe I was mistaken.

Maybe he wasn't really here.

Maybe he was just a figment of my sleep-deprived imagination, or…or…or a heat-generated mirage.

I squeezed my eyes shut, shook my head around a little,
wiped a trickle of sweat from behind my right ear and braced
myself for another look.

He was here, all right.

Terrific.

It had been a shitty day all around, capped off by an assignment from Janelle to come up with a list of ten possible wacky sidekicks before 9:00 a.m. tomorrow.

All I wanted to do now was hop on the subway and go home…alone.

But there was Mike, lounging against the subway entrance railing reading the *New York Post,* obviously waiting for me.

Would it be wrong to turn and run in the opposite direction?

I didn't have a chance to find out. He looked up, spotted me and folded his paper under his arm with a smile.

"Hey! There you are. I was afraid I'd missed you," he said, walking over to me and planting a kiss on my cheek.

"No…you didn't miss me," I told him, wondering why he had to be so darned good-looking.

"Actually, I did…miss you, I mean. Listen, I was thinking we could go see *Eddie and the Cruisers II* and then get Indian food."

"There's a sequel to *Eddie and the Cruisers?*" was the most scintillating response I could come up with at the moment.

"It's called *Eddie Lives.* Talk about giving away the ending," he added with a grin.

He was as charismatically sexy—and as off-limits, at least to me, from now on—as the black Jesus in that *Like a Prayer* video of Madonna's that caused such a big uproar a few months ago.

"Oh, hey…should I be worried that you didn't return any of my calls today?" he asked, peering down at me, as if he'd just noticed something might be seriously amiss in Beau-ville.

I quelled the urge to ask him how many calls, exactly, I didn't return.

Instead, I said, "Mike…we need to talk."

"We can go see something else instead if you want. I hear *Uncle Buck* is supposed to be pretty good."

"It's not about the movie."

"Uh-oh. That's not a good sign. I guess I should be worried, huh?" It sounded almost like a quip, but he wasn't smiling anymore. "Should I be worried?"

I evaded his question, pretending to hunt through my pockets for a subway token.

"Beau?"

God, I was exhausted, in desperate need of sleep or another dose of caffeine. Obviously, sleep was out of the question for the time being.

"Let's go get a cup of coffee somewhere," I said reluctantly.

"Make it somewhere with a liquor license. I have the feeling I'm going to need a drink after you say whatever you're going to say."

That was funny, considering that I didn't even know what I was going to say.

Not *funny ha-ha.*

I had the feeling that nothing at all about the evening ahead was going to be *funny ha-ha.*

I had to tell Mike that either he had to agree to share me with somebody else until I figured out what I wanted…

Or that he and I were as over as disco.

Since I doubted that the first option was even an option, I figured he and I were about to go the way of KC and the Sunshine Band.

But that wasn't what I wanted, dammit.

Was it?

It would certainly simplify my overly complicated life, but…

I wasn't ready to say a permanent goodbye to him yet.

Nor was I ready to say a permanent goodbye to the other Mike.

As we crossed the street toward one of Manhattan's ubiquitous Charley O's, I asked myself what I would be doing if the other Mike had been the one waiting outside the studio for me.

Would he and I be on the verge of becoming history instead?

Was this what it came down to? Was I making a choice based purely on chance?

Why, yes. Yes, I was. And it made about as much sense as any other scenario I could conjure at the moment.

The bar area was crowded with happy-hour patrons, all of whom looked as though they didn't have a care in the world.

"Would you like to go to the bar, or do you want a table?" the hostess asked Mike, who looked at me.

"A table," I said, aware that the conversation we were about to have called for privacy.

As she went off to check for a table, I jealously watched the cocktail-sipping, gossiping, not-a-care-in-the-world office drones.

Oh, how I wished that I didn't have a care in the world. What I wouldn't give to be standing at the bar sipping an Alabama slammer and dissing my boss with my co-workers.

"What if there aren't any tables free?" Mike asked, shifting his weight from one foot to the other.

Hmm. Good point. What *if* there weren't any tables free? I had already made one decision based on chance.

Why not another?

If there were no tables free, I decided, we would stand around and have a casual drink at the bar. And since standing around casually drinking at a bar was no way to have a serious conversation, our relationship would be spared. At least for tonight.

There. It was settled.

I felt a little better already.

The hostess reappeared, smiling.

I told myself that she was smiling because there were no tables and she, too, was relieved that there would be no breaking up tonight.

But she said, "We have a table opening up in back."

"Great," I said as my heart sank.

twenty-nine

The present

My suddenly sweaty palm maneuvers the mouse directly toward the e-mail from HappyNappy64.

Behind me, Tyler shrieks loudly from his Exersaucer.

"I know you want your toys again," I say without turning away from the computer. "Wait a minute, sweetie. I just need to check one thing."

Click, and there it is.

Subject: New York

Subject…New York? I frown, reading on.

Date: August 18, 8:09 pm Eastern Standard Time
From: HappyNappy64@websync.net
To: Beauandco@websync.net

We need to talk. I'll be in Manhattan on business the week of the twenty-second, staying at the Pierre. Call me there.

"No!" I say sharply…so sharply that Tyler, still babbling loudly in protest behind me, goes silent for a moment. Then he begins to cry.

That's it?

Not a word about the Don CeSar, the beach, the kiss?

No apology, no explanation?

I reread the e-mail.

Tyler cries louder.

"Oh, sweetie…" Reluctantly turning my back on the computer, I hurry over to hug my son.

I'll be in Manhattan on business?

Manhattan, of all places?

I pick up all the toys and gently replace them on Tyler's tray.

"Mama wasn't yelling at you."

His teary eyes twinkle instantly and he reaches for a big, pastel, stuffed block.

Why Manhattan?

What kind of business?

"Don't throw that block, Tyler."

He throws the block.

I pick it up and put it firmly on his tray.

"No throwing."

"Gote-dee-doo."

"I know it's fun while you're doing it. But if you throw, you won't have any toys to play with when you're done."

Business? I thought he didn't even have a job.

Tyler throws the block again.

"I'm not picking that up, mister."

Can seeing me possibly be the business he has in Manhattan? Or is it just a coincidence?

Tyler throws a rubber ball.

"That, either," I say wearily, sitting on the floor and resting my head in my hands. I rub my eyes.

Why didn't he mention that he was coming to New York when I saw him last week? Is it a last-minute thing? Maybe he was going to mention it but I didn't give him a chance. After all, I ran away.

Something soft and jingly grazes my shoulder on its way to the floor.

"Stop throwing, Tyler."

"Glah-bee-dot!" is Tyler's gleeful response.

This is the week of the twenty-second.

Maybe he's already in the city, waiting for me.

Does he actually think I'm going to call him?

There is no way I'm going to call him. Absolutely no way, I think, just before a wooden-rattle-turned-missile strikes me squarely in the forehead.

"Ow!" I yelp. "You little stinker!"

Tyler bellows in dismay.

"That hurt Mommy!" I scold, wincing as I touch the rapidly swelling spot above my eyebrow.

My son is now sobbing pitifully.

"I'm sorry," I tell him guiltily. "I'm so sorry. I didn't mean to call you a stinker. You're sorry, too, aren't you?"

He cries harder, his little lower lip vibrating with intense emotion.

"Shh. I know you didn't mean it, sweetheart. We never mean it when we hurt the people we love. Sometimes we just…we just can't help it."

I pick him up and rock him, but I'm crying too, bitter tears that have nothing at all to do with the painful lump on my forehead.

thirty

The past

"You didn't break up with him."

"No," I said flatly in response to Mike's question that wasn't really a question. "I didn't break up with him."

He sipped his beer and I sipped my gin and tonic, thankful that we had both opted for drinks instead of coffee.

"Are you still in love with him?" he asked, returning his mug to the paper coaster so violently that white foam sloshed over his hand. He didn't wipe it off; didn't even seem to have noticed.

"I don't know." I handed him my cocktail napkin. "But he's moving to New York."

"For you?"

"For a job," I said with a shrug, then looked him in the eye and admitted, "and for me."

"So that's it, then? You're back with him?" He seemed

incredulous, the unused napkin poised in his beer-covered hand.

I shrugged, feeling like a complete and utter fool.

"That's what you really want, Beau? To be with him?"

"I don't know what I want, Mike."

Oh, yes I did know what I wanted, I realized, looking into his eyes. I wanted *him*.

Just as fervently as I'd wanted Mike last night.

I was torn.

Torn between two lovers…

Feeling like a fool.

A giggle escaped me.

I don't even know where it came from. I mean, I was already well aware that there was nothing funny ha-ha about this.

But there it was, and I couldn't hold it in.

"Did you just laugh?" Mike asked, looking even more incredulous.

"No!" I said, and another giggle promptly burst forth.

"You just did it again," he accused, clearly hurt. "You're laughing."

Yes. I was. I was laughing. I gave up and gave in to another wave of mirth that was bordering suspiciously on maniacal. But I couldn't seem to help myself.

Maybe it was the lack of sleep, or the gin, or the stress of the moment, but all at once it seemed hilarious that my life could be summed up by an ultracheesy decade-old Mary MacGregor song.

"Why are you laughing?" he asked.

"I can't…explain." I reached for his cocktail napkin, since he was still holding mine, and wiped tears from my eyes.

Not the kind of tears you cry when you're about to break

somebody's heart, but the kind of tears you cry when you're laughing hysterically.

"Try me," Mike said, watching me. Those dimples of his were nowhere in sight, and somehow, I knew an attempted explanation wouldn't bring them out of hiding.

"You wouldn't get it."

How could he, when I didn't even get it myself? I heaved a sigh, trying to get hold of my unruly emotions.

"I'm sorry, I just…something just struck me funny. But…" I exhaled again, forcing myself to look at him. "I'm over it now."

"Are you sure?"

"Yes. I'm sure." I nodded somberly, remembering why we were here.

The lyrics to the sappy old song were still running through my head, but suddenly, they didn't seem comical at all.

"I'm sorry," I said again.

He didn't respond.

He just looked at me as though he didn't believe I was sorry at all.

But I was. For laughing. For everything.

"I was going to break up with him last night." I needed desperately to make him understand. "I really was. I was going to tell him all about you. I mean…about us. You and me. But I couldn't. I didn't have a chance before he—"

"Told you he was moving back?"

"Yeah." God, this was brutal. "I just never thought he would do that."

"Which means I was just your backup plan, huh? You were just keeping me around so you wouldn't be alone if he did move."

"No! You weren't my backup plan. You were…I mean you are…really, really special to me."

His dark eyes were filled with doubt.

"You have to believe me, Mike. I love you."

The words spilled from my mouth as easily as the laughter had moments before.

And I meant them. Truly, I did.

Mike just looked at me and shook his head sadly.

"Mike, please," I said, touching his arm. "I do love you. I just…I think I still love him, too. I can't help it."

"You can't love two people at the same time."

"But I do."

"Well, you can't," Mike said again.

Yep, as the song said I was torn between my two lovers…

How had that ever struck me as amusing? It was tragic, that was what it was.

"You have to choose, Beau."

He was right. I knew he was right.

I wiped tears from my eyes with a crumpled cocktail napkin.

Not the kind of tears you cry when you're laughing hysterically.

The kind of tears you cry when you're about to break somebody's heart.

thirty-one

The present

Two days have gone by since I got back home to Mike—
and to Mike's e-mail.

I didn't respond to it, if that's what you were wondering.

Partly because I figured he wouldn't read it right away, anyway, since he's in New York. Unless he has access to a computer and e-mail. Which he very well might.

But I'm not going to rush into a response…if, indeed, I'm
going to respond at all.

The main reason for that, I'll admit, is that Mike is home
this week, all week. Home on vacation, underfoot every second of the day—not in a bad way, really. Just…here. There.
Everywhere. I'm afraid that if I even dare to sit down at the
computer again, I'll turn around and find him looking over
my shoulder.

So I stay away from the computer.

But I don't stay away from Mike.

My husband, Mike.

Truly, there's something kind of nice about having him home.

Except when it sucks.

It only sucks when he and I disagree about how to handle disciplining one of the boys…or Melina, who's due this afternoon to clean.

But when everybody is behaving themselves, Mike is upbeat and helpful and as handy as Bob Vila. Mikey's school picture has been hung at last, the kinks are out of the garden hose, the broken oak limb has been transformed into firewood and neatly stacked behind the shed.

Now he's working on the pipes under the stairs, where the new half bath is going to go. And I hate to admit it, but I'm almost glad he's doing this instead of taking us on a fabulous New England beach vacation.

"I can't believe you know how to install a bathroom," I comment, peeking into the former closet to see him clanging away at a pipe.

"It's not hard," he grunts. "You just have to read the manual."

"That's what I always say about cooking," I point out. "But you still refuse to give that a whirl."

"When you learn how to install a toilet, I'll learn how to make a pot roast."

"Fair enough." I set a glass of homemade lemonade on the floor by his leg.

"What's that?" he asks.

"I thought you might be thirsty."

"You're kidding. Lemonade?"

"It's no big deal," I say, flashing a serene B.–Smith–meets–

Betty-Crocker smile. "Just squeeze lemons, add water, sugar and ice."

"Are you giving me the recipe so that I'll make some for you someday?"

"Maybe."

"You haven't made me homemade lemonade in years."

It's something I used to do with him back in the old days...the newlywed days. Back then, I loved to surprise him with lemonade, or his favorite oatmeal-raisin cookies hot from the oven, or spaghetti sauce made from scratch instead of poured from a jar.

I remembered that this morning for some reason, and felt guilty for too many synthetic cheese dinners from a box.

I watch him guzzle half the glass of lemonade, then make the same whispered "ah" sound both Mikey and Josh always make upon quenching their thirst. That brings another smile to my face.

"What's so funny?"

"Nothing, just...the boys are so much like you."

"Of course they are. I'm their daddy."

"I'm glad," I tell him, and I mean it.

At this moment, all is right in my little world at long last. There isn't a doubt in my mind that I married the right person, or that I did the right thing when I ran away from Mike on the beach last week.

I've built a life with this man. We're family. How could I even think that somebody else could possibly measure up?

"You *look* glad," he says, watching me. "Really glad. What's up?"

"What do you mean?"

"Just...you seem so happy all of a sudden."

"And you seem to be spending an awful lot of time gauging my moods all of a sudden." It sounds pricklier than I'd intended, so I smile brightly to show him that I'm just kidding around.

"I guess that's because they've been swinging so wildly it's hard not to notice."

"I guess it's just PMS," I tell him, because when you're a woman you can blame a lot of stuff on hormones without arousing suspicion.

"Yeah, that's what Jan said."

"What?" My jaw drops. "You're analyzing my mood swings with your secretary?"

"Not analyzing. Just…discussing." He's wearing the same expression Josh had yesterday when I caught him aiming one of his Blopen markers at a pile of clean laundry.

"I can't believe you would talk about me behind my back," says the woman who kissed another man.

"I'm sorry. I was just upset about it. And…worried."

"Worried about what?"

"I don't know… I felt like maybe you were having a midlife crisis."

"Midlife crisis?"

"Or maybe it's menopause."

"Menopause?"

"Jan said you're old enough to—"

"My age is none of Jan's business!"

I can hear Tyler starting to cry in the next room, where I left him on a blanket surrounded by toys.

"Calm down, Beau. You just woke up the baby."

"He wasn't sleeping."

"Well, then, you scared him with all this shrieking."

"Shrieking?" I shriek.

"I'm sorry." He puts down the lemonade, comes to stand in front of me, and reaches out to pull me into his arms.

I try to squirm away. "I have to go get the baby."

"Come on, Babs. Don't—"

"Please don't call me Babs."

"Why not?"

"Because I hate it."

"I didn't know that. Why didn't you tell me?"

"I was afraid of hurting your feelings."

"I'm not hurt. You should have told me." He's still holding me close. I can't see his face, but I know it's not angry, and that I have no business being angry, either. Not really.

How can I be angry? He cares about me. He's worried. He's looking for answers.

"I'm sorry," I say. For what, exactly, I'm not certain. But it isn't a lie.

"It's okay."

"And thank you."

"For what?"

I hesitate. "For the toilet."

He laughs. So do I.

I pull back and look up at him. "I'm serious," I say. "It's going to be great to have another bathroom."

"Yeah…and after it's done, we'll hire somebody who will actually clean it."

I don't say anything to that.

I can hear Tyler still fussing in the next room.

"Beau…"

"I know."

"I'm just reminding you. You have to fire her when she gets here today."

"I will. Just not today." I take a step back, as far as I can go in this tiny space without bumping into the slanted ceiling beneath the stairs or stepping into the open toolbox on the floor. I no longer want to be in the circle of his arms. "I have to go get the baby."

"It has to be today," he tells me. "You promised."

"No, I didn't. I said I'd fire her, but I never said today."

"Yes, you did."

"No, I didn't," I volley right back, not caring that we sound maddeningly like Mikey and Josh.

"Yes, you did."

"No, I said I'd fire her and I will. I'll give her a few weeks' notice, and—"

"You think that if you give her a few weeks' notice, she's actually going to clean anything in those few weeks? Why would she, when she's never bothered to clean in the past?"

"Well, I think it's the humane thing to do. She's a mother with children to feed in another country."

"I'm a father with children to feed in this house. This *filthy* house."

"Oh, please. It isn't 'filthy.' It's just a little dusty."

"It's filthy. And if Melina had done her job right in the first place, she wouldn't be losing it."

"I can't believe you're so coldhearted, Mike."

"And I can't believe you're such a sucker for a sob story. Where are you going?"

"To get the baby," I say, already in the hall. "And then, maybe out for a while."

"Out, where? Out with the baby?"

"No. Out alone."

"You can't do that. What about the kids?"

With that, this camel's back snaps in two.

"You're here," I snap. "You watch them."

"But where are you going?"

He follows me into the living room, where I step over the oblivious Mikey and Josh sprawled in front of Cartoon Network, and pluck a crying, squirming Tyler from his blanket. His tears and his drool are streaked with orange.

"What's all over him?" I ask his brothers, sniffing the orange goop.

"Cheese Nips," Mikey tells me, staring at the screen.

"You gave him Cheese Nips?" I ask in horror. Cheese Nips are too big for him to eat, and I never let him eat anything unsupervised.

"No, he found them. They fell out of Josh's pockets."

I hurriedly sweep Tyler's gummy wet mouth with my forefinger to make sure there are no stray Cheese Nip chunks. Safe. Thank God.

Thank God.

When I think about what could have happened…

And all because I wasn't watching him. All because I was distracted by this meaningless…stuff.

Distracted.

Ha. There's an understatement.

"Here," I say to Mike abruptly, and thrust the baby into his arms. "I have to go out."

"But out, where? For how long?"

"I don't know, and I don't know." I've grabbed my purse and my keys, and I'm already on my way out the door.

Mike is still following me, holding Tyler, whose arms are outstretched. "Look at him. He wants you, Beau."

"I'm sorry, sweetie…." I pause to kiss the baby's downy hair. He smells of old saliva and Cheese Nips. I swallow hard, thanking God again that he didn't choke.

"Mama will be back soon." I force the promise past the lump in my throat.

I drive away with no idea where I'm going.

Not at first, anyway.

Not until I find myself on the Sawmill River Parkway, heading south toward Manhattan.

thirty-two

The past

Mike had gone home to spend a day or two with his parents before they left on their cruise to Halifax. I had no idea that they were even going on a cruise to Halifax, or that Mike was going to Long Island, until I got home from the confrontation at Charley O's to find the note he'd left in my empty apartment.

Talk about relief.

After all I had been through in the last twenty-four hours, all I wanted was to crawl into bed and sleep until noon.

Of course I couldn't, as I had to be up and armed with a list of ten wacky sidekicks before 9:00 a.m.

But I could, and did, sleep a good ten hours, thanks to a hefty dose of Benadryl. I didn't have a cold; but until somebody came up with a better over-the-counter sleep medication, that was my drug of choice. Not that I wasn't technically exhausted enough to fall asleep on my own. But after what had just happened with Mike, I had the feeling I was in for a restless night.

I woke to find the sun streaming in the window and Valerie seated at her lighted makeup mirror opposite my bed. She was wearing acid-washed jeans, a white oversize men's shirt belted at the waist and one of my big black fabric bows clipped in her hair.

"'Morning," I croaked, sitting up and stretching.

"Hi." Busy outlining her eyes in thick black liner, she didn't turn around. "Boy, were you out of it last night when I got home. I shook you a few times just to make sure you were breathing."

"Oh…I was just tired."

"So what happened with Mike?" she asked, tossing aside the pencil and swiveling around to face me as I swung my bare feet over the side of the bed.

"Which Mike?" I asked.

"The Mike you were going to break up with the last time I talked to you."

"Which Mike was that?" I was still fuzzy from the Benadryl and not even certain, anyway, when we last talked.

"Beau! You said you were going to dump Mike when he got here from the airport the other night. Remember?"

"Oh. Right."

"You changed your mind?"

"Sort of."

"So you dumped the new Mike?"

"Sort of." Which wasn't exactly the truth, but I wasn't in the mood to explain what had happened last night. Truth be told, I wasn't entirely sure what had happened last night. I only knew what hadn't happened…and that I was in big, big trouble.

As if I hadn't been in big, big trouble before.

I got out of bed and headed for the bathroom with Valerie hot on my trail.

"Beau, at least tell me what's going on."

"I promise I will," I said, "just as soon as I know what's going on."

I closed the door on her protest and took a long, hard look at myself in the mirror.

Just what kind of person are you? I asked the girl in the ratty T-shirt and yesterday's smudged mascara, tousled brown hair sticky with day-old Aqua Net.

The girl didn't answer. She just turned her back and turned on the shower, getting ready to face another day.

thirty-three

The present

I change my mind about Manhattan by the time I've crossed into the Bronx, but I don't turn around and head north again. I just keep on going, and by the time I hit the West Side Highway, I've changed my mind right back again.

I mean, why shouldn't I go to Manhattan?

It doesn't mean that I have to see Mike.

I have plenty of friends here.

All right, two.

All right, one, with Gordy away doing summer stock.

But I promised Valerie I would come visit her in the city, remember?

I get off the highway in the West Seventies and head toward the park, reaching for my cell phone with my right hand as I steer with the left.

Yes, that's illegal in New York State.

But I'm the kind of woman who kisses another man behind her husband's back, remember?

At this point, it's fairly easy for me to cast aside any qualms about dialing while driving.

I dial Valerie's office number from memory. At least, I think I'm dialing Valerie's office number from memory.

But it isn't her snotty secretary who picks up, it's somebody who barely speaks English and is working at either the United Nations or a Japanese restaurant—I can't quite make out what she's saying.

Not that it matters.

What matters is that I'm on the winding road that crosses Central Park now. I have no idea what Valerie's real phone number is or where her office is located, but I know where the Pierre Hotel is located, and I happen to be heading right for it.

Of course, there are countless other fabulous potential East Side destinations. The Metropolitan Museum of Art. Saks Fifth Avenue. Le Cirque.

Valerie's office is also somewhere around here, and I can always dial 411 to find it.

But since I'm in the neighborhood, what the hell? I'm going to go to the Pierre and finish what I started last week.

No.

I'm going to finish what I started fifteen years ago, and it's about time.

thirty-four

The past

Mike returned from Long Island as abruptly as he left, showing up at my apartment just as I was changing out of the rumpled, rain-dampened rayon suit I'd worn to work.

"I didn't know you were coming back tonight," I said, letting him in the door, still adjusting my hastily donned long Coed Naked Volleyball T-shirt and black spandex stirrup pants.

"Didn't you get my note?" he asked, kissing me on the cheek. His hair was damp from the summer storm, his short-sleeved pale blue cotton shirt speckled with water droplets.

"I got it."

"Well, I said I'd be back in a day or two." He dumped his duffel bag on the floor of my room.

"It's been two. And I didn't even know you were leaving so soon in the first place."

"I didn't either. But when I called my mother, she made a big stink about wanting to see me before I left town, so…" He shrugged. "I'm sorry. And I tried to call you at work and tell you, but you never called me back. Didn't you get my messages?"

"No," I lied, idly wondering, again, how many messages he'd left.

Not that it mattered.

Why would it matter if he left three messages and the other Mike left only two, or vice versa?

It would only matter if I were going to use that information to arbitrarily choose which Mike I should stay with and which Mike I should leave behind.

And I wasn't. I had already made my decision based on far more relevant criteria.

Yeah. Sure I had.

I had made my decision based purely on which Mike happened to be standing in front of me. Or so it was starting to seem.

"So…do you want to go get something to eat?" he asked, checking his watch. "I'm starved."

"But it's only six-thirty." I said it even though I knew what his response would be.

Oh, hell, maybe I said it *because* I knew what his response would be.

"Yes," he said tersely, "and normal people eat dinner at six-thirty."

"New Yorkers are normal people—"

"Some might beg to differ," he inserted with a wry smile.

"—and most New Yorkers don't eat dinner at six-thirty," I continued as if he hadn't spoken, "so if you're going to be a New Yorker, you're going to have to adapt."

That said, I smiled to show him that I was kidding around. Except that I wasn't.

"Why are you acting so bitchy?" he asked. No more Mr. Nice Guy. Clearly, I had pushed the wrong buttons....

Or the right ones, considering my mood.

I was trying to start a fight.

Why?

Who knew?

Maybe because I was a spoiled brat.

Feeling guilty—but probably not as guilty as I should have—I reached for Valerie's pack of cigarettes and conceded, "I'm sorry. I've just had a really long day."

"Since when do you smoke?"

"I don't." I lit up and took a deep drag.

"You're smoking now."

"I know."

He seemed to be waiting for further explanation.

"It's because..." I began, and trailed off. I gazed at the rain-spattered window and the grim gray dusk beyond it, trying to figure out if I wanted to appease him...or piss him off further.

"Because why?"

I settled for the truth, suddenly tired of this game we were playing.

Or rather, this game I was playing. He was more of a spectator, really—which didn't seem fair. And that wasn't all that didn't seem fair.

"I'm smoking because I'm a nervous wreck, Mike."

"You're a nervous wreck? Why?"

I inhaled smoke deep into my lungs, so deeply that it actually hurt. I was glad. Maybe I needed to punish myself.

I shook my head, released the breath in a white mentholated puff, and said slowly, "There's something I have to tell you before…well, there's just something I have to tell you."

When, exactly, had I decided to come clean about Mike?

I had no idea. For all I knew, it had popped into my head mere moments before I blurted it out. Or maybe I had known all along that I would eventually have to be entirely honest with this man. I guess maybe I thought I owed him at least that.

Maybe I owed him a hell of a lot more than that.

Or maybe I didn't owe him anything at all.

I was more confused than I'd ever been in my life.

Which, if you'd been following my life up to that point, was pretty extreme.

"What do you have to tell me?" Mike asked, watching me closely, his nose wrinkling from the acrid smoke wafting its way.

"I've been seeing somebody else, Mike."

There.

I'd said it.

I didn't know what I expected him to say in return. Certainly something other than what he actually said; that's for sure.

What he actually said was the last thing I ever thought I'd hear from his lips.

What he said was, "Marry me, Beau."

thirty-five

The present

He could very well be out at a meeting or lunch in the middle of a business day.

In fact, the odds that I will find Mike here, in his room in the Pierre Hotel, are slim to none.

That, at least, is what I tell myself as I make my way into the lobby after parking the SUV at a garage over on Lex.

But then, I also once predicted that Madonna would vanish along with fingerless gloves and panty-hose-as-headbands, and that INXS would be the next Beatles.

Funny how fifteen years can really put things into perspective.

A lot of things, and not just pop culture.

Mike is in his room when the hotel desk clerk calls upstairs to check.

"He says that you can go on up," the man informs me, smiling in a businesslike, but not particularly friendly, way.

Looks like you're not in Florida anymore, Dorothy, I think as I murmur, "Thank you."

"You're welcome," he says, and tells me the suite number.

I want to ask him how Mike sounded when he heard that I was there, but he seems a little stiff. If he were a woman, I might ask. Or if this were a Holiday Inn.

But he isn't a woman, and this sure as hell isn't a Holiday Inn, so I merely thank him and make my way through the elegant lobby to the elevators.

This place is just as grand as the Don CeSar was. I wonder, not for the first time, how Mike can afford it.

But that doesn't matter, really.

Nothing matters now, except that I do what I came here to do.

Steeling myself for whatever lies ahead, I approach the elevator.

The operator greets me and politely stands aside.

I pause. Can I really do this?

Suddenly, I want to bolt for the street.

But my feet carry me over the threshold and into the elevator instead.

"Which floor, ma'am?" the operator asks.

I hesitate only a moment.

"Fourteen," I say firmly, and watch the doors slide closed in front of me.

thirty-six

The past

"*Marry* you?" I echoed in disbelief. "What are you talking about?"

"I'm talking about getting married."

I just gaped at him.

Outside, thunder boomed, as if to punctuate the drama.

"I guess I'm not saying it right, huh?" He laughed nervously. "I had this whole thing planned out, this whole rad speech I was going to give you when I gave you the ring, and you caught me off guard."

"Mike…" For a moment I was at a loss for words.

He was going to give me a ring?

A ring, and a whole rad speech?

He thought I deserved a ring and a whole rad speech after what I'd done?

Maybe he hadn't heard me correctly.

Maybe instead of *I've been seeing somebody else, Mike,* he thought I'd said, *I really need you to propose to me right now, Mike.*

What? It *could* happen.

All right. It couldn't happen.

So, pardon my French, but…what the fuck?

At last, I found my voice. "Mike, didn't you…I mean… well, did you hear what I just said?"

"You said you've been seeing somebody else. I know."

"You know that I said it? Or you know…that I've been seeing somebody else?"

"Both."

Another shocker. Christ, they were dropping like Tetris blocks tonight.

"How did you know?" I demanded, wondering who'd told him. Valerie? Gaile? Pat, the senior wench at work who hated me?

"Well actually, I didn't, for sure," he said, even as I reminded myself that (A) Pat didn't know I was cheating on my boyfriend, and (B) Pat didn't even know I had a boyfriend, so (C) Pat couldn't be the one who had spilled my secret.

Paranoid much? my inner voice asked sarcastically as my wan outer one asked, "You mean you just figured it out on your own?"

"Pretty much."

"How?" I collapsed onto the nearest seat before my wobbly legs could give way. "When?"

"Over the last few weeks. I'm not stupid, Beau."

No, he wasn't stupid. Even though he had adopted the annoying habit of speaking like a Bill-Ted hybrid, he wasn't stupid.

More guilt. I couldn't believe I never gave him enough credit to think that he might realize something was up.

"Listen, I know that you're a beautiful woman. I know other guys aren't blind. And I know you're only human."

Hey, that was true. I was only human.

Suddenly, what I had done didn't seem quite as unforgivable.

"You were starting to seem more and more distant," he went on. "And you were never home lately when I called. So I put two and two together. It was about time, don't you think?"

I opened my mouth to tell him that it hadn't been going on for that long.

But somehow, that seemed worse. I didn't want him to think I had fallen this hard for somebody else in the space of a few weeks.

"Maybe," he said, his voice laced with regret, "I just never realized until lately that I was actually going to lose you if I didn't grow up and step up to the plate."

"But, Mike…you *did* step up to the plate. You turned down the job in California for me—a great job that I know you really wanted. And you're moving back—"

"That isn't enough for you. I could see that the other night. It's obvious. You want more. And you deserve more. That's why I went out to Long Island, Beau."

"What are you talking about?"

"Here…I'll show you."

I felt numb as I watched him cross the room and bend over to reach into his duffel bag.

Something told me that another Tetris block was about to fall.

He rummaged through his bag, then returned to the chair.

"I went out there," he said simply, softly, "to get this."

This was a velvet ring box. He snapped it open and I found myself gaping at a diamond engagement ring.

"No," I said in hushed disbelief as he sank onto one knee at my feet and reached for my hand.

"No?" he echoed, stopping short belatedly as if he'd just heard what I'd said. "No, what?"

No, a lot of things.

No, this can't be happening.

No, you're not allowed to propose to me.

No, I can't possibly marry you.

I took a deep breath. "Mike…"

"Beau, will you marry me?" The question spilled forth in an earnest rush. "I love you. Please."

thirty-seven

The present

The door to the suite opens before I can knock, leaving me standing there with a raised fist and the realization that it's absolutely too late to back out now.

Not that I planned to.

All right, I *was* tempted to ask the elevator operator to make it a round trip. But I didn't.

So here I am, face-to-face with Mike once again.

And stunned, once again, to see that he's aged.

No, not since last Tuesday.

Just…I don't know if I'll ever get used to seeing him with graying hair and crow's-feet.

"I'm kind of surprised you're here" is all I can think of to say as middle-aged but still drop-dead-gorgeous Mike steps back and motions me inside.

"I was about to say the same thing to you." He closes the door behind me with what seems like a deafening click.

"I got your e-mail."

"Obviously."

"Obviously?" I echo, feeling as though my brain stopped functioning properly back at home, before I picked up my keys.

"You're here," he explains.

"Oh, right. I'm here."

Here is a spacious suite with old-fashioned moldings, tall, drapery-framed windows, European furnishings and a stunning view of Central Park.

"What do you think?" he asks.

"It's beautiful."

"Eh," he says with an unimpressed wave of his hand.

"Eh?"

"You never did get to see the presidential suite at the Don CeSar. If you had, you'd be saying 'eh,' too."

"I doubt that."

"Can I get you a glass of wine?"

"No, thanks." I gesture at his casual black slacks and white linen shirt, wondering why he isn't wearing a suit and tie, and, again, why he's here in his suite midday. "Do you have…I mean, aren't you busy with…business?"

He laughs. "Not at the moment."

"I thought that was why you were here."

"It is. Why?"

"You don't look like you're dressed for it. That's all."

"The kind of business I'm here to do doesn't demand any particular style of dress."

"Oh. Well, actually, I thought you didn't have a job in the first place."

"I don't, per se. My job these days involves some investments and holdings, and from time to time I come up to New York to deal with them."

I want to ask him more about that, but he cuts me off with a brisk, "Sit down."

I sit down.

He sits next to me on the couch. Not right next to me, but close enough that I can smell his cologne.

He never wore cologne when I knew him.

"The last time I saw you," he says in a tone that's hard to read, "you ran away, Beau."

"You don't mince words, do you?"

"I never did."

"No," I agree, thinking back. "You never did."

His expression is wry. "As I recall, neither did you."

thirty-eight

The past

"I can't marry you, Mike."

The words were blunt, yet even as I said them, I wasn't entirely certain that I meant them.

I still loved him. I still thought we could work it out somehow.

He swallowed hard, asked, "Because of *him?*"

That was the last thing I wanted to admit.

I wanted there to be another reason, a noble reason.

Like, I was secretly dying of a terrible disease.

Or, I couldn't bear children.

In my narcissistic, youthful ignorance, I almost thought that either of those things would be easier to live with than what I'd done.

"Yes," I said quietly, staring down at the diamond ring I was positive then that I would never wear. "Because of *him.*"

"I can't believe you're going to throw away everything we have because of a...a fling."

Frankly, I couldn't either.

There were so many things I suddenly wanted to say to Mike.

But not *this* Mike.

I just hoped it wasn't too late.

I stood up and headed for the door.

"Where are you going, Beau?"

"I just...I'm sorry."

"Wait a minute. You can't just walk out. Beau, come on. Stay here and talk to me. You owe me that, at least."

Yes. I owed him that, at least.

I was crying. Hard.

But I didn't turn around, and I didn't stay.

thirty-nine

The present

No, I never did mince words, and I'm not going to start now.

"That's why I'm here, Mike." I look him squarely in the eye. "Because of the way I ended things with you that summer. It wasn't fair to you."

"Gee, you think?" He laughs softly, bitterly.

"Just…listen, Mike. I'm sorry for that. And I'm sorry for what happened last week. I didn't mean to run away like I did."

"Yeah, well, I don't know why I expected anything different from you, Beau."

"What do you mean by that?"

"Just…I guess I figured you might have grown up a little over the years. I thought, when you came down to Florida, that you were ready to pick up where we left off."

"I know you did, and…"

I wanted to tell him that he was wrong about that. But it was time I stopped lying to him…and to myself.

"Maybe that *is* what I wanted, somewhere in the back of my mind," I admit reluctantly. "But when I realized that was what you wanted, too…and that it could actually happen…"

"You chickened out."

"Yes."

"But you're here now." He reaches for my hand, grasps it tightly in his, just the way he used to.

"Only because I need to tell you something."

"I'm all ears."

"I came here to tell you that I'm truly sorry. For everything. And I came to say goodbye."

"A proper goodbye?" He put his arms around me. "Do you mean…?"

"No," I say, pushing him away with a sad smile. "I really do mean goodbye, Mike. I love my husband. I've loved him all along. So, to answer the question you never did give me a chance to answer, no."

"No…?"

"No, I don't regret that I married Mike. This is it. This is my life. The life I chose…."

For better or for worse, for richer or for poorer, in sickness and in health, until death do us part.

"This is my life," I say again, firmly, all grown up at last. "And…I'm going back to it."

forty

The past

He wasn't home.

I stood in the crummy vestibule of his crummy building in Chinatown pressing the call button beside his name for a long, long time.

There was no answering muffled voice on the intercom; no reassuring buzz-click as he unlocked the inner door from upstairs to let me in.

Where the hell was he?

Why wasn't he here when I needed him?

I stared miserably out at the rainy, darkened street, wishing I had stopped to grab a slicker, at least. Wishing I didn't have to venture back out there so soon. Wishing a lot of other things, too late.

Maybe if I just waited here long enough, he would show up.

No. I couldn't do that.

For all I knew, Mike was out on a date with another girl.

Or maybe he had left New York and was on his way back to the Midwest.

No. He wouldn't do that.

He wouldn't leave without saying goodbye.

Would he?

Actually…why *wouldn't* he? Would I really blame him if he'd fled without a backward glance?

No. But I couldn't accept that we might never see each other again.

He was probably just…out.

I could tell him what I had to tell him later, over the phone. Or tomorrow. It didn't have to be said tonight.

I just wanted it to be.

Now that I knew what—and whom—I wanted, and needed…

Well, I wanted and needed everything settled.

Too many things could happen between now and tomorrow morning. Especially if Mike—and his whole rad speech and his totally unexpected engagement ring—hadn't left my apartment by the time I got back.

What if he tried to talk me into marrying him?

What if I said yes?

That, after all, was what I had wanted from him all along, wasn't it? A commitment.

And now that he was offering one, I was just going to walk away?

You already did, I reminded myself.

But it might not be too late. He might still be at my apartment. Or at Penn Station, waiting for a train. Or on his way to his parents' house on Long Island already…but I knew where they lived. I knew where to find him…

If that was what I decided to do.

One thing was certain…I couldn't stand here all night in a crummy vestibule waiting for somebody who might never come back.

forty-one

The present

"I'm back," I call, walking into the house, then pausing to sniff the air.

That's odd. It smells like bleach, and flowers, and onions frying in olive oil.

Melina was here, I remember belatedly. Which might explain the bleach, though it isn't something she uses on a regular basis, despite my requests.

Well, maybe Mike stood over her making her scrub the place from top to bottom. I wouldn't be surprised if he had. Right before he told her to get lost.

C'est la vie. He's right about that. He's right about a lot of things.

In the remarkably dust-free and uncluttered living room, I find five children—three of them mine, two of them Laura and Kirk's—lined up on the couch, captivated by an episode of *Dragon Tales.* Only Tyler, propped on pillows at the end of the row, looks up and smiles happily at the sound of my voice.

"What's going on in here?" I ask and pick him up, cuddling him close, inhaling deeply.

This morning when I said goodbye, he reeked of old saliva and Cheese Nips. Now he smells like fabric softener and Johnson's Baby Shampoo.

"Did you have a bath, sweetie?" I ask him, surprised. "Boys, did Daddy give Tyler a bath?"

"Shh…we're s'posed to be good and quiet," Mikey informs me, not even looking away from the television.

I set Tyler back on the couch and marvel that he doesn't protest, just snuggles in contentedly next to his big brothers and returns his attention to Ord's on-screen birthday party. My baby is starting to grow up.

Everybody does, sooner or later.

Walking into the kitchen, which is as shockingly spotless as the living room, I find Mike standing at the stove, his back to the door.

For a second I just stand there, watching him.

He stirs the contents of the skillet, consults the cookbook propped open on the counter, pours a measuring cup filled with amber liquid into the pan.

Then I notice the source of the floral scent: a huge bouquet of stargazer lilies on the table.

"Mike?" I say quietly, walking toward him. "I'm home."

He turns, and the relieved expression on his face confirms the question I answered back in the hotel.

No, I don't have any regrets. None at all.

This is my life. The life I chose.

forty-two

The past

I stepped back out into the pouring rain, looking up and down Canal Street.

Naturally, there wasn't a cab in sight.

I was going to get drenched walking to the subway, but what did it matter? My T-shirt, stirrup pants and black canvas high-tops were already soaked through, my sticky hair was matted to my head and smelled strongly of wet Aqua Net, and my eye makeup must have been somewhere around my chin by then.

I walked down the street with my head down, because of the rain and because, quite simply, I could no longer hold it high.

That was why I didn't see him first.

That was why I didn't see him until I felt a hand on my arm, heard him say my name, looked up to see a familiar pair of dimples.

forty-three

The present

He doesn't ask where I've been.

Someday, I'll tell him. But not now. There's nothing to hide, but it doesn't seem nearly important as it once was.

All that matters now is that I'm back where I belong.

"Hey," he says, pulling me close and hugging me.

"Hey," I whisper back, leaning my head against his shoulder. "What are you doing?"

"Cooking dinner. You hungry?"

"That depends. What are you making?"

"Arroz con pollo. It's Mexican."

I grin and look up at him. "I know it is."

"I know how much you love Mexican food."

"I do. And so do you."

"Yeah."

"Thank you," I say. "For dinner and for the flowers. And for getting Melina to actually clean the house."

His smile fades. "About that…I have something to tell you and you're not going to like it."

"What is it?"

"I…well, I fired her. This afternoon."

I'm silent, waiting for the rest; sensing, somehow, that there's more.

"I went out and bought a Spanish-English dictionary so that I could communicate with her. So when she got here, I brought the kids over to Laura's to get them out of the way, and then I told her…and she…she…"

"What?" I prod as he trails off, looking distinctly unsettled. "What did she do, Mike? Cry? Beg for her job? Refuse to leave?"

"No. She…" He takes a deep breath. "She slapped me across the face."

"What?"

"I told her she was *caliente,* which I thought meant that she was fired, and it turns out that it meant—"

"You told our cleaning lady that she was *hot?*" I ask in disbelief.

"Unfortunately, yes. Yes, I did."

I start to laugh.

So does he.

"I think she thought I was hitting on her," he says.

"*Ya* think?" I ask, still giggling.

"She started screaming at me in Spanish, and I may not know the language, but it isn't difficult to figure out that *bastardo* isn't a compliment."

I laugh harder.

So does he.

"Then she gestured that she was quitting, and she stormed out of here."

"How did she gesture that she was quitting?"

"Oh, trust me, that's universal in any language," he says ruefully. "So you're not mad?"

I shake my head, still giggling. "I'm actually relieved that it's over. But how did you replace her so fast?"

"What do you mean?"

"The house is so clean. What did you do, call one of those services that advertises in the *Penny Saver?*"

"I cleaned it myself," he informs me. "I left the kids over at Laura's for the afternoon, and I cleaned everything. Oh, and I finished in the nick of time. Laura's water broke and she's in the hospital. We may have their kids overnight. Kirk promised he'll call as soon as there's news."

"She's having the babies *now?*" I'm so happy. So, so happy. For them.

For us.

"She's having the babies now." Mike holds me close again. "Remember when you and I went to the hospital?"

"Which time?"

"All three. But for some reason the first time stands out more than anything else. You were so scared. I was trying to keep you calm, telling jokes, going on and on about that stupid couch to make you laugh, when all the while I was probably even more terrified than you were."

"You were terrified?" I ask, stunned.

"Of course."

"Of what?"

"Of something happening to you. Or the baby. Or failing as a father. Or as a husband. Sometimes, I'm still terrified of those things."

"Don't be." I kiss him. "You aren't a failure."

"Not in the things that count," he says. "But…"

"But?" I hold my breath.

"I still don't have my own sitcom."

I laugh. "Do you wish that you did?"

"Nah," he says, looking down at me, flashing his dimples. "I have everything I need."

"So," I say contentedly, "do I."

forty-four

The past

"Where are you going?" Mike asked me, pulling me beneath his black umbrella as the rain poured down around us.

"I...um...home," I stammered. "I was going home. I didn't know where you were, and—"

"I'm right here. Are you okay? You're soaked." He leaned in and brushed the raindrops mingling with teardrops on my cheeks, using his thumbs as mini–windshield wipers. "Hey...you're crying."

"I know. It's because I thought you were gone."

"I was gone. And now I'm back. I went to see *Eddie and the Cruisers II.*"

He went to see *Eddie and the Cruisers II?*

He went to see *Eddie and the Cruisers II!*

I had never been so relieved in all my life.

"Thank God," I said, clutching his shirt in both my hands.

"You mean because now you won't have to see it with me?"

"I mean because you're here."

"Where else would I be?" He looked around at the stormy night and said, "Actually, I can think of a few other places I'd rather be, but—"

I cut him off with a kiss, standing on my tiptoes and pulling his face down to mine.

"I broke up with him," I said when we stopped kissing.

"You did? For good?"

"For good."

"Are you sure?"

"I'm positive, Mike," I said, and I meant it. "I don't want to be with anybody but you."

forty-five

The present

You know, if I've learned anything lately, it's that everything comes around again sooner or later, if you wait long enough. Chandelier earrings. Paula Abdul. Strawberry Shortcake dolls.

Even old boyfriends you've written off for good.

I got one last e-mail from Mike after that day at the Pierre.

Subject: Me again
Date: October 5, 9:32 a.m. Eastern Standard Time
From: HappyNappy64@websync.net
To: Beauandco@websync.net

I just wanted to let you know that it's okay. Really. I'm glad you're happy. You deserve it. Don't we all? :-) Take good care of yourself and that family of yours.
www.palmbeachpost.com\accent

That's it.

I click on the link, and am promptly transported through cyberspace to the newspaper's Web site.

It takes me a few minutes to find the item, partly because I'm not sure what I'm looking for, and partly because I almost skip right past his face.

I told you I'll never get used to seeing Mike as a middle-aged man. But he looks good in the picture, very handsome, very…rad, I think with a smile.

And he's posing with a beautiful brunette in pearls.

I read the engagement announcement through a few times—particularly the last part. About how the groom founded a software company in Silicon Valley over a decade ago with two fellow researchers, one of whose names was familiar. Bradley Masterson was Mike's old computer-engineering professor. And I might not know much about computers, but even I recognize the name of the software company that they founded.

Websync.

As in HappyNappy64@websync.net.

Or Beauandco@websync.net.

I was in business with a few other guys, but we sold it.

I smile at his newspaper photo, wishing him well with his new bride.

Then I sign off and go upstairs to find my husband, who's watching the Yankees beat the Mets on television.

"You're never going to believe this." I sit next to him on the couch.

"Tyler just took his first steps?"

"Mike! He's barely crawling. And anyway, he's asleep. All three of the boys are." I snuggle into his side as he puts an arm around my shoulder. He knows of course about Mike having been in touch with me over the summer; about my having seen him in Florida. I didn't tell him about the kiss…only because it would have hurt him. I can't bear to hurt him.

"So what am I never going to believe?" he asks.

I tell him. About Mike getting engaged, and about Mike founding—and then selling—Websync.

"I bet he walked away with a million dollars," I say, shaking my head.

"A million? Are you kidding, Beau? He walked away with a *billion*. Probably more. I remember reading about that deal in *Business Week*. I just didn't realize he was the one who made it."

"Just think," I tease, "if I had chosen him instead—"

"You could have been a billionaire's wife?" he cuts in.

"No, if I had chosen him, he wouldn't have taken that job and he wouldn't be a billionaire. I was going to say maybe you would have been the one to walk away and become one of the wealthiest men in the world."

"That," he says smugly, "is exactly what I did. And I wouldn't trade places with him, or anyone else, in a million years."

I smile, admiring his dimples. Then I say, "Don't you mean a billion?"

forty-six

The past

"Nervous?" Mike asked in a low voice.

I shook my head.

"Yes, you are," he hissed, and squeezed my trembling left hand in his. Both our ring fingers were bare, but not for much longer now.

In my right hand, I clutched a bouquet of stargazer lilies. Their heady perfume billowed around me, old-fashioned and romantic as the layers of white illusion and lace that shielded my face.

I was wearing Grandma Alice's veil, my mother's pendant and a gorgeous gown that was sixty percent off at Kleinfeld's.

Something old, something new, something borrowed.

The something blue was tucked into my bouquet with the lilies, barely visible to anybody but me.

Two months was not enough time to throw together a formal church wedding with a big reception.

I had always wanted to get married in the fall, wearing a white gown with a train and veil. And as my big brothers liked to say, *Whatever Beau wants...*

Well, you know the rest.

But that isn't always the case.

I'm not *that* spoiled.

I mean, I also wanted to get married in Saint Patrick's Cathedral; I had settled for Central Park beneath a canopy of October foliage.

I wanted a reception at Tavern on the Green with lobster bisque, filet mignon and an orchestra; I had settled on a midtown Mexican restaurant with kickass chimichangas and a live mariachi band.

I wanted a three-week Hawaiian honeymoon; I had settled for a weekend in the Poconos.

But when it came to the thing I wanted most of all, I hadn't settled.

I smiled up at Mike as the pastor began, "Dearly Beloved..."

forty-seven

The present

"Nervous?" Mike asks in a low voice.

I shake my head.

"Yes, you are," he hisses, and squeezed my trembling left hand in his. Both our ring fingers are bare again, for the first time in fifteen years.

In my right hand, I clutch a bouquet of stargazer lilies. Their heady perfume billows around me, old-fashioned and romantic as renewing our wedding vows on our anniversary beneath a canopy of October foliage in our own backyard, with our three children at our side and family and friends looking on.

I don't have on a long white gown this time, but I am wearing a pretty ivory dress I bought last month when I spent a weekend in the city shopping with Valerie. I'm also wearing her lucky pearl bracelet and the earrings I wore on my wedding day.

Something old, something new, something borrowed…

And something blue. The same something blue as the first time around, once again tucked into the fragrant bouquet of lilies.

Nobody knows it's there but me.

Oh, and Mike, of course.

This whole thing today, the vows renewal and the party, was my idea.

The week in the Caribbean, just the two of us, was his. He made all the arrangements, and his parents are here to stay with the boys until we get back. They arrived from the airport last night armed with migraine medicine and several bags filled with toys.

"Did you remember to bring my fire truck, Grandpa?" Josh had asked eagerly.

"I'm sorry, Josh…we must have forgotten it."

If I'm not mistaken, I can hear crunching sounds coming from my middle son right now. I'll have to remind my mother-in-law to check the pockets of his Gap Kids khakis before she washes them.

I can also hear Tyler babbling in his stroller, and one of Laura's infant twins starting to fuss somewhere under the shade tree where she's sitting.

It will be good to have a week of peace and quiet alone with my husband in Aruba, I think. But it will be good to be home again, too.

This, after all, is what marriage is all about.

Marriage.

And life.

I look down at my bouquet, just to make sure it's still there.

The blue business card that didn't get thrown away after all that long-ago July.

Do I believe in fate?

Do I believe that my life was preordained?

Do I believe that what happened would have happened even if I hadn't settled on the only vacant stool in an airport bar back in the summer of eighty-nine?

Absolutely.

I smile up at Mike as the pastor begins, "Dearly Beloved…"

New from Ariella Papa, author of
On the Verge and *Up & Out*

Q: What are the two most dreaded words that a single
girl can hear from her married best friend's mouth?

A: We're trying.

And that's just what Voula's best friend, Jamie, tells her,
quickly ending their regular drinks-after-work tradition.
So with Jamie distracted by organic food, yoga and
generally turning her body into a safe haven for her
impending bundle of joy, Voula sets out in search of a
bundle of joy to call her own—an apartment. In the
New York real estate game, though, she's more likely
to stumble upon an immaculate conception than an
affordable one-bedroom....

**Available wherever
trade paperbacks
are sold.**